RIDE THE WAVES

THOMAS MCDONALD

To order additional copies of this book, contact:
Bookwhip
1-855-339-3589
https://www.bookwhip.com

Punky grumbled, "Just what we needed, a back seat driver.

"Hey don't forget, you get to baby sit, all of this cruise."

"Somebody up there hates me. I got to go back to a clean living.

They had their backs to the door. "Gentlemen, could you tell me where I could find Lieutenant Punky Wilson?" Punky knew that voice. He turned and was face to face with the redhead. He stared at her and she stared back. You, they both said at the same time.

"Who wants to know?"

"I do, I'm Charlie Crow and I have been assigned to him for the cruise."

"I'll take the assignment off your hands," whispered Jerry.

"Forget it, I got it covered."

When Punky finally found his voice, he said, "I'm Lieutenant Punky Wilson. I thought you were a man."

"Well you can see I'm not a man."

"Yes ma'am, you are a woman, but where did you get the name Charlie? How many people call you crow?"

Her temper started to show, "Where did you get the name Punky? I guess your mother thought you were a punk."

CHAPTER ONE

Pensacola, Florida May 1963

Punky turned off highway 90 on the road to Saufley Field Naval Air Station. He was excited to begin advanced flight training. This was time to separate the men from the boys. This was a tail hook squadron. A flight of T-28C aircraft circled overhead, the lead plane banked to start his approach to land. Punky smiled at the sight. He knew soon, he would be up there with a flight.

He had his top down on his blue and cream 1959 Ford Skyliner. He felt a surge of excitement go through his body. It was make or break time in this stage of training, having to land on an aircraft carrier. Punky thought of the friends he left back in Texas, the banker job he had turned down and Connie, the girl he had left behind. Had he made the right move, it was too late to have any regrets. He wanted to be where the action is. He wanted to see the world.

At the main gate, he stopped to show his identification card, got a sticker for his car and got directions to the Administration building to check in. The base was small which made it easy to find your way around. He parked his car close to the building and looked the base over.

A pretty Wave in Navy uniform, blue skirt and white blouse greeted Punky up front at the record counter. He handed her, his service records to process. She turned around to get check in forms out of a set of file cabinets, bending over to reach the bottom drawer her skirt rode high on her thighs, showing a lot of skin which Punky took advantage of. "Did you see something you like?"

"As a matter of fact I did."

"Well you can forget it. I don't date students."

She gave him the cold shoulder. Well he would try again later because he did like what he saw. She was a delicate blonde with blue eyes, hair cut short, cute little nose with a few freckles over it and a smile that bowled you over.

Punky read her nametag which read Patterson, nametags only had last names. "What's your first name?"

Susan, but I told you I don't date students."

"Why don't you date students?"

"They are too much like kids and try to intimidate you. They are full of themselves."

Punky didn't know where to go from here. He wanted to date her, but he was losing ground. "Tell you what, any time during our date if you want to go home, I'll take you home." She stared at him for a long time, trying to decide if she wanted to go, licking her dry lips and feeling her body go hot.

"Do you promise not to try anything?"

"Only, if you want me to."

"I will only go on one date with you. Pick me up Saturday night at my trailer. I live in the trailer park on the left just before you hit the main highway lot number three. Pick me up at seven o'clock and we can decide what we want to do."

Punky knew what he wanted to do. He grabbed his check in papers and left before she saw the effect she was having on him. His pants were getting too small for him. He checked in at the flight training office, the infirmary, the duty office and his living quarters, which was shared with another student. The student was gone so Punky took the extra bunk and locker. He stored his gear and went to find the mess hall. He was hungry and it had been a long trip.

He was in luck, the mess hall was open. He had steak, a baked potato and a salad, plus cherry pie for desert. He had tea to drink. After finishing off his meal, he went back to his living quarters.

"Well it looks like I have a room-mate."

Punky walked in and shook his hand, "Punky Wilson at your service."

"Jerry Adam, welcome to Pensacola, Florida, the home of the brave, tail hook time."

"It's time to separate the men from the boys. I hope I turn out to be one of the men," replied Punky.

"I think you are the last one in this class because we start flight training tomorrow."

"Well I guess it's better late than never. I didn't know I was cutting it this close."

"Well we had better turn in. Tomorrow will be a long day."

The next morning after breakfast they reported to their first class. Lieutenant Commander Brown gave them their welcome aboard speech.

After that the Chief gave them the rundown on what to expect in the coming weeks. "Your first week will be class, learning the aircraft, learning the runways and flight patterns. We don't want any accidents with this class. One word of warning, all the women in the area is looking for an officer for a husband. They will tell you anything you want to hear just to get a wedding ring, so be on your toes. Are there any questions? Take a break and your first class will begin in an hour."

Their first class was on navigation and lasted the rest of the day. The routine started, eat, sleep and go to class. They started to do exercises first thing each morning before class. Punky would be glad when Saturday came. He needed some rest and relaxation and some loving, he hoped.

They threw in a first aid class on Friday. Punky got to play the part of a man with a broken leg and arm. They put splints on his arm and leg. They even put him in an ambulance. They carried him to the hospital. It was late before he finally got back to his classroom. Class was over so Punky went back to his quarters. Jerry was getting cleaned up to go out.

"You want to come to the Officer's Club with me tonight?" asked Jerry.

"Sure, why not, might as well enjoy our last night out before we start flying."

They went to the Officer's Mess and had a good meal, chicken with all the trimmings. When they finished, they went on to the Officer's Club. They entered and found the rest of their class seated at a large round table drinking beer. They joined them and ordered beer. Punky scanned the club, girls, girls, and more girls were everywhere.

Punky asked, "Where do all the girls come from and how do they get in the club?"

Jerry said, "They get a visitor pass at the gate and nobody stops them from coming in the club. I think the high ups know we will go off base to find girls, so they let them come to us. You have been warned that most of them are looking for a husband."

Punky scanned around the club, a band was playing at the head of the dance floor. Officers were mingling with the girls. The club had a long bar with barstools on one wall, the dance floor had tables and chairs around it. Then Punky saw her sitting at the end of the bar. She was beautiful with long wavy black hair, a short evening dress showing off her long legs and a low cut front showing off the top of her full breasts.

"Jerry, see the girl at the end of the bar?"

"Forget that one she is off limits. She is the Captain's daughter."

"She is a woman, women like men and I like to live dangerously."

"You are crazy you must have a death wish."

"No, but she is someone I would like to meet, so I'll see you later."

Punky slid out of his chair and walked over to the bar and sat on the barstool next to her.

She turned to face him and starred at him. He starred back at her. "Do you know who I am?"

"You are the Captain's daughter, but I don't know your name."

She smiled at him, "My name is Cindy Moore and you have a lot of nerve talking to me." She smiled at him again, liking he wasn't afraid to buck her father.

"I saw a pretty girl and I wanted to meet her. I like to live on the edge."

"If my father saw you talking to me, he would make it rough on you."

"I'll take the chance. Would you like to dance?"

Nobody ever ask her to dance, they were afraid of her father, "I would love to dance."

Punky led her to the dance floor where there was a slow dance playing as she stepped into his arms. They fit together like a matched pair. She laid her head on his shoulder and enjoyed the dance. They danced several more dances before they sat one out.

Jerry watched Punky and couldn't believe his eyes. How lucky could a guy be? They had their heads together like a couple of lovebirds. Punky told her his life story leaving parts of it out. He told her about leaving a girl behind and not taking a bank job. Cindy told him about growing up as a Navy brat and how strict her father was on her. She didn't have many close friends. She had to be home by eleven o'clock, being on a curfew, but she promised to get together with Punky again.

"Where did you get the name Punky?"

"I don't know, but at least I wasn't named Sue."

"I got to go, but I'll see you soon." She kissed him lightly on the lips as she left.

Punky walked back over to the table and sat down with Jerry. "I don't believe what I saw and you were lucky her old man didn't come in while you were with her."

"Her name is Cindy and I plan to see her again."

"Man you are crazy."

The class sat and starred at Punky. "You are a maverick, aren't you?" said one of his classmates. "Yes, I have been called one. All my close friends are mavericks."

They broke up the party at one o'clock in the morning and went back to their quarters. Jerry and Punky went straight to bed. Punky dreamed of Cindy until another face crossed his mind.

He remembered he had a date with Susan Patterson tonight. He was lucky, having been here only a few days and had two girls already. He dreamed about both the girls the rest of the night.

He slept in late Saturday. He didn't leave the base, but did his laundry, went to the Navy Exchange to shop, shined his shoes and got his uniforms in order.

Saturday night, Punky left the base to pick up his date. He arrived five minutes early and knocked on her trailer door. The trailer park was small so he didn't have any trouble finding it. Susan opened the door and let him in. Smiling at him, she was only wearing panties and a bra. "I'll be ready in a few minutes, you can make yourself at home, there's beer in the refrigerator. Punky thought how she answered the door. Was she telling him something? Like tonight is the night and bringing on an instant erection. Susan came back a few minutes later wearing a short black dress that clung to every curve. She stopped in front of him.

"Do you like my dress?"

"Yes very much. Where do you want to go tonight? I don't know the town yet."

"How about we go out to eat and then go dancing."

"That sounds good to me."

Punky opened the car door for Susan, went around to the driver side and started the car. She gave him directions down town to a small restaurant. It had high backs on the booths. Candle light and soft easy listening music gave an intimate touch. A waitress came and took their order. Punky had steak with all the trimmings and Susan had a large salad. As they waited for their food they stared at each other and sparks flew. They knew how the night would end. After they finished their dinner, Susan gave him directions to a nightclub. It had a large dance floor and a live band. The waitress showed them to a table by the dance floor. They ordered drinks and sipped them for a few minutes. Punky looked at her and knew what she wanted to do by her body language.

"You want to dance?"

"You bet I do, I love to dance."

Punky pulled her chair out, led her to the dance floor as she went into his arms. He guided her around the floor to a lively two-step. He liked country western music and liked to dance to it. Finally a slow dance started and Punky pulled her in close. Heat from her body caused him to have a hard on. Susan could feel a hard ridge pressing against her belly and she became hot. She pulled Punky closer to her and moaned in his ear.

"Let's go home and do what we both want to do."

"I'm ready to go if you are."

By the time they made it back to the trailer they were both burning up. As soon as they were inside the trailer Punky reached for her, sliding the straps off her shoulder and letting her dress drop to the floor. He unhooked her bra, pulling it off and then slid her panties down. He stepped back to look at her.

He kissed her lips, slipping his tongue in her mouth as she opened to him and touched tongues. He broke the kiss and moved down to her breast to suck on her nipple. She moaned and grabbed his head pulling him closer. Punky moved over to the other nipple giving it his full attention before moving down her body to her core and touching it lightly.

"Punky, I want you in me now, I can't take any more."

She started to pull at his clothes, but he backed off and took his own clothes off. When he was naked, he led her to the bed. Susan lay down and watched as Punky covered her, spreading her legs, covering her mouth with his, he entered her in one swift movement. He wanted to hold back and make it last, but they were both out of control. She bucked and he rode her hard until they both went over the edge.

"That was good, but next time I'll try to make it last," said Punky.

"Well hurry up, I'm ready to go again."

"Give me a minute, guys aren't like girls, they need a minute to get it up again."

The next morning, Punky went back to the base with his butt dragging. All she wanted to do was have sex all night. He had never run across a girl like her before. He felt used, but what a way to go. She had duty and had to go to the base. Punky went back to the base, ate breakfast, showered and went to bed. He slept Sunday away.

Monday morning came, Punky was still tired from Saturday night, but he was up and running. After breakfast and exercises, he went to his class. Jerry shook his head when Punky sat down beside him. "I see you have a bad hang over," laughed Jerry.

"No, I had a tough date."

"Let me guess, Susan Patterson." He laughed again. "Oh, didn't I tell you about her?"

"No you didn't, so tell me what I'm missing."

"She goes with a guy one time and scores him on his performance on a scale of one to ten. It's a game with her. She only goes out with you one time."

"Now you tell me."

Jerry laughed as the class started. They were told they would report to the flight line to learn how to preflight their aircraft since it was their first time to fly the T-28C aircraft.

The Plane Captain does the preflight on the aircraft first before the pilot comes to the flight line. The pilot does the preflight on the aircraft again and then it's a go.

The Plane Captain instructed the students how to preflight their plane for the rest of the morning. They went to lunch and came back to the flight line. They would go on their first flight with an instructor. There were seven instructors and each one would take up a student. The students were told to go to the ready room and draw their flight gear which they would use the whole time they were there. They returned to the flight line in flight gear. They would now pair off with a Flight instructor.

Lieutenant Commander Brown paired off with Punky. He would be flight leader. The rest of the class paired off with other flight instructors.

"Mr. Wilson our plane is 01, preflight it while I watch you."

"Yes sir, I'm on it."

Punky had to get used to being called by his last name again. He finished his preflight in record time. "Preflight is complete sir."

"Very good, you take the front cockpit and I'll take the back."

The Plane Captain helped them strap in and slid off the wing. The T-28C had three wheels, two main wheels and a nose wheel or called a tricycle landing gear. Another sailor put his foot in the step on the wing and pulled himself up on the wing. He had on a headset. "Good evening sir." Punky read his name on his shirt, McDaniel his rank was first class aviation electronic technician. He walked out on the tip of the wing and sat down to wait for any radio problems. The pilot would signal to him if any of the planes had trouble. "Ok Mr. Wilson, start your engine." All the planes started their engines.

"This is the flight leader, start the radio check down the line."

"02 sir"

"03 sir"

"04 sir"

"05 sir"

"06 sir"

"07 sir"

"08 sir"

The Plane Captains pulled the chocks on a signal from the pilots. The tower gave the permission to take the duty runway. "01 roger, all chicks prepare to taxi and follow me.

McDaniel slid off the flap as the pilot raised the flap. The Plane Captains signaled the planes out of their slots and saluted the pilots as they passed them. The flight taxied out next to the duty runway and turned up. After a check of the engines all planes were good to go. "Saufley Tower, 01 with seven chicks, ready, to take-off."

"01 tower, you are clear for take-off." The tower gave them altimeter settings, wind conditions and altitude of five thousand feet.

"Ok Wilson, take-off and climb to five thousand feet."

"Roger sir."

Punky made a smooth take-off, climbed to five thousand feet and circled the field, waiting for the flight to join on him in formation. They joined up one each side behind him, one behind each of them and two in the slot. "Flight 01, we will be flying different formations so you will get used to formation flying and get the feel of your aircraft. We will break formation at my command, change altitude and join back with a different formation."

They flew around and made several turns until they did them perfect. "Saufley Tower 01 request change to three thousand feet."

"01 Tower roger you are clear to three thousand feet."

"Flight 01, break formation now and join back in formation at three thousand feet."

The flight practiced more formations and altitude changes before they returned to the base. They flew over Bronson Field and Baron Field on their way back to the base. They would be their practice fields for landings and take-off. The flight circled the field for a landing. "Saufley Tower 01 with seven chicks for a landing."

"01 Tower you are signal Charlie."

"Ok Mr. Wilson, take us home."

"Roger sir." Punky made a smooth three point landing and taxied off the runway to the spot he left. The other planes followed and parked down the line. The Plane Captains choked the aircraft. The pilots and students left their aircraft and went to the ready room to debrief and see how well they did on the flight.

The fight leader took the notes from all the instructors and started to debrief the class. They had done real good on the flight and the flight instructors were well pleased. Punky had a perfect score on the flight and he was so happy he could shout. They were dismissed for the day. They changed back into uniform and left the ready room.

Jerry and Punky ate dinner and went back to their quarters. As Punky was about to enter his quarters a sports car pulled up at the curb. Punky made an about face.

"Hi fly boy, what are you up to?"

"I just finished my check ride and from now on I fly solo."

Cindy looked Punky over as if making up her mind about something. She knew it was probably a bad idea to start a relationship with Punky, but her body wanted to feel him touching her, wanted much more, like him inside her. She shook her head, now where did that come from? She was trying to figure out how they could spend time together without her father finding out. She decided to live dangerous. Hadn't that been what Punky had told her when they met. Well she was ready to take him up on it, dam the consequences, full speed ahead.

Punky could feel something was about to happen. "What's on your mind?"

"You are," she leaned over so he could see almost all of her full breast.

Punky had an instant erection. "What do you have in mind?"

"How about I pick you up Saturday and go to the beach. We could find an area with very few people. Then we could swim and mess around," she giggled.

"Sounds like a plan which I like."

"Good, I'll pick you up at nine Saturday morning and we can make a day of it. Now kiss me, I got to go home." She was testing him to see if he would do it.

He reached over and cupped her head between his hands and kissed her until her heart rate raced and her toes curled up. He set her body on fire. She had asked for it and got what she asked for.

Jerry stood in the open door, "Wow, I wish I had your nerve."

Punky glanced over his shoulder and back to Cindy, "See you Saturday."

She started her car and drove off. Punky went inside and confronted Jerry.

"Don't say it, I know I'm in trouble if we get caught, but I think it is worth the risk."

"Well if I had a girl as pretty as that chasing after me, I would take a chance too, but I don't so I can give advice."

Tomorrow was the big day, they would fly solo so they ate and went to bed early. They were in the ready room for briefing at seven the next morning. There would be one instructor and seven students on each flight now.

Punky was assigned to plane 02 and would be the wingman for the flight instructor. They were told to man their aircraft. Strapped in, he glanced over at the flight leader and saw McDaniel on the wing of the flight leader's plane. They started their engines. They started their radio check down the line. Punky couldn't get his radio to work. He saw McDaniel slide off the wing of the flight leader's aircraft and come over to help him. He plugged in the back and asked Punky what was wrong.

"My radio is out."

McDaniel unplugged his headset and came to the front, reached in and turned the radio to the right channel. "Now try it sir."

"Thank you." Punky was embarrassed, but he would probably make more mistakes before he finished training.

They taxied out to the duty runway, turned up and took off. They were on their way to Bronson Field for landings and touch and go practice. The base had been closed for a long time and only the runway was used. They took up a landing pattern over the field. The L. S. O. gave them signal charley and they started to do touch and go practice. They would touch down at the beginning of the runway and then add power to take off again. The L. S. O. was set up beside the runway with a mirror landing system and a charley cart with a radio in it. The pilot would come around on the runway and call meat ball, then they would fly in on the glide path. If he came in right he got a green light to touch down and take off, but if his approach was bad, he got flashing red lights, added power and went around again. They did touch and go until the end of the flight.

"Flight 01, we will now make a complete landing, taxi off the end of the runway and back to the front of the runway beside the L.S.O. After everybody has landed and lined up, we will take off and head back to Saufley Field." The fight followed the flight leader. One of the students had a problem. He couldn't line up properly on glide path.

"05 Fight leader, if you don't get down on the next pass, I'll come up there and shoot you down." "Flight leader 05 roger sir."

The next pass he made it and the rest of the flight landed behind him. The flight leader led the flight out and took off. They took off and climbed out to their assigned altitude for the trip back to Saufley Field. They all landed without any problems and went to the ready room for debriefing. The flight leader told each student what if any problems he needed to work on. Punky had one little problem, to remember to put his radio on the right channel.

Are there any questions? Ok then, dismissed."

The next four days were routine, class one day and fly the next day. Punky was not looking forward to Friday night. He was assigned Shore Patrol Officer for the Pensacola area.

He had never been on Shore Patrol before. A navy van took all the ones assigned to Shore Patrol down town to the office used next to the police station. Each base had to send men to make a force of Shore Patrol. There was a few permanently assigned, but the rest came from the military bases around Pensacola. Saufley had sent the people for Friday night.

The Lieutenant at the desk gave them their instructions for the night. Punky was told he was in charge of the roving patrols and the men would be paired off, some would ride and some in the downtown area would walk. Punky looked around the men and spotted First Class McDaniel. He told McDaniel he would be coming with him on patrol. Walkie-talkies were passed out to each team along with flashlights and nightsticks. They were given a list of out of bound places and maps. If they had a problem with a military person they could cancel his liberty pass and return him to the base, but if they had trouble with a civilian they would call the

Police and let them handle the problem. Punky and McDaniel were issued 45 automatics in case they had a real problem.

They used military vans for patrol and walking patrols rode with Punky to their area for their watch. McDaniel drove and Punky rode shotgun. They dropped off the walking patrols downtown and started their patrol. They checked nightclubs, eating places and anyplace they thought a military person would visit.

Punky picked up the big flashlight, "Why do they issue such a big heavy flashlight?"

"To use as a club in case you don't have time to draw your weapon or nightstick."

"Well I guess that makes sense. Have you stood shore patrol before?"

"Yes sir, many times. I don't have long before I will be transferred back to sea duty."

"Where do you want to go when you leave?"

"I want to go to a squadron where I can fly. I want to become a combat aircrew man."

"Well I would like to fly jets, but you know the military they always send you where you don't want to go."

"Well time to do our job."

McDaniel pulled over to the curb where two sailors were falling down drunk. McDaniel took their liberty passes and they drove them back to the base, Pensacola Naval Air Station and let them out at the barracks. They went back on patrol. Punky called each patrol, but everything was ok and nothing they couldn't handle on their own.

"Are you getting hungry sir?"

"Yes, my stomach thinks my throat is cut."

'Fine, I know a good place to eat and I think you will enjoy the scenery."

McDaniel hung a left and headed to a quiet part of town. It looked like a resident area, but Punky didn't say anything since McDaniel knew where he was going. He pulled in at a large old house. It had two floors with stairs up the back of the house.

McDaniel got out and Punky followed him to the back door inside into a large kitchen. There was a large table and chairs in the middle of the room, all modern appliances around the wall with a large island to the side to prepare food for cooking. An old black lady was fixing a large salad on the island.

"Well look what the cat's drug in."

"Hi Mama, what's for dinner?"

"We got fried chicken, mash potatoes, corn, peas, green salad, cornbread, tea to drink and apple pie for desert."

"Mamma meet LTJG Wilson, sir meet the best cook in Pensacola as you will soon find out."

She got two plates, filled them with food, two glasses of tea, side salad and set it in front of them. She then got silverware for them. A few minutes later a big fat lady walked in and greeted them. She sat down and McDaniel told him she owned the house, but he didn't know what the house was used for. He would find out soon enough.

"Have you had any trouble with the military tonight?"

"No Mac, they behave or I throw them out."

Punky was dumbfounded. He didn't have a clue what was going on. The fat lady and McDaniel pulled the joke on any new Shore Patrol that he was with. The three of them sat there eating when five young girls walked into the kitchen and was served food. They knew McDaniel by name and said hi to Punky. There was something wrong with this picture. The see through clothes they were wearing didn't hide anything. Punky was looking at a full breast with cute nipples and a bush down below on all five girls. He got an instant erection and couldn't do anything about it. Everyone stared at him and laughed. The joke was on him, but he didn't care. They could pull the joke on him anytime. The five girls finished eating and left. Five more girls walked in and sat down dressed the same way. Punky wanted to ask how many girls worked there.

One of the girls let her front fall open, a breast and nipple stated at Punky. He had an instant erection. She smiled, "You can do more than look anytime you want to." It was embarrassing, his face turned red and everyone laughed at him. She got up and came around to the back of Punky's chair. She laid a breast on each shoulder and rubbed them against each side of his neck. That was all he could take, turning his head he covered a nipple with his mouth and sucked on it.

She sucked in a breath and moaned. She hadn't expected him to do that. She slid her hands in his hair, pulling him closer. Everybody sat there and watched the show. Punky finally let go of her nipple and she backed off. The joke was on her now, but she would have the last word. "You come to my room anytime and I'll do a number on you." Punky knew what she would do to him.

McDaniel and Punky thanked them for dinner. They went back on patrol. Punky called the other patrols for a report. They were lucky with nothing to report.

"McDaniel, payback is going to be sweet."

"Yes sir, but didn't you have a good time?"

"As matter of fact I did. If I wasn't an officer I would take that young lady upon her offer and I may do it anyway."

The rest of the night was easy with only picking up two more drunks which they drove back to Saufley Field with them when they got off their watch. Punky was starting to have a bond with McDaniel. Officers and enlisted men didn't run together, but Punky still liked him. He took a quick shower and hit the sack, he had a date tomorrow. He knew he was playing with fire, but he was still going.

At nine o'clock sharp, a horn sounded out front. Punky burst out the door with a coffee cup in his hand. Cindy looked so good he wanted to eat her for breakfast. She was smiling at him knowing what he was thinking. "Are you ready for a fun day?" She giggled.

"Bring it on let's get out of here before someone calls your Father."

"They wouldn't dare because he's not up yet and later he will play golf."

Cindy turned right when she hit the main highway. She drove straight through Pensacola and headed east along the coast until she found a section of beach without anyone on it. She killed the engine and turned to Punky. They came together in a heated kiss. He could feel her hard nipples digging into his chest. He reached down and cupped her bottom pulling her between his legs so she would feel his hard erection against her. She moaned and wiggled against him, but then she pulled away.

"You got to be kidding."

"Come on party pooper, we got all day to play around."

Something wasn't right, she was hot and ready to go, but she backed out for a reason. Now why would she do that unless this was her first time and she was embarrassed? Well he would have to work on that. He pulled off his clothes having a swimsuit on under his clothes. Punky ran to the water and dove in. It was cold and his erection died. He came up looking for Cindy.

She grabbed him from behind and ducked him. The fight was on. They played in the waves until they were tired, before coming back to the beach. Cindy laid a blanket on the sand and they lay down to get a sun tan.

After they got their tan, Cindy brought a basket of food and they ate their fill. They talked about their life problems before going back in the water. They decided to swim some more. Punky held out his arms and she went into them. He just held her awhile before he said, "This is the first time isn't it?"

She looked at him shyly, "Yes it is my first time."

"I thought so, are you afraid?"

"Yes."

"Well, we will take it slow and I'll make the first time good for you. That is if you want to make love."

"I want you to be the first, but I am scared, I was told it would hurt."

"It will hurt for a few seconds and then it will feel good. Trust me."

"If I change my mind again, will you stop?"

"Yes, but you won't want to stop."

"Are you sure?"

"Yes, trust me."

Punky slowly pulled off her swimsuit top, eased her bottom over her hips and pulled it down to her feet where she stepped out of it. She stared at him as he slid his swimsuit off. She went into his arms, flesh to flesh, the water wasn't cold anymore. She clung to him and waited for him to show her what to do. She could feel his hard erection between her legs and her body caught fire.

"Put your legs around my waist and your arms around my neck."

Cindy did as she was told. She could feel the heat from his erection on her folds. Punky pulled her tight against his body so she could feel the heat between them.

"Now I'm going to lower you slowly onto my shaft. When I break your cherry you will feel just a little pain. When you have all of me in you I'll stop until the pain goes away."

"Where is my swimsuit?"

"Our swimsuits will float back to the beach on the waves."

"Sorry, but I wanted to know I would have a swimsuit when we get out of the water."

Punky laughed, "You will. Now are you ready to make love?"

"Yes, let's go for it."

Punky slowly lowered her until he was fully sheathed. He stopped to let her pain ease. "Does it hurt?"

"Not now it doesn't."

"Ok, hang on for the ride."

Punky kissed her. Cindy opened her mouth and he plunged in with his tongue. He slowly started to move inside her. It felt so good she started to buck against him. He wanted to make it last, but she was too hot to slow down. She had a climax first, squeezing him and shuddering against him. He couldn't last with her throbbing around him. He put his hands on her buttocks and pulled her tight against him as he had a throbbing climax.

"Oh Punky, that was fantastic."

"You were fantastic too," he said as they waded out of the water. Picking up their swimsuits and putting them on. Dropping down on the blanket they would let the sun dry them off.

It was getting late so they gathered up their things and headed back to the base. Cindy didn't want to push her luck by staying out too late because she wanted Punky again. He got out looking around and kissed her. He watched her drive off before he went inside.

Punky walked in with a big smile on his face. "How was your weekend?"

"Well believe it or not I picked up a girl at the club, but we didn't get to go out. She had to go to work at the hospital in town. She is a nurse."

"Do you think she is one of the women looking to marry an Officer?"

"I don't think she is, but I will be careful."

"What are you doing tomorrow?"

"I have a date with the nurse to take her to church. What about you?"

"I have been asked to go to the swamp and go snake hunting. Sounds like fun."

"Are you crazy?"

"Some people say I am," laughed Punky.

Sunday morning found Punky down by a muddy slew with McDaniel. They had a flat bottom boat and 38 pistols with plenty of ammunition. They put on life vests and shoved the boat into the water. Punky wasn't too sure about this snake hunting, but he always said he liked to live dangerous.

McDaniel asked, "Are you ready to kill some snakes?"

"I'm as ready as I'll ever be."

They got in the boat and shoved off, the boat cutting through the water powered by a small motor. About ten minutes they saw their first big snake. McDaniel took the first shot taking out the big snake.

"What kind of snake was that," asked Punky.

"That was a water moccasin which is a poison one."

"That's just great. I thought you said this was fun not dangerous."

McDaniel laughed, "I guess I told a little white lie. It's hard to get someone to hunt with you."

"I can certainly see why."

"Look out here they come."

Snakes popped up everywhere as they took aim and fired, but finally they had to snap shoot to keep up. Punky had never seen so many snakes in his entire life. When you killed one snake two popped up to take their place. Finally McDaniel turned the boat around and headed back. "I've never seen this many snakes out at one time."

"Now you tell me," said Punky. "Let's get the hell out of here."

They were half way back when Punky saw a large black snake hanging down from a limb in front of them. He raised his weapon and fired. Wrong move, the snake fell in the middle of the boat. They both turned and fired at the snake. They killed the snake, but they shot holes in the bottom of the boat and now they were sinking. Punky looked for a bucket and started to bail out water. They were sinking fast, but they made it back to shore. They could laugh at how stupid they were, but at the time all they had on their mind was to kill the snake.

"Well we made it back in one piece, didn't we?" argued McDaniel.

"Yeah right, I guess we did."

They put the boat away and went back to the base where they checked in their weapons. Punky wasn't going snake hunting again. "How about next time we just go to the range for target practice like we were supposed to do."

"Yes sir, target practice it is," laughed McDaniel.

Jerry was back from his date when Punky came in the quarters. Well, how was church."

"Just fine and we went out to eat after church. How was snake hunting?"

"Don't ask I should have gone to church."

"Now I am curious as to what did happen."

"Well, besides a large snake falling in the boat, shooting holes in the bottom of the boat and the boat almost sinking it was cool."

"Sounds like you had a good time."

"Yeah right, we had a blast."

Monday came too soon and they were back to their old routine. One thing Punky always liked was watching the Navy Blue Angels practice. Pensacola was the home of the famed Blue Angels. He watched them every chance he got. He would love to be a Blue Angel.

Friday an instructor took them to Barin Field to show them where they would finish their flight training. He took them down to the runway to show them the mirror landing system, the same as was used on the carrier. Each time the wind changed the system had to be moved to a different runway. The aircraft had to take off and land into the wind. The L. S. O. was working a flight of aircraft when one aircraft had a problem.

"Air Control 05, sir I have a sump light and I think my engine is going to quit."

"05 Air Control, maintain level flight and slowly bring your bird around and land."

"Air Control 05, I got to land now."

He banked sharp trying to land on the nearest runway. The aircraft spun in, his engine breaking off with hot fuel leaking it burst into flames. The fire truck was on the scene in a couple of minutes hosing down the aircraft with foam, but the pilot's legs were pinned in the cockpit and the firefighters couldn't get him out in time. He burned to death.

It was a horrible sight to see a man being burned alive. Some of the students got sick watching the scene. They cleared the runway and went back to operating. It would be the same aboard a carrier. Push the plan over the side and keep operating. The instructor formed the students in a circle around him. It was time for a lesson hard learned.

He instructed the class, "I'm sorry about what happened, but what you witnessed was a pilot killing himself. It was pure pilot error. He was told the proper way to handle the problem and he panicked. He made a sharp turn to the left too close to the ground, lost his lift on the wings and fell like a rock."

"If he had followed flight procedure from the operation manual he probably wouldn't be dead. We lose a lot of pilots due to pilot error, but we lose some to failed parts on the aircraft. Monday you start your training here at Barin Field. The planes stay here and you drive out each day or ride a van. The base is closed except for one hanger we use and the firehouse. Do you have any questions?"

"How long will we train before we go to the carrier?" asked Jerry.

"When you are ready and a lot depends on the weather. Bad weather slows down our flight ops. It may take as much as a month longer to finish training. Since there isn't a mess hall out here the food isn't great. They bring food from Saufley."

Punky saw McDaniel standing by the L.S.O. and went over to talk. "Good evening sir and welcome to Barin Field or what's left of it."

"What are you doing out here?"

"We get moved around and it's my turn out here. I set up the runway equipment and work on the planes."

"Well, I guess I'll see you Monday."

The class was leaving so Punky loaded on the van for the trip back to Safley. Barin Field was across the line in Alabama. Punky was off the weekend so he was going to try and hook up with Cindy. Last weekend was great and he wanted to repeat it again. He knew he wasn't in love with Cindy, but they had a good time. He didn't think she was into serious relationships. She knew he would be shipped out soon and they would probably never see each other again. When he got back to his quarters he was trying to figure out a way to contact her. He knew he couldn't call her home so he decided to wait for her to contact him. Jerry had Shore Patrol on Saturday so they decided to go to the Officer's Club that night.

Punky decided to call home before they went to the club. He hadn't called since he got to Pensacola.

Jerry and Punky entered the Officer's Club and found their class there as usual. Most the guys had a girl and they were dancing most of the time. Jerry waved to the nurse he was trying to date and she came over to their table. Punky scanned the club and found what he was looking for. Cindy was at the end of the bar at her usual place. She waved at him. He left the table and joined her at the bar. "I was hoping you would be here since I couldn't call you at home."

"I have been waiting for you. I've missed you all week. How are we going to have some time together this weekend?"

"How about we go out to eat tomorrow, take in a movie and then come back to my quarters. My roommate has Shore Patrol tomorrow and won't be in till late tomorrow night."

"It sounds good to me. What time do you want me to pick you up?"

"How about eleven o'clock tomorrow morning?"

"You got yourself a date. Now, I want to dance."

Punky led her out to the dance floor, pulling her into his arms as they danced to a slow love song. She felt Punky's erection pressing against her belly and it made her hot all over. Cindy liked the power she had over him and wished his erection was inside her, but she didn't think the club would go for that. A girl could dream, couldn't she? Cindy giggled and smiled at him.

Punky stared into her passion filled eyes, "What are you thinking?"

"I'll never tell or you would think I'm crazy."

"I do crazy, remember."

"Not this crazy."

Punky was curious, but he knew she wasn't going to tell him what she was thinking. They liked to dance and danced the night away. Jerry scanned the dance floor and shook his head, Punky had a death wish. He would get caught with the Captain's daughter sooner or later and it would be hell to pay. Cindy had to leave early.

She quickly kissed Punky and went home. He came back over to the table and sat down to have a beer. Everyone stared at him. "What is going on?" asked Punky.

One of the students answered, "You got balls playing around with the Captain's daughter."

"I don't know about that, but I like going with her and we click together."

They shook their heads around the table and went back to partying.

At eleven o'clock on the dot, Punky heard a horn out front. It was warm weather and Cindy dressed in a short blue skirt and a white blouse. She had her hair in a ponytail. Punky scanned her from head to toe and thought she looked like a sixteen-year-old. She was wearing just a trace of makeup. She was beautiful and Punky told her so. Cindy drove to downtown Pensacola.

"What do you want to eat?" asked Punky.

"I want some junk food. How about we eat at Whataburger?"

"It sounds good to me."

"I think there is one about two blocks over from here."

Cindy pulled in and parked. They decided to eat inside. They got out and went inside. They ordered hamburgers, fries, and drinks. Punky brought their order to a table. The hamburgers were huge. Punky picked up his hamburger and grinned at Cindy. "It takes two hands to hold a whopper."

She wasn't sure he was talking about his hamburger, "Are you being bad?"

"Not me, you must have your mind in the gutter."

She guessed she did, but she wasn't sure. She did remember Punky did have a whopper and it made her hot thinking about it. They finished their food and left to go to a movie. They didn't argue on the movie, Cindy wanted to see a chick flick, but Punky wanted to see a western, so they flipped a coin and she lost. They went to see Rio Bravo staring John Wayne.

"For me not seeing my movie I want popcorn, candy and a coke."

"I can handle that to keep from going to a chick flick."

Punky got her goodies and they found seats half way down to the screen. By the time the movie started it was sold out. Everybody had bought popcorn. They didn't call John Wayne the popcorn king for nothing. When the movie ended they drove around town before heading home.

Punky said, "I worked in a movie theater when I was in high school."

"What did you do?"

"I sold popcorn, drinks and ran the projectors."

"It must have been fun working at the theater."

""It was, you got to meet all the girls."

"And you went out with a lot of them."

"Maybe a few since I worked I didn't have much time going to school and working."

"Poor baby, my heart bleeds for you."

She stepped on the gas. She wanted as much time as possible with Punky before they had to call it a night. She parked in front of his quarters and they went hand and hand inside. Punky turned around to lock the door. When he turned back around Cindy had pulled off her skirt and was pulling off her blouse. She was ready to make love. There were two beds, two dressers, two desk and two chairs in the room. Cindy asked, "Which bed is yours?"

"That bed in the corner."

Cindy walked over to the bed, taking off her bra on the way and turned to face him with nothing on, but her panties. "What are you waiting for or do I have to start without you?" She slid her panties slowly down her legs letting them drop to the floor. She sat on the bed and spread her legs inviting further intimacies. Punky shed his clothes as fast as he could and joined her on the bed. He slid between her legs resting an arm on either side of her head, staring into her passion filled eyes and waited.

As she arched her back, she murmured, "I want you inside me now."

"Your wish is my command." He plunged deep inside her throbbing passion.

"Faster, faster, I'm burning up." She arched her back to meet each thrust.

"Wait for me to catch up." Punky gave it to her fast and hard.

"I'm coming, I'm coming. I can't wait."

Punky kissed her while sliding his tongue in her mouth and kept slamming into her until he had a shattering climax. It took a while before their breathing returned to normal. He rolled off and lay beside her." Oh Punky, "That was so good. I want to do it again as soon as you can."

"Give me a few minutes to get hard again."

"I read somewhere if you eat raw oysters you increase your sex life."

"I think that's an old wife's tale."

Cindy reached over, taking his organ in her hand, started stroking him softly and it started to rise up in all its glory. She giggled, "Looks like you are ready." She turned over on top of him. Rising up over him, she lowered herself until she had all of Punky inside her. She started to rock and roll, twisting and grinding until Punky thought he would die of pure pleasure. They both went over the edge at the same time and she fell forward on his chest her breast flat against his chest. She didn't get off. Punky was still inside her.

"Are you going to be up to go again?" She still wasn't satisfied.

"I don't know, but I'll try. Just lay still for a while."

"Ok, but don't take too long. I have to go home shortly."

"I'm not going to promise anything."

Cindy covered his mouth with her own as he opened to her she plunged her tongue deep in his mouth. His hair on his chest tickled her nipples and they became hard. She leaned back and took one of his nipples in her mouth and sucked on it. She could feel him growing inside her. She waited until he was completely hard before she started to bounce and grind. This time it lasted a long time before they both had a climax. This time she was content having her fill of sex. Their bodies were wet with sweat and smelled of pure sex. They took a shower together and had cokes to cool off.

Cindy had to leave at eleven. Punky walked her to her car, kissed her and she drove off. He went inside since it was not too late he decided to study until Jerry got back from shore patrol. When Jerry came in, Punky wanted to know where he ate dinner.

"We ate at a Dairy Queen, why do you want to know?"

"Just curious, I ate at a cat house when I was on shore patrol."

"Get out of here, you're putting me own."

"No, the Sailor I stood Shore Patrol with took me to an honest to goodness cat house. We sat in the kitchen and ate with the girls, who buy the way had little or nothing on." He left out the part with him and the girl.

"Who was the sailor with you?"

"I can't tell you that. I don't want to get him in trouble."

They decided it was time for bed. Sunday, Jerry went to church with his nurse, while Punky stayed in the quarters and studied.

Monday, Jerry and Punky drove to Barin Field together. This was their last phase of flight training. They would soon be carrier pilots. They arrived as the Plane Captains were finishing their pre flights. They went to the ready room for their briefing. They would take off and land there. It would be fast and furious from now on until they were ready to go to the carrier.

Lt. Scott took the podium, "Gentleman welcome to Barin Field where you will complete your flight training or fail your flight training. As you know we lost a pilot last Friday. It was due to pilot error, which shouldn't have happen. He panicked under stress, killed himself and destroyed an aircraft. I don't want this to happen on my watch. If you have any problems come to me for help. We start our last phase of training before we go to the carrier. It will be at a fast pace so if you have trouble keeping up tell me and I will slow down a little. When I give an order do it, don't hesitate. An example is, when flying formation and I say break, do it or you may have a mid-air or get run over. If there aren't any questions the first flight will man your aircraft."

Jerry looked at Punky, "That's us, let's do it."

"Yeah man, let's show the other classes how it's done."

Lt. Scott took his flight out to man their aircraft. They did a pre-flight and climbed into their aircraft. He gave the sigh to start aircraft to his Plane Captains which gave the signal down the line. With all engines he asked for a radio check down the line. After the radio check was complete he gave the Plane Captain the signal to pull chocks. After the chocks were pulled he guided the plane off the line followed by the other aircraft. They taxied down to the duty runway to turn up and check the engines.

"Barin Control 09 has a flight of seven chicks for takeoff."

"09 Barin Control you are clear for take-off and climb to an altitude of five thousand feet."

"Barin Control 09 roger"

Lt. Scott taxied onto the duty runway, took off followed by his flight. He circled the field as the flight joined on him. Making a large circle he called Barin Control. "Barin Control 09 roger we are ready for landing and take-off practice."

"09 Barin Control you are signal charley."

"Flight 09 we will break formation on my command, make a low pass over the field, then come around and start our landings. Call meatball when you see it and stay on it all the way down until you receive a cut or a wave off. Break formation now."

The flight followed Lt. Scott down across the runway and turning into a landing pattern. He called meatball and followed it all the way in. He received a cut from the L.S.O. After touching down he gave his plane full power and took off climbing back into the landing pattern. The flight would stay in the landing pattern taking off and landing until their fuel ran low, then they would land.

"Barin Control 09 our next landing will be final. Thank you for putting up with us."

"09 Barin Control roger, it was our pleasure."

The flight landed and taxied back to the flight line where the Plane Captain guided them to park and chucked the aircraft. The planes would be fueled and made ready for the next group of students. Punky and Jerry walked to the debriefing together. Lt.

Scott gave the debriefing for the flight, each pilot was told of any errors he made and how to correct them in the future.

"Gentlemen, today is the way we will do our day until you are ready to go to the carrier. Are there any questions? Dismissed, see you first thing in the morning. Stay out of the club during the week, get a good night's sleep, you will need it."

Jerry and Punky made it back Saufley Field in time for dinner. They decided Lt. Scott gave them good advice so they were going to bed early. As they came back from the Officer's mess, there was a car parked in front of their quarters. Punky walked over to the car.

"Hi Punky," said Cindy, "You want to have some fun tonight?"

"I can't go out during the week."

"You mean you won't. A lot of the students go out and to the club."

"I'm sorry, but I want to pass my flight training without an accident and to do that I need a good night's sleep."

"Well if you won't go out, then I will find somebody who will."

"I'm sorry, but do what you got to do."

Cindy burned rubber, leaving Punky at the curb watching her go. "Such is life," he bowed his head and went inside.

"Are you alright?" asked Jerry.

"I guess I'll live, I don't have a good track record going with girls. I don't have any trouble picking them up, but I don't seem to hold on to any of them."

"Well, that was the smart thing to do. You don't have time for girls now."

"I guess it would be hard to leave her when I left to go to my next duty station."

"I'm sure she would never leave here and go with me. I don't make a big enough paycheck for her to be satisfied. After all, her father is a Captain."

"Now all you have to do is pass your carrier qualifications."

"I hope I can do that. I want to be a jet pilot."

"Well, I had just as soon fly props myself."

"What happen to the nurse you was seeing?"

"We go out together, but there's nothing serious going on. We just like to hang out."

"We had better hit the sack tomorrow will be another long day."

"Punky drove the next day. The routine was the same every day except when the wind changed direction and they had to move the mirror landing system to another runway. They lost flight time waiting for the change.

The next couple of weeks were fast and furious. They were doing excellent and if they kept it up they would go to the carrier soon. The flights became easy. Punky swore he could fly them with his eyes closed. It was Friday. They had to debrief and they were off for the weekend. Jerry and Punky walked side by side to the ready room. Lt. Scott said, "Gentlemen you are ready to go to the carrier. Next week we separate the men from the boys. Have a good weekend and I'll see you Monday, dismissed."

Jerry and Punky decided they had earned a night of fun so they decided to go to the Officer's Club. They entered the club and found their class at their usual table. They joined them at the table and ordered beer. Punky scanned the club and saw Cindy at the bar as usual, but she had a young Officer with her. She looked at him, turned her head and went back to talking to the young Officer. It hurt a little, but he knew it was for the best. Such is life, you move on.

Punky got a big surprise. Two of the girls from the house walked in and looked around. He waved to them and they came over to the table. They were good looking and it got everyone's attention at the table. Jerry pulled out chairs for the girls and they sat down.

"I would like you to meet two girls I met while on Shore Patrol." Punky didn't say where he met them. After introductions the girls ordered drinks and stayed to party.

"Are the girls from where I think they are from?" whispered Jerry.

"Yes they are," replied Punky.

"Which one were you messing around with?"

"The girl I am staring at." She smiled at Punky and he knew what she had on her mind.

"Wow" Jerry stared at her.

"How would you like to bed one of the girls tonight?"

"Would I? Are you kidding?"

"Ok, we go for it."

"How do you know they will go with us?"

"Trust me I know."

Punky got up and asked her to dance. Ginger smiled at him, "I thought you would never ask. Remember what I told you I would do to you?"

"I remember I want you to try it."

"Where and when?"

"How about after we dance and drink awhile. Would your friend go out with Jerry?"

"I'm sure she would."

"Good, we'll take you to our quarters and party when we leave here."

Jerry asked the other girl Pam to dance. Punky gave Jerry the thumbs up sign. They danced for an hour and then Punky asked if they were ready to leave. They were ready to leave. Ginger couldn't wait to bring Punky to his knees. She had never had a guy that could out last her.

Punky opened the door for them. As they stepped inside, Jerry turned on some soft music. Punky got drinks for everyone. The girls looked around the apartment. They were hot and ready to make love.

"Which bed is yours?" Ginger asked. Punky pointed to the bed in the corner.

"It's time to party." She walked over to Punky's bed and turned to face him. Pam went over to the other bed and faced them.

"Boys sit down and enjoy the show," teased Ginger.

Both girls started to dance as they pulled off their clothes. Jerry and Punky sat there with their tongue's hanging out. They got down to their bra and panties.

Jerry yelled, "Take it all off."

"I second that," yelled Punky.

"Why don't you do it for us?" giggled Ginger.

Punky and Jerry were on their feet at the same time. They went for the girls.

Punky turned out the lights on the way to his bed. Ginger turned her back to him so he could unhook her bra. He flipped the catch, tossed the bra on the floor and reached for her panties. She turned and faced him, putting her arms around his neck, molding her body to him. Punky lowered her onto the bed with him on top. She spread her legs to welcome him inside her. He didn't have to foreplay with Ginger. She was hot and ready so he took the plunge. Punky rode her hard as she bucked and twisted, pulling him deep into her passion heated body. They both came together and she pushed him off. Ginger straddled his hips and stared at him. "It's my turn now. We will take turns being on top until one of us cries uncle. I told you I would take you down."

"But it isn't fair a girl can keep going where a guy needs time to get it up again."

"I'll give you time in between, but I will wear you out."

"I'm ready when you are."

Ginger raised her buttocks up, slowly came down and sheathed all of him. She didn't take it easy. She bounced up and down giving Punky great pleasure. They both came again. After the third round Punky was almost on the ropes.

Jerry and Pam had sex two times and went to sleep, but Ginger was still ready to go again. As he rested she curled up beside him like a contented cat. They made love two more times that night before Punky cried uncle. He was so tired he couldn't move, but Ginger made him take a shower with her to remove the sex scent from their bodies. They went back to bed and slept like a log. The next morning the girls were up and dressed, before Jerry or Punky woke up. Ginger shook Punky.

"We have to go, but it's been fun and anytime you want a rematch call me."

"Lover, you about gave me a heart attack last night."

"Yes, but what a way to go," giggled Ginger.

"Thanks for a fun night and you take care."

"Being good isn't any fun unless we are talking about something else."

Punky let the girls out and went back to bed. Jerry and Punky slept until noon before they finally managed to drag themselves out of bed.

Jerry grinned, "Well, that was a very arousing night."

"You can say that again, but I'm so beat I'm not sure I will survive the day."

"What was that thing between you and Ginger?"

"I had a thing happen while I was on Shore Patrol. She said she would put me down."

Jerry laughed, "You know you can't out last a girl."

"No, but it sure was a pleasure to try."

"Let's get something to eat I'm starved."

They went to the Officer's mess for lunch. After lunch they decided to go work out and try to get their strength back. After a good workout Punky thought he would live. They went to the club and watched television the rest of the day.

The next two days their training was hard like they were in combat. At the end of each day they were dead on their feet. Lt. Scott told them they would go to the carrier tomorrow. Some of them were glad and some were worried about the flight. Punky and Jerry was ready. They wanted to get it over with and go to their new duty station. They had fun in Pensacola, but it was time to move on.

Jerry and Punky was at the field early the next day raring to go. They would be the first flight to the carrier. Lt. Scott would lead them. He stepped upon the podium to give them a briefing.

"Gentlemen, today we take a little trip to the U.S.S. Lexington for fun and games. We will fly in formation out and back. I know the ship will be moving, but follow the meatball and you will be fine. Does anyone know what they call a landing on an aircraft carrier?"

"They call it a controlled crash sir," replied Punky.

"Right you are and you get the prize. You get to be my wingman for the flight."

"Thank you, sir."

"Ok, it's time to man your aircraft."

They did a preflight, started their engines, did a radio check down the line, taxied to the duty runway, checked their engines and took off for the carrier. It took thirty minutes until they had the U.S.S. Lexington in sight.

"Lexington Tower 06 with seven chicks for carrier qualifications."

"06, Lexington Tower, take angels 2,000 while we turn the carrier into the wind."

"Lexington Tower 06 changing altitude to 2,000 feet."

They took a wide circle over the carrier while it turned into the wind. The carrier looked like a postage stamp from several thousand feet up. The carrier was now headed into the wind.

"06 Lexington Tower you are signal charley."

"Lexington Tower 06 I am taking signal Charlie."

CHAPTER TWO

"Flight 06 here we go, follow me and make me proud."

Punky thought, this is it as he banked behind the flight leader. They would land and take off until the flight leader gave them a passing grade or a failing grade. After many landings, Lt. Scott was well pleased with his students. "Flight, 06 join on me for the flight home. You looked great."

In formation, they made a fly over of the carrier. "Lexington Tower, 06 thank you for your time."

"06 Lexington tower it was our pleasure. You are cleared to angels 5,000."

"Lexington Tower 06 roger and good day to you."

"Flight 06 you can rest easy now. You have all passed your advanced flight training."

The flight back to land was normal, but then the flight leader's engine started to overheat and he got a sump light indicating metal in his engine. He started to lose power and slowly started to lose altitude. Lt. Scott called Punky and told him to take the flight home. He then called mayday as he went down. He was too low to bail out.

The engine quit and Lt. Scott went in on a dead stick. His right wing hit a tree and tore half of it off spilling fuel as it finally came to a stop. He tried to open the canopy and couldn't get it open. Punky made a quick decision. "02, 05 Jerry take the flight home. I'm going back."

"05, 02 Punky he gave you a direct order."

"02, 05 Jerry just do it. I got to know if Lt. Scott is alright."

Punky banked away from the formation and headed back. He made a low pass over the other plane and didn't see Lt. Scott. He had to be hurt or couldn't get the canopy open. He noticed a small fire in a distant from the plane and it was burning its way toward the plane. Punky made another quick decision.

"02, 05 Jerry there is a fire burning toward Lt. Scott's plane and I don't see him. I'm going in."

"05, 02 Are you crazy?"

"02, 05 probably, wish me luck."

Punky looked for a place to land, but there wasn't any. He decided he would have to land close to the other plane or he wouldn't be there in time before it caught fire. He came around and lined up beside the other plane. This is going to be a rough landing.

Punky left his wheels up, dropped his flaps, prop full forward, cut his power almost to a stall and prayed he would make it. He came in hitting small trees and bushes doing a number on his aircraft. By the time he stopped his plane was torn to pieces, but the cockpit. Punky was out of the plane in a few seconds and running over to the other plane. He grabbed the canopy latch and pulled hard. The canopy opened and Punky helped Lt. Scott out of the aircraft. They just made it away from the aircraft, before the fire reached it and it exploded.

"Man that was close sir."

"You know you are in a lot of trouble for crashing that aircraft, but I'm glad you came back for me. My wife will thank you to."

"I couldn't leave until I knew you were alright, to hell with the rules."

"I always knew you were a maverick, but I'm glad you are. You can be my wingman anytime."

"I believe in the code of not leaving a man behind."

Search and rescue finally made it to the crash scene and put out the fire. They gave Lt. Scott and Punky a ride back to Barin Field. The salvage crew would come and investigate the crash.

Lt. Scott and Punky went to the ready room where the students waited for them. "Gentleman we had a little excitement today, but thanks to Mr. Wilson everything came out ok. I owe him my life." Everyone gave a round of applause.

"All of you will be leaving for your new duty station, but Mr. Wilson. He will have to stay until after the investigation of the plane crash is over. I am sorry about that. Good luck to all of you and one day you may come back to Pensacola as an instructor."

They said in unison, "Thank you sir."

"Class dismissed."

Jerry and Punky drove back to Safley Field. They went to the Personnel Officer to check the list for their new duty station. Jerry had orders to HS-8 Ream Field in California. He would be flying helicopters. Punky had orders to a jet outfit, but beside it was canceled.

"Flying helicopters won't be so bad," said Jerry.

"Well at least you get to leave. I don't know how long I will be delayed and they will probably give my billet to someone else. Oh well, such is life."

"I'm real sorry man."

Jerry shipped out next day leaving Punky alone in his quarters. Lt. Scott told him to report to the ready room that he would be attached to VT-5 until the investigation was over. He would fly test hops and work as instructor when needed with the students. They didn't waste any time putting him to work. He was assigned a test hop that afternoon. Punky went out to preflight his plane and found McDaniel already working on it.

"What have we here?" asked Punky.

"I got moved back from Barin Field. I fly test hops along with my other duties, sir."

"Well let's fire this hog off and see if it will fly."

The Plane Captain waited while they got in the aircraft, Punky in the front cockpit and McDaniel in the back. Punky started the engine. The Plane Captain removed the chocks and signaled him out. He taxied down to the duty runway, checked the engine and called the tower. They gave him permission to take off. Air born he turned north away from the fields.

McDaniel had his own test to do. He had to check for carbon oxide and other gasses. He finished his test and told Punky. Now it was time to put the aircraft through the passes.

"Hang on back there, time to see if this crate will hold together."

"Roger sir."

Punky took the aircraft into two rolls, a sharp roll to the left, dived toward the deck, pulled out and went straight up. He took the aircraft almost to a stall before he leveled off. He did a few more rolls and turns.

"McDaniel, are you ready to check the back cockpit controls?"

"Yes sir."

"You have the controls."

"I have the controls sir."

McDaniel started making turns and change in altitude, but nothing fancy. They finished their test and headed back to Saufley Field. For the next couple of weeks Punky flew test hops and gave lectures to the students.

Finally he was told to report to a room where they were holding a review board of the crash. They questioned him and Lt. Scott about the accident. They cleared Lt. Scott of pilot error and following procedure. Then it was Punky's turn.

They read him the riot act about not following orders and destroying a Navy aircraft, but he saved a life, so they cut him some slack. He received a reprimand for not following orders and destroying the aircraft. He received a citation for saving a life. With the review board over Punky was told to report to personnel to pick up his orders. He was finally leaving Pensacola.

When Punky asked for his orders he was not surprised to find they had been changed. He was going to HS-8. One good thing it was the same squadron Jerry went to. He took a week's leave to visit his family and friends.

Punky pulled up to the gate at Ream Field, changed base stickers and drove around the base. It was a small base used for the helicopter squadrons. The base was located in the small town of Imperial Beach just five miles from the Mexican Border. Punky found the hanger that housed HS-8. He entered the hanger and saw four SH-3A helicopters being worked on. He walked around one and looked it over.

"Good morning sir," there came a familiar voice. Punky turned around to face McDaniel.

"Where did you come from?"

"I decided you needed someone to watch over you sir. You seem to always be in trouble."

"Yeah right, I probably do need a keeper."

"Mr. Adam is here also."

"Well look who's here." Jerry said.

Punky was beginning to like Ream Field with old friends to greet him. "Jerry, are you assigned to a flight crew yet?"

"No, but let's try and form our own, McDaniel do you want to be our first crewman?"

"Yes sir."

"All we need now is another crewman."

"Sir let me pick the other crewman, I have someone in mind."

"You do that. Get me a name to submit for our crew."

Jerry walked with Punky to check in. They caught up on what had happened since they parted in Pensacola. Jerry was already checked out on the helicopter, but wasn't assigned to a flight crew.

This was the perfect time to form a new flight crew.

"This will work out good, you and me as pilot and copilot, McDaniel in the electronic shop supervisor. Most of your problems are electronic. If he comes up with another rating we will have two things covered."

"Sounds good to me," said Punky as McDaniel walked up.

"Sir I have our other crewman. His name is James Morgan and he is a first class mechanic. He is black. Will that be a problem?"

"No problem."

"Thank you, sir. Morgan is a good mechanic and you never know when you will need one."

Jerry said, "Let's go submit our flight crew to flight ops."

The scheduling officer didn't have a problem with their request. Some wanted on the same crew all the time while others like to swap around.

"Are you living on base?" asked Punky.

"No, I live a few blocks outside the base. It is a two bedroom apartment. Would you like to share it with me and share the expenses?"

"I guess we are roommates again."

Jerry gave Punky the address and a key. Jerry was the new Ordnance Division Officer so he went back to check on things while Punky went to finish checking in. Each shop had a division officer, but a Chief or First Class ran the shop. Punky was assigned the new Electronic Shop Officer. He liked that assignment if only he was flying jets. He was flying jets in a way since the helicopter had two T58 jet engines to turn the rotary wing and tail rotor, but it still wasn't a jet fighter. That's what Punky wanted to fly.

Punky found the apartment and was unpacking when Jerry came home. The apartment wasn't big, but it was live-able. It came furnished with everything they needed including a television and stereo system. They wouldn't be there much to use them anyway. They would be out to sea a lot.

"Have you found a woman yet?" asked Punky.

"Not yet, but I have been too busy to look for one. Is that all you think about is girls?"

"I like good food. There's nothing like good food and a hot woman."

"You are still as crazy as ever."

"Jerry, you only go around once in life enjoy, it to the fullest."

"I would like to be like you, but I usually play everything as safe as I can. I try not to take to many chances."

"It's time to you changed your way of life. I live one day at a time. Only God knows when your time is up."

They stayed home and caught up on everything. The next day they were scheduled for a training flight. Jerry would be the pilot with Punky as copilot in training for pilot, while Morgan would be in training as second crewman. On a training flight they could fly anywhere in the area. They would be just a flight of one aircraft. Pilots and crewmen did a preflight together. Jerry started one engine, then the second engine, spread the rotary wing and engaged it. McDaniel checked the sonar while Morgan was checking the rescue hoist for proper operation. When the pilot was sure everything was good, he gave the Plane Captain the signal to taxi. Chocks were pulled and they were clear to taxi. The copilot handled the radio calls while the pilot handled most of the flying.

"Ream Field Tower aircraft 15 request liftoff."

"Aircraft 15 Ream Tower you are clear for liftoff."

"Ream Field Tower aircraft 15 clear for liftoff."

Punky pushed the power forward while Jerry came up on the collective and worked the rest of the controls. They made a smooth liftoff and turned east toward the mountains. Punky pulled the control up to raise the wheels.

"Where are we going?" asked Punky.

"I thought we would fly over the mountains for a little fun and games."

"What exactly are you referring to?"

"Just wait and see. I think you will enjoy."

Jerry skimmed the top of the mountain and dropped down into a small valley. He flew about two hundred feet off the deck and slowed down. He stopped the helicopter in a hover.

People was playing volleyball and swimming in a pool below them. They looked out the windows to see what was going on.

"They don't have any clothes on," declared Punky.

"They usually don't at a nudist colony," laughed Jerry.

"Wow, look at the one by the swimming pool with the big boobs."

"Sir I hate to say this, but we better beat feet out of here. There comes a guy out of the house and he has a shotgun," warned Morgan.

Jerry pulled out fast as they heard the shotgun go off, but they were out of range.

The aircraft climbed high over the mountain in the direction of the Salton Sea. It was a body of water inland from the ocean, but was still salty. They received a call from Ream Tower wanting to know their location. Punky told them they were approaching the Salton Sea from the southwest and would be over it in ten minutes.

"Aircraft 15 Ream Field Tower we have a distress call from the south end of the Salton Sea. There is a boat sinking with two men on board. Could you assist?"

"Ream Field Tower we should have them in sight any minute."

Punky took care of the radio and navigation while Jerry flew the chopper. They spotted the boat as it was sinking. Punky glanced over his shoulder, "McDaniel and Morgan prepare for rescue."

"Roger sir," replied McDaniel.

They went to the back, put on gunner belts and opened the back hatch. Jerry put the chopper on automatic approach, setting it for a hover at fifty feet over the water. The chopper could be flown from five different stations, pilot, copilot, and crewmen positions. It had a joy stick at the back hatch so the crewmen could fly the chopper from that position. The pilot set the altitude, but you could fly in any direction. The chopper stopped at fifty feet in a hover. The chopper was close to seventy five feet from the men in the water.

Jerry said, "McDaniel you have control of the chopper."

"Roger I have control." He eased the chopper forward and over the men.

"Hoist going down sir," said Morgan. "The hoist is at the water and a man is getting in the sling. Hoist is coming up and now we have the man on board." Morgan repeated his rescue with the second man.

"You have control and the back hatch is closed sir."

"Roger I have control."

McDaniel went forward while Morgan dropped the bench seat and strapped in the men. They were wet but happy to be alive. They said their pickup was on the east shore so Jerry turned east. They found the spot and started an approach. Punky dropped the handle for the wheels and took control of the power while Jerry landed the chopper.

Morgan dropped the front hatch so the men could go down the steps. The men were happy to be back on dry land. They thanked the crew for their rescue. The men bent over and walked under the blades to safety.

"Ok Punky, time for you to be pilot. You take the controls. I got the radio, power, and wheels."

"Roger I got the controls."

"Take us up."

Punky made a smooth liftoff and turned west over the water. Jerry called Ream Tower and gave them the news that the two men from the boat were safe. They climbed higher to make it over the mountains. They flew until they reached the Pacific Ocean and turned south to fly along the beach. It was a little cold for swimming, but there was a few surfers riding the waves. Further out, they could see some big sharks. It made Punky shiver just looking at them. When they reached Coronado Punky turned, flying over it and down the peninsula to Ream Field. They flew over the Navy Seal training base located about half way down the peninsula. There was a group of men carrying a log on their shoulders. The Navy Seals were one tough outfit. Punky flew over the base as Jerry called for permission to land. They landed and taxied back to the hanger.

They flew a hop every day for the rest of the week. By then Punky was trained as a pilot, but Morgan would have to wait until they were out to sea to qualify on the sonar. They were going on a short cruise to prepare for the coming West Pack Cruise. The carrier would go on several training cruises before the big one. By Friday Punky was ready for some fun and games.

"What is there to do for entertainment around here?" asked Punky.

"Are you kidding? There are lots of things to do here," replied Jerry.

"Yeah like what?"

"Night clubs everywhere, world's largest zoo, football, camping in the mountains, Sea World and just up the coast is Disney Land. Is that enough for you?"

"What do you want to do tonight?"

"I don't care as long as we have fun."

Punky thought about it for a few minutes. "How about we go out to eat and then go night clubbing."

"What kind of club?"

"All of them. We can pick up a couple of girls along the way."

"You are sure of yourself, aren't you?"

"Yep, you got to think positive and you can make things happen."

They dressed in slacks and shirts for their night out. Punky drove his Ford and they headed for San Diego. They stopped in Chula Vista and ate dinner before they went on to San Diego.

"Where do you want to start?" asked Jerry.

"How about the worst bar first and work our way up to the most expensive."

"It sounds good to me."

"You see that old tin building called the body shop."

"You got to be kidding."

"No I'm not." Punky turned off into the parking lot and parked. They got out and entered the building. The bar extended the full length of the building. There were pool tables and shuffleboards for the customers. They sat down at the bar and ordered beer. After they got their beer they went and played shuffleboard. As they finished their game a fight started at a pool table.

"Time to go," said Punky.

"I'm right behind you."

"Maybe we better go for a little better place," said Punky as he started the car and pulled back out into traffic.

"Yeah I think you are right."

Punky drove around for a while until he spotted another club. They didn't know their way around since they hadn't been there long. Punky pulled into the parking lot. The name of the club was Deon's Bar of Music. They went in and looked around. It had a large bar, a dance floor and tables. It was more like a club. They sat at the bar and ordered beer. The price was high. Shortly the found out why, several topless girls climbed upon the bar and started to dance up and down the bar.

"Now that's more like it," said Punky.

"You can say that again."

"See the red head on the end with the long hair?"

"What about her?"

"That's what I want to be in tonight."

"Punky you are crazy. She is working and I doubt she would go with you anyway."

"It doesn't hurt to try all she can do is say no."

"I still think you are crazy."

The music stopped after a while and the girls got down off the bar. They started to mingle with the customers. Punky eased his way to the red head at the end of the bar. She was sitting at the bar drinking a glass of water. She was hot from dancing, but Punky was hot from watching her. He sat down next to her. She turned to face him and looked him over. She could see passion in his eyes and her heart skipped a beat. She usually never had an interest in customers, but this one caught her attention. He looked like a man on a mission and knew what he wanted. She stared at him and he stared back.

"I liked your dance."

"You did." She lost her voice with him staring at her. She only had on hot pants, but she felt like she was naked.

"My friend and I are making all the clubs tonight and I sure would like you to come with us."

"I can't go out with customers when I'm working."

"Tell them you are sick. I promise you will enjoy yourself."

"I can't afford to lose the money."

"I'll pay your wages for the rest of the night."

She thought for a long time about it before she decided to go. "Are you in the Navy?"

"Yes, I'm a pilot stationed at Ream Field."

"Then you are an Officer."

"Yes, now have you decided to go?"

"Yes I have."

"Do you happen to have a girlfriend that could go with my friend?"

"I think I do." She waved at her friend at a table and she came over to the bar. The girl was happy to go out with an Officer. Punky motioned for Jerry and he joined them at the bar. They said they would meet them outside in a few minutes. Jerry and Punky left the bar and waited beside their car. The two girls joined them in a few minutes. They got in and Punky pulled out into traffic.

Punky introduced himself and Jerry. The red head introduced herself as Sandy and her friend as Betty. They were ready to party. Punky asked where another club was located. Sandy gave him directions to a club called The Mirror.

Punky wandered where the club got the name. He found out when they were seated at a table not far from a dark stage. The stage lights came on and a girl's reflection could be seen in a mirror dancing. The girl was in a pit and her reflection showed on the mirror. They would never actually see the woman. She was dancing to strip music. It was different. Punky had never seen anything like it before. She stripped down to a thin strip of cloth covering her private part. She dropped to the floor just as the stage lights went dark.

"Now that was a different kind of show," said Punky.

"You guys would like anything that showed skin," giggled Betty.

"You are probably right," agreed Jerry.

"You guys have seen enough skin for now, let's go dancing," argued Sandy.

She grabbed Punky by the hand and pulled him up out of his chair. Sandy led Punky to the exit with the rest following behind them. They talked rock and roll or country western and country western won out. Sandy gave Punky directions to a club called Cowboy Country. They entered the club and waited a few minutes for a table. It was a huge club with a live band, a large dance floor and a bar down one wall.

The girls ordered mixed drinks, but Punky and Jerry stayed with beer. They were small town boys and they drink beer most of the time. After they got their drinks it was time to dance. Both couples hit the dance floor and the band was playing a fast dance. They played a slow number after that and Sandy melted into Punky's arms. She could feel something hard pressing on the lower part of her belly and smiled. She squirmed on his organ and knew it would drive him crazy. "Stop that or you will drive me crazy."

"That's what I had in mind to do." She looked up into passion filled eyes and smiled at him. His body also had an effect on her. She became hot all over, her breast standing at attention, her heart beat faster, her nipples digging into Punky's chest and her legs were weak. She thought she might have a heart attack. Sandy pulled back from him to cool off. Punky grinned at her. She knew he saw right through her. Her face was flushed and a tremble in her body. They danced a few more dances, but kept a distance between them. After they danced the Cotton Eye Joe Sandy whispered in his ear, "Let's pick up my car and go to my apartment to continue our party."

"I didn't think you would ever ask."

"We have just started to party," she giggled.

"I'll round up Jerry and Betty and meet you at the front door."

"Don't take too long."

Punky rounded up Jerry and Betty. They headed for the front door, "Let's get out of here."

Punky woke up about four in the morning with a hand stroking his shaft. Her face was flushed as he looked at her. He knew she was hot to go another round. Then she did something he didn't expect her to do. She lowered her face over him and took his erection in her mouth and sucked on it. He thought he would pass out with pleasure.

Saturday they all slept in not having to work. Sandy was the first to wake up. She let Punky sleep while she took a shower and dressed in a short dress. She went to the kitchen and made coffee. Punky came in the kitchen and made for the coffeepot.

"Do you know how to cook?"

"I can boil water."

"Good, you can help me cook breakfast."

"I'll make the toast and set the table."

Sandy cooked eggs and bacon. The smell drifted into the other bedroom. Jerry and Betty showed up ready to eat. They were hungry and ate a big breakfast. Since Sandy and Punky cooked breakfast, Betty and Jerry volunteered to do dishes.

"I don't have to go to work until seven tonight so what do you all want to do today?"

"We could go to the Zoo or Sea World," suggested Betty.

"Let's vote on it," said Jerry.

They voted and Sea World won out. They took Sandy's car since she knew the way. It was located north of San Diego. It turned out to be a pretty sunny day. Sandy finally found a parking space. Jerry bought tickets for everyone and they went to the first show.

They had a pilot whale doing tricks. A trainer had a large toothbrush brushing his teeth. The whale gargled after brushing. He checked his heart with a stethoscope and the whale acted like it was cold. The trainer then motioned for the whale to jump high out of the water. The whale bounced up and down until he had enough momentum to make a high leap out of the water to take a fish out of the trainer's hand. After a few more tricks they moved on to another show.

The seals show was about balance. They would balance items on their nose and swim around while maintaining a balance of the items. After a while they moved on to the main attraction.

The main attraction was the dolphin show. They could jump high out of the water and twist all shapes while still in the air. To open the show a dolphin took a rope in his mouth and swam away from the dock attached to the house. He pulled the rope raising the American flag. The dolphins jumped through hoops over the water and tossed things around. A dolphin pulled a boat with a girl dressed in a hula skirt out to the dock. She got out and kissed the guy.

She started to dance while five dolphins danced in the water and tried to sing. Then the dolphins did some large jumps and twists out of the water. After a while they moved on. They viewed large tanks with every kind of fish imaginable. They finally seen it all and made their way to the parking lot. They picked up fast food on the way back.

Punky went to work with Sandy while Jerry stayed home with Betty. He sat at the bar and watched Sandy dance. When she was on break she would sit with him. He loved to watch her dance, but it made him hot and hard. Sandy got off work at midnight and they went home.

Sandy was tired from dancing, but not tired enough to miss out on making love. They made love two times before they curled together and went to sleep. Sunday morning Betty woke up first. She punched Jerry in the side and woke him up before she got out of bed. She jerked the sheets off him.

"Get up lazybones it's our turn to cook breakfast."

"I can't cook."

"Well it's about time you learned."

Betty dressed in shorts and a t-shirt and headed for the kitchen. Jerry followed a few minutes later.

"You set the table, make coffee and toast while I cook."

"How much coffee do I use?"

"One scoop is enough."

Jerry made coffee and set the table, but waited on the toast until the eggs and ham were almost done. Betty glanced at Jerry, "Go wake Punky and Sandy so their food won't get cold."

"You got it."

Jerry went and knocked on the bedroom door and called out that breakfast would be ready in a few minutes. He could hear feet hitting the floor. He went back and started the toast. A few minutes later Punky and Sandy joined them at the table. They made it just as Betty was serving the food. Jerry told the girls they would be out at sea for about a week for training exercises. They would call when they could get together again.

They left the girl's place at noon and went back to their apartment. They spent the rest of day packing for the cruise. Monday was a busy day. The squadron loaded trucks with gear and tools. They had to take all the equipment to maintain the aircraft. The ship furnished a space for them to work out of. When the trucks were loaded, the men loaded aboard busses for the trip to Long Beach.

They arrived at the USS Bennington CVS-20 docked in Long Beach at three o'clock and started to load equipment on the carrier. They set up their shops and found their sleeping quarters.

The enlisted were crammed into small spaces with bunks stacked three deep end to end and side by side. The Officers had it better with two to a small compartment. The carrier was taking on stores to last a week. The Air Group consisted of three squadrons, three detachments, rescue choppers and one cod. The cod was the most important aircraft on the carrier. The cod brought mail and personnel. The ship took on a full load of fuel for the ship and aircraft.

Tuesday morning the carrier pulled out of port and headed southwest out to sea. The squadron aircraft would fly aboard. Punky and his crew did a preflight and waited to take off. Commander Owens the HS-8 C.O. would be the flight leader. He called the tower for permission to lift off with his flight. Thirty minutes later the flight was over the carrier and asking permission to land. Jerry was told to assume plane guard position for the landing of the fix wing aircraft.

He flew the helicopter around to the starboard side of the carrier and flew a long side at sixty feet. After all of HS-8 helicopters were landed and stored they waited for the fixed wing. The carrier made sure it was headed into the wind.

VS-33 Screw Birds flying S-2E aircraft arrived. They were two engine prop aircraft. They flew over the carrier and turned into a landing pattern. They used the mirror landing system to land. The helicopters didn't need the system to land.

VS-38 Red Griffins landed next. VA-93 Blue Blazers flying A-4B aircraft landed next. The carrier was starting to get packed on the flight deck and the hanger deck. Hu-1 Pacific Fleet Angels flying UH-2A helicopters landed last. The Cod C-1A was already on board. The Air Group was all on board except for the plane guard.

Jerry flew around to the port side, eased the helicopter in sideways and set down across from the island. He folded the blades and cut the engine. "Well Punky, how do you like flying helicopters?"

"Alright I guess. It is a lot easier to land."

"Just think you go forward, backward, sideways and angles. Let me see a fixed wing do that."

"Ok Jerry you sold me. I guess I can live with flying helicopters."

The helicopter was chucked and tied down where they landed. Punky and crew went to the forward ready room under the flight deck. They changed from their flight gear and waited to look at their flight schedule for their first hop. They had an eight to twelve flight the next day. Punky and Jerry were off until then so they went to their room which was together. McDaniel and Morgan went to their shops to work. They worked a shift and flew also sometimes during their shift, but sometimes when they were off. They worked twelve hours on and twelve hours off around the clock. Flight ops were around the clock when in a training exercise. McDaniel and Morgan both worked nights, seven at night to seven in the morning. They had a flight at eight the next morning which would make for a long day. At seven thirty Punky and crew was in the ready room for briefing and manning their aircraft. Punky was the pilot and Jerry copilot.

They lifted off one by one and turned to port away from the carrier in a flight of four. There would be four helicopters in the air all the time until the training exercise was over.

The helicopters would hunt for a submarine with sonar until they found one. The four helicopters would bracket the sub and one bird would do a bombing run on him. The destroyers, S-2E and a patrol plane would hunt the submarine also. They worked together to catch the sub.

"Crew pilot we are going in after a sub."

Punky put the helicopter on automatic approach set at fifty feet above the water. The helicopter came into a hover at fifty feet.

"Crew pilot you have control."

"Roger we have control, answered McDaniel. "Down Sonar," He hit the down button dropping the transducer into the water. He let the cable out to one hundred feet and hit active sonar. Morgan used pots on the console to adjust the helicopter to center the sonar cable. McDaniel watched the scope for a contact. All four birds were dipping their sonar looking for a submarine. They all searched for the silent enemy, our subs playing the bad guys. They didn't have any luck the first hour. "Pilot, sonar, I have a contact at 090 degrees 500 yards and closing."

"Sonar pilot stay on him."

"Pilot sonar 490 yards and turning away from us. Morgan was tracking the sub on a plotting board. Jerry called the other helicopters and started a bracket around him. They would play leapfrog on the sub until one of them made a bombing run.

"Pilot sonar I lost him."

"Sonar pilot bring up the sonar."

"Pilot sonar roger," McDaniel hit the up button and brought up the transducer and turned it off before it broke water.

"Pilot sonar you have control."

"Sonar pilot I have control."

Punky climbed out to a hundred feet to leapfrog on the sub when the lead helicopter called and told them to take a shot at the sub. They had him nailed down.

"Sonar pilot, man the back hatch for a bombing run."

"Pilot sonar roger," McDaniel and Morgan put on a gunner belt and opened the back hatch.

"Pilot sonar we are manned and ready."

The lead helicopter gave them range and bearing and Punky lined up on the target. "Sonar pilot stand by to drop on my command."

"Pilot sonar roger," Morgan pulled the pin on the PDC and handed it to McDaniel.

"Sonar pilot drop, drop, drop," McDaniel dropped a smoke, PDC and a smoke.

"Pilot sonar drop away"

"Sonar pilot roger," McDaniel closed the back hatch. They pulled off their gunner belts and went forward. They would wait and see if the submarine would UQC that they were sunk. Sometimes the sub would play like he wasn't hit. They didn't like to admit they were sunk. The sub was honest and sent out a UQC.

"Sonar pilot we just sunk our first submarine."

"Jerry glanced at Punky, "Now wasn't that fun?"

"Yeah, kind of like chasing as fox."

All the helicopters left the area and gave the sub a chance to get away. After that they would hunt him again. It was everybody's job to keep the submarine away from the carrier. The submarine's number one target was the carrier.

Everything was expendable to protect the aircraft carrier. The submarine beat feet and didn't try to penetrate again on their flight. They returned to the carrier and landed. They went to the ready room for debriefing. They had a good hop and a submarine kill. Teamwork is the name of the game and it will get the job done.

For the next three days it was hot and heavy, fly, work and sleep when you got the chance. Punky and his crew had a four until eight in the evening. They took off at four and started a search for a submarine.

"Sonar pilot the patrol plane got a mad contact at 030 degrees 6,000 yards from us. Let's check it out."

"Pilot sonar roger that."

Jerry called the flight, "Tally ho the fox." The flight came running and the hunt was on. Punky set the automatic approach for fifty feet. It stopped at a fifty foot hover.

"Sonar pilot you have control."

"Pilot sonar I have control down sonar." The transducer cable was stopped at one hundred feet in the water and the sonar went active.

"Pilot sonar target bearing 035 degrees fifty yards away speed twenty five knots and we are tracking."

"Sonar pilot stay on him help is on the way."

The helicopter suddenly dropped and bucked around. Punky glanced at Jerry, "What the hell is going on?"

"Pilot sonar we are taking a bath in hot hydraulic fluid, sonar coming up."

"Sonar pilot roger let me know when the sonar clears the water."

"Pilot sonar the sonar is up."

Punky pulled the helicopter out of a hover and leveled off at one hundred feet. It started to buck Jerry called a mayday and gave their position to the carrier.

"I can't hold it we're going down, prepare for a crash landing."

"Sonar pilot roger," McDaniel ejected the window next to him and they pulled their seat belts tight. They were going into a nose dive and if they couldn't bring the nose up before they hit they would disintegrate on impact. Punky was pulling back on the stick and up on the collective, but none of the controls were responding. Finally just before they hit Punky got the nose part of the way up and they hit hard skipping across the water like a rock.

The helicopter settled in. They kept the rotary wing and tail rotor turning. The helicopter had floatation to stay afloat, but if the engines stopped they would flip over on their back. The flight stayed close to assist. Punky ordered McDaniel and Morgan to abandon the helicopter. They went to the back hatch and slid it open. They inflated a small raft, jumped in it and bowed low as they paddled away from chopper. There was a foot of water in the floor when they left the chopper.

A whaleboat from one of the destroyers picked McDaniel and Morgan from the water and took them back to the ship. The carrier came to the crash scene. It was decided to try and save the aircraft. The carrier pulled in front and backed down close to the helicopter. Punky lifted off straight up to about seventy feet. The carrier backed down until it was under them. Punky let the helicopter drop to the flight deck with water streaming from it. They wanted to find out what caused the crash. The chopper and equipment was ruined by salt water. There had been other crashes, but they had never been able to save the aircraft.

One of the helicopters picked McDaniel and Morgan up from deck of the destroyer. They went up the cable and were returned to the carrier. There would be a review board on the crash. This was the second crash Punky was in and he had only been in the Navy a short time. They went to the ready room for debriefing.

"McDaniel did you see what caused the crash?" asked Punky.

"As far as I can tell the hydraulic servo package in the broom closet blew up."

"That would explain why the helicopter went crazy."

"We were lucky to get out of that one alive," said Jerry.

"Yes we were and we got the bird back to study."

"Jerry did you know we are the first to save the aircraft?"

"I hope the review board will see it that way."

McDaniel and Morgan went to work. It was turning dark and they had a long night ahead of them. Punky and Jerry went to their room.

The next day Punky and crew had to go before the review board. "Well Mr. Wilson I see you like to crash Navy aircraft. Is it a hobby of yours?"

"No sir sometimes things just happen that way."

"From what the review board has decided is you couldn't help crashing."

"The ruling is faulty equipment caused the crash. There have been several crashes and we still don't know what caused them. Maybe with the crashed aircraft we can get some answers. The helicopter will be sent back to the factory. This board is adjourned."

McDaniel and Morgan went to bed since they had to work at night. Punky and Jerry went to the Officer's mess for coffee.

"Punky, you are one lucky son of a gun. You have walked away from two crashes in a short time without getting hurt or killed and the review board still let you fly."

"Maybe it's my lucky rabbit foot I carry, just kidding."

"We don't have a hop today, guess they cut us some slack, but we have a four o'clock take off in the morning."

"Jerry old boy, want to take in a movie? It's a John Wayne war movie."

"No, but I would like to go to the First Class mess and watch a movie."

"Why is that?"

"They show XXX movies down there."

"Forget it, I'm going to our room and read."

Four o'clock the next morning they were manning their aircraft. Four helicopters lifted off and four landed. Commander Owens was flight leader for the flight and assigned a search area for each aircraft. Punky and crew was assigned the starboard side of the carrier out in front. The flight before them warmed them a contact had tried to get close to the carrier.

The sun came up, the water was blue the carried plowed gracefully through the waves. It was a beautiful sight to see. All was peaceful, but not for long. Punky flew the helicopter into a fifty foot hover.

"Sonar pilot you have control."

"Pilot sonar I have control down dome." The cable stopped at eighty feet. The water had layers of different temperatures caused the sonar beams to bend and give false readings. It was hard to pick up a submarine in those conditions. You had to pick the best temperature to operate in. McDaniel turned the sonar to active, watched for a contact on the scope and listened for one. Morgan sat with plotting board in hand.

"Pilot I have a contact at 095 degrees three hundred yards and closing, speed ten knots."

"Sonar pilot stay on him while I call for backup. He is trying to get close for a shot."

Flight Leader 05 we have a contact trying to get close enough to fire on the carrier."

"05 Flight Leader keep the coordinates coming. I'm going to make a bombing run on our little friend." He flew over 05 and lined up on the contact. The PVC landed right on top of the cunning tower. Punky called and gave a direct hit. The submarine changed course and speed, but didn't give the signal he was sunk.

"05 Flight Leader well we got one that doesn't want to play fair. I'm making another run on him."

The second run nailed the submarine again and again, but he refused to give the signal he was sunk. By now the Commander was pissed off.

"05 Flight Leader stay on the sub, the rest of you join on me for a pass over the sub." The Commander circled and they joined on him forming a wedge.

"Flight, Flight Leader, prepare to drop scats, all your scats."

They flew over the submarine and dropped all the scats they had onboard. A funny thing happened. The submarine sent a signal it was out of action and would surface. A scat was like a leach which clung to the submarine with a magnet. A clapper beat the side of the sub as it moved through the water. It was covered in scats. The submarine would have to send divers in the water to pick off the scats.

"Flight, Flight Leader, I guess the sub will play fair next time." They had made a laughing stock of the sub.

"05 Flight Leader give that sonar operator a pat on the back for a job well done."

"Flight Leader 05 roger will do."

"Flight, Flight Leader, Return to your assigned area and screen for the carrier."

The submarine made a bold move trying to sink the carrier, but a sharp sonar operator saved the day. If he had got close enough to get a shot off it would have been worth him getting sunk. In World War two German submarines hunted in what was called wolf packs to destroy allied shipping.

When the flight was over and they were in debriefing, the Commander praised his flight for a job well done. "Don't mess with the Eight Ballers." The training exercise would be over today and they would all get some needed rest. One more day out and they would be headed home.

CHAPTER THREE

The next day a bunch of big wigs flew aboard on the cod. They were going to watch a show. Punky and crew was standing by the cherry picker waiting to see what the show was about. A destroyer pulled to the starboard side of the carrier and dropped back. A helicopter was on a raised pad on the back deck. An Officer stood beside the platform with a remote control in his hand. The unmanned helicopter was launching from the platform. It flew along the starboard side of the carrier and made a wide circle.

"That helicopter has a torpedo attached and it looks like it is going to launch it."

Jerry glanced at Punky, "I think you may be right. He is lining up for a run."

"Here he comes, what the heck, everyone duck," yelled Punky.

Just before the helicopter passed the carrier it turned toward the carrier, launched the torpedo and struck the cunning tower. The torpedo went into the wheelhouse and the helicopter, burning, fell down the side of the carrier.

Punky and crew crawled out from under the cherry picker. "Well that was entertaining," said Jerry.

"You can say that again," responded McDaniel.

"I would hate to go to the review board for this crash," said Punky.

"They shouldn't be too hard on him, he sunk a carrier," laughed Jerry.

"Well back to the drawing board," murmured Morgan.

They watched the shipboard damage control team remove the torpedo. They had to patch the hole in the bulkhead. The idea of using the unmanned helicopter to launch a weapon was great, but some kind of noise interrupted the signal to the aircraft and the operator lost control. Maybe in the future they would come up with a better mousetrap. The training exercise was over so the crew lounged around on the flight deck.

Punky checked out shotguns and a skeet launcher. Punky and crew went to the stern of the ship and set up. They spent a couple of hours shooting skeet before the air boss wanted the aircraft set up for fly off. The next day the aircraft would fly off and go back to their land base. The carrier would pull into Long Beach to unload the Air group. Hs-8 would unload back on trucks and busses for the trip back to Ream Field.

Punky and crew manned their aircraft at eight o'clock. Commander Owens, the Commanding Officer was flight leader for his squadron. He asked permission from Bennington Tower to lift off with his flight. He lifted off first followed by the rest of the flight. They formed a formation and made a pass over the carrier.

Then flight landed at Ream Field in an hour greeted by wives and girlfriends, there weren't anyone to greet Punky and crew. They were single and hadn't had time to build a relationship with anyone. Punky said, "Maybe we can find some waves to ride tonight."

McDaniel glanced at Jerry and Morgan and back to Punky, "You want to go swimming tonight?"

"That's what Punky says when he wants to make out with a Wave," laughed Jerry.

"I want a big steak with all the trimmings the food aboard the tub wasn't so good," complained McDaniel.

"I second that," agreed Morgan.

"I like to ride the waves too." Everyone looked at Punky and laughed.

They unloaded their gear, went to the ready room and changed and went home. Jerry called Betty, but she wasn't home so he left a message for the girls. "I guess tonight's not the night," complained Jerry.

"You never know, let's go to the club here on the base and check it out. I want a wave to ride and tonight I'm not choosy. I just want to have sex."

"You are crazy as usual."

They went out to eat off the base and went back to the Officer's Club. They entered the club and found it crowed, probably because the carrier had come in. Almost all the pilots from HS-8 were there and greeted them. They were all after the same thing, a woman. They worked hard and liked to play hard. There were several Wave Officers in the club, but they were already taken. It was slim pickings tonight.

Two girls sat at a table across from them, one was fat, one was skinny as a toothpick and they had their legs spread. Jerry glanced their way and under the table he could see up their dresses, they weren't wearing panties. They smiled at Jerry and he looked away. He wasn't that hard up yet.

He had always heard that the girls always looked better at closing time. Well it wasn't closing time and he wasn't drunk yet.

"Did you see something you like?" teased Punky.

"You got to be kidding."

"You could put a paper bag over her head. Turn girls upside down and they are all sisters."

"I'll wait and see if I can hook up with Betty tomorrow."

"Are you in love with her?"

"No, but she is fun to be with."

"Did you ever go to bed with a ten and wake up with a one?"

"Yeah I did a couple of times while I was in high school."

They decided to shoot some pool since there weren't any girls to choose from. Jerry turned out to be a pool shark. He beat Punky every game. They went back to table and continued to drink beer. They had bet on each game and Punky wanted his money back.

"Since you are an Officer and a gentleman I bet you ten dollars you won't ask one of those girls to dance."

"For ten dollars I would dance with the devil. Get ready to pay up."

Jerry left the table and went over to the girl's table. He couldn't decide which one to ask. He finally picked the skinny one and asked her to dance. She was hot and ready. They danced a slow song she was holding Jerry so tight he couldn't breathe. She reached down and grabbed him by his buttocks and slammed him against her. He could feel her heat against his shaft. He didn't want to have a hard on, but he couldn't help it. She looked up and smiled, "That feels good."

"Sorry I didn't mean to do that."

"Honey I could make it, feel a lot better if it was inside me."

Jerry knew Punky was laughing his ass off. Better to get even than to get mad. When they finished their dance Jerry told the fat one Punky is shy, but he would like for you to join us at our table. Jerry had played the game before where the one with the ugliest date won a bet and the money. He was going to do a number on Punky. The girls followed Jerry back over to their table.

The fat one made herself at home beside Punky. If looks could kill Jerry would be dead. The fat one grabbed Punky by the hand and pulled him out on the dance floor.

Punky vowed he would kill Jerry the first chance he could push him out of their aircraft. He decided the only way to make it through the night was to get drunk which he did. Jerry decided he had better stay sober enough to drive.

Punky knew what was coming next Jerry invited the girls to go home with them. He also noticed at closing time and him drunk that they started to look a lot better. Punky was so drunk by now he didn't care what was happening. Jerry parked the car and they staggered up to their apartment.

"Come on in girls and make yourself at home," said jerry.

"We will," they said in unison. They shed their coats and shoes. They both had on short skirts and deep-v-blouses which showed a lot of skin. They were staring at Jerry and Punky like they were a piece of meat and they were ready to eat.

"What would you girls like to do?" asked Jerry.

"You know what I told you at the club."

"Yeah I remember let's go to my room."

"No, you don't even know our names."

"Ok I'm Jerry and my pal is Punky now what's your names?"

"I'm Linda and her name is Lee."

"Now can we go to my room?"

"No, we like to do it together and watch each other. It's more fun that way."

Jerry though what had he got them into Punky was going to kill him. Linda stood in front of Jerry and pulled her blouse off. She wasn't wearing a bra and her breast were firm with hard nipples. She let her skirt fall to the floor. Jerry starred at the dark patch of hair. Linda walked over to Jerry and grabbed his belt buckle and unhooked it.

"I can take it from here." He stripped off all his clothes and stood naked before her.

"That's more like it." Linda grabbed him by his erection and pulled him to the floor on top of her. She spread her legs and guided him in. She took all of him and started to bounce and grind. She wrapped her long skinny legs around Jerry. It didn't take long until they both came. She kept her legs wrapped around jerry so he couldn't move off her.

"Now it's my turn," said Lee. Punky undressed the same time she did. He crawled in between her fat thighs and positioned himself. Lee grabbed his buttocks and arched up to take all of him. It didn't take long for them to come.

She reached under Punky and pulled him over with her on top with him still inside her. Linda pulled Jerry over so she was on top. The two couples lay side by side.

"Now we play a game," explained Linda. We do all the work. You guys lay back and enjoy the fun."

"Yeah let's ride them," Lee bounced up and down on Punky. Lee finished off Punky first. He couldn't get it up anymore. She wanted a turn with Jerry. Linda got off and Lee finished him off.

Jerry and Punky lay side by side dead to the world. They were down for the count. They wouldn't have any more sex tonight.

Linda glanced over at Lee, "Let's go home there won't be any more action here tonight."

"You got that right. I thought these guys would have lasted longer. Well it was fun while it lasted, let's go home."

They dressed and left Jerry and Punky on the floor as they closed the door. They never moved all night. The next morning they woke up with big hangovers. They went to their bedrooms and went back to sleep. They stayed in bed all day until late in the evening. Finally they got up, showered, shaved and went out to eat. They didn't call Sandy and Betty because they were too tired to go to San Diego. They took in a movie that night and stayed home all day the next day. Thursday they had to be back at work. They got a shock when they went to the ready room. Their names were on the list to go to survival school next week. They were not happy campers, but they knew they would have to go sooner or later. They had missed Christmas while out at sea. It was January and it would be cold.

Jerry looked at the flight schedule, "We have a flight at four this evening training for navigation."

"What you mean is bore holes in the sky." They had to use up their fuel allotment for the month or they wouldn't get as much next month when they would need it.

"We can use it to teach our crewmen how to fly."

"Yeah it's time, but you know it is against regulations."

"Punky since when did you go by regulations? You have always been a maverick. You only follow regulations when it's to your benefit."

"I just like to do things my way."

Four o'clock they lifted off and turned east toward the mountains. Jerry was the pilot and Punky was doing navigation. He had punched in their takeoff on the navigator and watched it track their flight. As long as the navigator worked everything was simple until the navigator quit working.

"Sonar pilot McDaniel we are starting a new training exercise today. You and Morgan will get stick time on each flight."

"Jerry and I want both of you trained as pilots. If anything happens to one or both of us I want you to be able to fly us home."

After passing over the mountains Jerry turned north. It was flat land and a good place for beginner to learn to fly. He leveled off and put the helicopter on automatic pilot. He set the altitude to four hundred feet.

"Sonar pilot McDaniel come up front, Punky will take your seat."

"Pilot sonar roger," He went forward and took the copilot seat.

"Are you ready to learn to fly?"

"Yes sir."

The helicopter was on automatic pilot. Jerry instructed him on all the controls, collective, rudder peddle, stick and wheels. He showed him how to read his instruments. Just by moving a knob he could change course or altitude. Then he showed him what would happen when the automatic pilot was turned off. The aircraft went crazy if you didn't know how to handle the controls. McDaniel didn't and it would take time to learn.

After an hour, McDaniel and Morgan swapped places. Morgan got an hour as the pilot. It wouldn't be long before they would be good pilots. They both wanted very much to fly as pilots. Punky liked the idea of everyone on board having the skill to fly the aircraft.

Morgan and Punky swapped places. It was time for navigation training. Punky turned off the navigator, now he would have to use other means. They had a directional finder on the aircraft. It wasn't too reliable, but it would get you close and you could use landmarks. If all else failed, they could use the sun, moon and stars to navigate like in the old days before electronics.

"Punky, do you know where we are?"

"Give me time, I'm working on it."

"Well I hope you figure it out before we run out of fuel."

"Turn left." He finally picked up the Ream Field beacon.

Jerry increased altitude to get over the mountains. They picked up highway 80 and followed it to San Diego.

"Punky I hope you can do that well when we are out to sea and don't have landmarks."

"No sweat, I got you covered anywhere we go."

"Let's see you find the survival school in the mountains. The one we will going to."

"Turn left go back toward the mountains, turn north now and hold that bearing."

"Punky you are taking us over the nudist camp."

He grinned at Jerry, "I know, might as well do some sight-seeing on the way."

They flew over the nudist camp, but there wasn't anyone out. It was too cold. Punky gave a slight correction to their heading. They passed over what they thought was the survival school. It had a barbwire compound and some small buildings. That had to be it. Jerry circled and made another pass over the compound.

"I saw some movement next to one of the buildings," said Jerry.

"They probably heard us coming and made the prisoners hide or go inside."

"They want the place to look deserted."

"Jerry I don't like the looks of that place, I don't think it will be fun, more like hell."

"Old buddy I have to agree with you on that one. The place gives me the creeps."

"Let's get out of here."

Jerry turned left and headed toward the ocean. When he was out over the water he turned south and went along the beach. There were a few brave surfers surfing on a cold day. When Ream Field was in sight Jerry turned southeast to the field and landed.

Friday they had another training flight. They flew out to sea where McDaniel and Morgan got an hour each at the controls. Then Jerry decided Punky should learn to auto rotate down in case their engines quit or they ran out of fuel.

"Punky old friend, this is your first time to try this so I'll do it first."

"This is like coming in on a dead stick right?"

"Not exactly, unlike a fixed wing aircraft your tail rotor is your rudder and when the engines quit you lose your rudder. The helicopter will start to spin around and around with the rotary wing unless you are good you will be dead."

"You really know how to perk a guy up."

Jerry leveled off at three thousand feet, pulled the engine power back to idle and the helicopter began to drop. As soon as the tail rotor stopped the helicopter started in a spin and kept dropping. At one hundred he gave the helicopter engines full power and the tail rotor started to spin and stopped the spin. At fifty feet he pulled out and climbed back to three thousand feet.

"As you can see if you let the helicopter ease over and you lose control, you will tumble and never get control again."

"Ok I get the point."

"Are you ready to try it?"

"No, but I guess I have to."

Punky pulled back the power and started his auto rotation. He was always good at anything to do with an aircraft. He made it look so easy. He pulled out at fifty feet and climbed back to three thousand feet.

Jerry looked over at Punky, "Show off."

"I can't help it an aircraft feels like part of my body and responds to each touch."

"You are definitely a superior pilot and I'm glad I'm flying with you."

"Thanks that means a lot to me."

Punky turned east back toward Ream Field and landed. They read the bulletin board and saw a change. They would start survival training Sunday. They had Saturday off. They decided to stay home, run, exercise and sleep. They wanted to be in shape. They knew what was coming.

They reported to the ready room Sunday morning at seven o'clock for a briefing. They were told to dump everything they had on them in a bag and put it in their locker. They were issued a small knife, string, one hook, and a canteen of water. Today and tonight they would stay on the beach close to Coronado. They would live off the land.

They loaded aboard a bus for the trip to the beach. It was cold when they unloaded and looked up and down the beach. They were told they could eat anything they could catch. They weren't hungry, but were told they had better eat what they could find because they wouldn't get any food for a long time.

"I was afraid he would say that," grumbled Jerry.

Punky looked at Jerry, McDaniel and Morgan, "We work together, one of us has food we all have food."

"Let's find some food," Jerry said.

They searched up and down the beach until McDaniel found a couple of clams. They decide to cut one up for bait and try to catch some fish. Morgan cur his finger and squeezed the blood on the bait to make blood bait. Everyone lost their bait except Morgan. He seemed to be the better fisherman.

Finally he got a strike. He played the fish slowly wearing him down. He pulled the fish out of the water and they dragged him up on the beach. The fish turned out to be a shark. He was big enough to feed them and some of the other guys. They still had to eat the shark raw. It was a cold night and they slept on the cold sand. They slept huddled together for warmth.

They woke up the next morning cold and hungry. Morgan found some baby shrimp in a pool of water. They were small, but food was food. He caught eight of them and brought them over to the rest of the guys.

"Breakfast is served," he gave each of them two shrimp.

"Where is the shrimp salsa?"

Morgan glanced at Jerry, "Beggars can't be choosy."

They ate their raw shrimp and did some exercise to get warm. It was time to leave for the fun part of the training. They loaded on the bus for the trip to the mountains. It took time to climb the mountain on an old dirt road or more like a pig tail. They finally came to a stop in front of an old building and unloaded. A man dressed in a Russian uniform and carrying a short quirt came out to welcome them. There were twenty students in the class. They followed him into the old building.

"You are about to begin one of the hardest training courses of your life. There is nothing in your power you can do. The only good thing is you know it will end. Within the next couple of days you will hate me and you will think you have been transported to some other country. All classes are treated different so if you know somebody that has been here it won't do you any good. Some of you will make it through and some will be given a second chance. Believe me when I say welcome to hell."

The first day wasn't so bad. They trained you in navigation on the ground, how to use the compass, maps, and how to find your best route from one place to another. Everyone was given a compass and map. You had to go point to point, dropping off mountains and through bad terrain, making all the check points on your way home. There wasn't any food, only a little water left in your canteen.

Punky and crew made it through, but was exhausted. All the class made it back and sat resting by the old building. An instructor walked by with a big black dog. The guy's eyes followed the dog. "You guys get your eyes off my dog. If one of you gets lost he will find you." Like in the cartoons when the big bad wolf looked at the sheep and saw dinner the men looked at the dog and saw dinner. People will say I won't eat that, but when it comes down to starving you will find out you will eat anything to survive. Before they had time to rest they were taken out and dumped. They were told to find their way home before dark. Punky and crew made it back before dark, but were tired and hungry. They were given two small pieces of rabbit and told to make jerky strips.

By the time they cured the pieces of meat they were small, it was only two bites. Punky stared at his small strips. "Think big guys, I don't think I can eat all of this," but he did and washed it down with a swallow of water.

"Tomorrow is going to get tough," said Jerry.

"Punky scanned the crew, just a walk in the park. They can kill us, but they can't eat us, we are too tough."

The next day they were taken into rugged country and dumped out. They were dumped behind enemy lines trying to get back to their own lines. As a reward if you made it through enemy lines, you got a ham sandwich and a glass of milk. Very few ever made it. Punky was the first one caught half way through the escape and evasion course. Some men dressed in uniforms like the man who welcomed them there slammed Punky to the ground. One put a foot on his head and pushed his face into the dirt. They caught the rest of the crew and marched all of them to an old truck. They were treated just like prisoners of war. They shoved them, punched them and called them bad names. They finally pulled up in front of the compound and were unloaded.

One by one they were forced into a barbwire holding pen where they had to undress and stand on the outside naked. It was very cold outside. They were given a prison number to remember and herded into the compound which they had flown over the week before. They could finally put their clothes back on. They took their knife, fishhook and string. They were cold, hungry and exhausted. They were told to try and escape, but they moved them around so much there wasn't a chance in hell they could plan anything.

They put Punky and Jerry in black boxes for hours on end. Punky beat the black box. He flexed his toes, fingers and dreamed of girls. They finally let the group out of the black boxes. Everybody except Punky crawled out of the boxes, their bodies numbed from like of blood circulation. Punky stood up and walked out of the black box. He had made a big mistake. They punched the men on the ground crawling and called them pigs. Two men dragged Punky off to a small building where another man met them at the door.

"We got a smart ass here, have fun with him."

"I like a live one now and then I'll give him some special treatment."

"Call us when you are finished with him."

"It won't take long."

As soon as Punky was inside he was thrown across the room hitting the floor hard. Next thing he knew he had a broomstick behind his knees and was bent over backwards.

He took hard blows to his chest and stomach. It was funny how they could beat you half to death and not leave a mark on you. They were good at what they did.

"What's your name?"

"John Wayne."

"What's your service number?"

"12345678."

"What's your squadron?"

"Bluebirds I think."

"What do you fly?"

"We fly kites."

After an hour of interrogation he called the guards to come get Punky. He threw him out the door into the dirt. He tried to get up, but couldn't. He was dazed and didn't know where he was. They drug him to the other part of the compound and threw him inside. Morgan tried to help Punky. The guards hung him up on the fence by his fingers.

The one in charge walked outside the compound with a mean look on his face. He beat the quirt against his hand. He glanced at Morgan, "Why do you help this piece of white trash? You are a free man. You don't have to answer to him."

"Yes I do we are a team."

"You are nothing, now shut your mouth."

"Go to hell."

"That's where you are. Bring me the smart ass."

Two guards dragged Punky out of the compound. The two men held Punky while a third man worked him over. They beat him until he almost passed out. The man with the quirt walked back and forth in front of the compound. "You see what we do to troublemakers. Look at these two, now does anyone else want to be a hero?"

"No," Punky cried out, but it was too late.

"Go to hell," yelled McDaniel and Jerry. They couldn't stand to see Morgan and Punky treated that way

"Bring me those two men now."

All the prisoners blocked the gate and the guards couldn't get in. The order was given to lock down the compound. Jerry and McDaniel helped Morgan down off the fence. Punky was thrown back into the compound. For their effort they didn't get any food or water, but everybody had worked as a team. That got them high marks. They were suppose, to defy the enemy anyway they could. All the prisoners huddled together and talked until they dropped a tear gas canister in the middle of them. They had to scatter to get away from the tear gas. There was a hole in the ground for them to get out of the weather, but the door had a lock on it. They were being punished for being bad.

The next morning Punky could hardly move. He felt like every bone in his body was broken, but he got up and moved around anyway. They put part of the men on a work detail, dig a hole and fill it back up. One man flunked out of the course that day. He was put in a black box and went bananas. He didn't know he couldn't stand to be closed in a small space. He would be dropped from the flight program.

The next day while the prisoners were out in the compound they heard a helicopter in the distance. The guards rushed into the compound and unlocked the door for the hole. They were herded into the hole and the door was locked.

Punky said, "We were right about this place. When a plane comes over they hide everything and make it look deserted."

"Why do they do that?"

"It's a game they play just like the real thing. This camp is like in a foreign country."

"I get it they play air raid."

When the helicopter left the area they let them out of the hole. They took three of the prisoners out of the compound, Punky and two others. They were made to dig another hole, but this one was the size of a grave. The integrator and two guards brought a pine box out to the grave and sat it down.

Two guards grabbed Punky and forced him into the box. He kicked and tried to get free, but the guards were too much for him. They nailed the cover down. "Ok smart ass now will you answer my questions?"

"Go to hell."

"Fill the hole."

""You can't do that," said one of the prisoners.

"Watch me."

One of the guards took a shovel and started filling the hole. The interrogator checked his watch. Punky thought this wasn't real, they would let him out in any minute, but they didn't. His air supply in the box ran out and he passed out.

The interrogator yelled, "Get him out of there." He couldn't believe Punky hadn't broke and called out. As soon as they opened the box Punky slowly came to. The two prisoners were allowed to take Punky out of the box and back to the compound. He was still pale when he finally got to sit down on the ground.

"What happened to you?" asked Jerry.

"You don't want to know, it was horrible."

"What did they do?"

"They buried me alive."

"You got to be kidding."

"Believe me they did. I passed out and woke up with the lid off."

The rest of the prisoners were afraid they would be next, but they never came for them. That night they finally got something to eat. Not much, just cornbread and water. They wolfed it down. Jerry said, "Just think how much weight we are losing."

Everyone was beginning to smell. They were still in the same clothes and hadn't had a bath in almost a week. It would take more than one bath to get them clean. Punky could see why the guards called them pigs.

They stopped beating on the prisoners and started the mind games. They would start rumors one prisoner told something on another prisoner to start hate and discontent among the prisoners. The interrogator would tell the married men their wife was running around and single men their girlfriend was messing around.

Once again they were playing the mind game trying to break a man down. They even told a married man his child was hurt or his wife was pregnant by another sailor. Anything to stir up trouble even to the point of telling a prisoner his girlfriend had a disease. Punky wasn't married and didn't have a girlfriend so they told him his mother died. He almost took the bait, but kept his mouth shut.

Their time there was almost over so for nothing g better to do the next day they were forced to do exercise until they dropped. The prisoners were weak from like of food and water. They were then forced to crawl around on their hands and knees while the guards made fun of them calling them pigs.

The next day was D-Day, the school was over and they got to go home. They were let out of the compound and escorted to the old building by one of the guards in a sailor uniform.

All the staff was in Sailor or Marine uniform. The prisoners stared at them. They were the enemy. The man with the quirt was a Lieutenant. He said, "Have a seat and eat all you want. We will debrief while we eat." There were tables and chairs for the staff and prisoners. The tables were covered with food and drink. Everybody was starved to death, but they couldn't eat very much. Their stomachs had shrunk until they were small from like of food, but they ate as much as they could hold.

The interrogator a Marine Sergeant started the debrief he praised Punky for his resistant to everything. He told them they had a good example of what it was like to be captured by the enemy. He also explained the mind game they play. They never wanted the prisoners to bond which made them dangerous. If you kept them divided it didn't take as many guards to control them.

The staff shook hands as they loaded on board the bus for the trip home. They all slept on the way home. The bus felt like heaven compared to sleeping on the cold ground. They unloaded at the hanger and went to see what was going on.

There was a list of promotions on the bulletin board. Punky and Jerry both made Lieutenant. They were ready to celebrate being back and making Lieutenant, but they were told to get their gear together they were going on another short cruise to pick up an Apollo shot. Take off was seven in the morning. They went home to pack.

Seven o'clock the next morning they lifted off for their flight to the carrier. The carrier turned into the wind and the Air Group landed. After the Air Group was on board the carrier headed toward Hawaii.

During the trip practice pick up was done with a dummy capsule. The dummy capsule was dropped overboard. Punky and crew flew Navy Seals out to the capsule and dropped them near the capsule. The Seals put a ring and harness on the capsule to keep it afloat for pickup. Punky and crew then picked up all the Seals, but one that was left to attach the capsule to the crane. The carrier maneuvered in close to the capsule. The crane operator lowered carrier's number 3 elevator. He stopped it at the hanger deck level.

He swung the crane out over the water and lowered the cable. The Seal attached the cable to the capsule and it was hauled up with him. He kept the capsule from turning and twisting on the way up.

The capsule was swung on to the elevator and the pickup was complete. They waited a short time and started over again. After two practice pickups they decided to knock off. The carrier cruised toward Hawaii. The rocket was not manned, but hope was to put a man in space soon using the rocket and capsule they were using on this flight.

The carrier passed Hawaii and headed for the pickup point. The next day the capsule was suppose, to come down close to the carrier. It went off course and landed far from the carrier. It landed close to Australia. A cargo plane carried the Seals from Hawaii to where the capsule landed. They bailed out and landed close to the capsule. They put a flotation ring and harness on it.

The carrier steamed at full speed to reach the capsule. All the practice and nothing went down like it was practiced to do. The Seals had a long wait before the carrier finally arrived, but everything went smooth loading the capsule aboard.

The carrier was close to Australia and the crew hoped to pull in there, but the space crew wanted the capsule back as soon as possible so the carrier headed back to the states. It was a big let-down. Hardly any of the men on the carrier had ever been to Australia.

By the time the carrier got back and the squadron off loaded, Punky and Jerry were ready for a night out. Jerry called the girls, Betty was off, but Sandy was working. Jerry told Betty he would pick her up and they would go out to eat.

Jerry drove his car, picked up Betty and went to Steak and Ale to eat. Jerry and Punky was starved for some good food. Shipboard food would keep you alive, but it liked the taste. Punky wandered how the cook could take a beautiful steak and destroy it. There were a few good cooks in the Navy and a Commanding Officer would kill for a good cook. Punky and Jerry had T-bone steaks with a baked potato and a salad plus ale to drink.

After they finished dinner, Jerry dropped Punky off at the club where Sandy was working and took Betty home for some loving. As soon as they entered the apartment they were tearing at one another's clothes. Jerry was sex starved. His erection was throbbing when he entered her.

Meanwhile back at the club Punky sat at the bar drinking beer while Sandy danced topless on the bar in front of him. His eyes were locked with hers and he knew she was doing moves just for him as she danced.

It seemed like hours before she would get off work. Punky drank more beer than he intended to, but the house wouldn't let a person stay and watch the show if they didn't order drinks. Finally at midnight Sandy got off work. She drove as Punky sat close to her and slipped his hand up her dress between her thighs.

Sandy glanced at him, "You better move the hand or I may have a car wreck."

"I'll take the chance." He inched closer to his target.

"Don't touch me like that." Her body trembled at his touch.

"I want you hot and ready when we get home."

"I am hot and ready I've been wanting you, all night."

"I guess I'm just a horny old man."

"Well I guess that makes me a horny old woman," Sandy giggled, "I want you to."

She drove as fast as she could without breaking the speed limit. As soon as they entered the apartment Pumky pulled her into his arms and kissed her until she melted against him. Sandy hadn't had anything to eat all night and she was starved. They went to the kitchen for a midnight snack.

Good food and good sex went together. They stared at one another while they ate. Punky never realized the effect a girl licking her finger could have on the body until now.

"What are you thinking? You look like you want to eat me."

"I do," he grinned.

"Let's go to the bedroom and find out."

They left their dishes on the table and Sandy led him to the bedroom. The door to Betty's bedroom was closed. Sandy turned to face him and started slowly removing her clothes. Punky did the same. They stood staring at each other until he opened his arms. She walked into them and melted against him. He kissed her as their naked bodies burned against one another. Her hard nipples dug into his chest and his erection dug into her belly. She opened her mouth to him and he explored the inside with his tongue.

She wrapped her tongue around his and sucked on his tongue. He broke off the kiss, nibbled her neck on down to her breast as he covered a hard nipple with his mouth and sucked it. He then switched to the other nipple giving it the same attention until he moved on down her body. She was trembling and grabbed his hair and pulled him closer.

Punky went down on his knees and eased her back against the bed. She lay down with her legs over the side. He eased between her thighs, placing her legs on either side of his head. He spread her folds and lowered his head. Sandy came unglued. She couldn't believe anything could feel so good. She was bucking and twisting when Punky braced himself above her. He slid into her and she took it all.

"Punky, don't stop, do it all night."

"That's a tall order, but I'll do the best I can."

They both went over the edge and came at the same time. Punky turned over pulling here on top. He was still inside her.

"That feels good with you still inside me," she giggled, "But now I'm going to put the squeeze to you."

"Oh baby you're going to kill me."

"At least you will die happy."

"That's for sure."

They lay there for a while until Punky could get his strength back. Sandy could feel his organ growing inside her. She started to move up and on his shaft.

"It's my turn to be in charge," She giggled as she rode him.

"I don't care have your way with me."

She had an earth shaking orgasm and lay there trembling as her inner muscles squeezed Punky until he thought he would die of pure pleasure. He slammed upward and came deep in her body. They lay there in the smell of sweat and sex then drifted off to sleep with her on top and him still inside her. Sandy liked to sleep that way. She knew if he got his strength back he would get hard again and it would wake her up.

Sure enough at five in the morning his hard erection woke her up. He was still asleep so she lay there and enjoyed it. Punky started throbbing inside her and woke up.

"Good morning sunshine, how do you like waking up like this?" She squeezed him.

"I love it." He would like to wake up like this every day.

She leaned over and kissed him as she started to move. "I want you on top."

"No problem." He flipped her over and slammed into her hot body.

"Faster give it to me faster."

"How does it feel?"

"Oh yes it feels so good."

They both had a big climax at the same time. When their breathing finally came back to normal they got up and took a shower together. Sandy went to fix breakfast and Punky went and woke Jerry and Betty. They had to get back to the base and work.

After they had breakfast Punky and Jerry said goodbye to the girls and left for the base. They had a good time that night, but there were no strings attached. Everybody was out for a good time.

The squadron was preparing to go on a Westpac cruise. They only had a few days left. They were leaving toward the end of February. The main priority was that the maintenance be done an all aircraft. The next priority was to get the men all their shots which were a lot of shots. Punky hated shots, but he didn't have a choice.

The day before they were to leave they got a briefing from their Commanding Officer. Commander Owens stepped up to the podium.

"Men we are going to be gone for a long time which puts a hardship on the married men, but we have a job to do. We have advisors in South Vietnam at this time and we may be involved in a war at any time. We will be in the area for the next six months or longer. I want to remind you of the part we play in the big picture. Our primary mission is antisubmarine warfare using our sonar to find, track and destroy submarines. We have a lot of other missions. They include angel work, picking up downed pilots, holy hello on Sundays, mail and personnel transfer to the destroyers plus many varied photo missions. Our Medical team would like to say a few words."

Doctor Robinson stepped up to the podium. "Men I only have a few things to say. If you are really sick don't wait until you are dying before coming to sickbay. We have a good Dental and Eye department. One word of warning if you have sex, put on a condom. If you catch something come to sickbay immediately. There will be condoms on the hanger deck when you go on liberty."

Jerry glanced at Punky, "I guess skinny dipping is out."

"Yeah I don't like to use a condom, but I don't want to bring something back I don't want."

"I don't think I will have sex while I'm overseas."

"Right and elephants fly," laughed Punky.

"Tonight is our last night here. What do you want to do?"

"How about, we go to Coronado to the Officers club."

"It sounds good to me. I heard it is a big club with lots of girls," replied Jerry.

Seven o'clock they entered the Officer's Club at Coronado and it was full. There were girls everywhere. A lot of the women were called Westpac widows since their husband was overseas and they were bored at staying home. Most of them came to drink and dance or have people around to talk to, but a few wanted more. It was hard on married couples in the military to keep a marriage together since they were apart so much and would get lonely. A lot of the couples used the saying, what you don't know don't hurt you. Punky didn't like that and decided he wasn't going to get married.

"We might get lucky tonight."

"Yeah I know you want to ride the waves."

"I would like to if I find the right wave."

Punky scanned the club, "Do you see what just walked in the door."

"Wow, now that's what I call a beautiful woman."

"Dubs mine I saw her first."

The woman wore a simple skirt and blouse, but something about her said a woman with a lot of passion. Punky couldn't keep his eyes off her. She was about five feet eight inches, firm breast, hard nipples that strained at the material of her blouse, red hair hanging to her shoulders turned under. Her skin was flawless and she wore just a small amount of makeup. She took a seat at the bar. Punky couldn't keep his eyes off her. He wandered what color her eyes were. His whole body tingled with anticipation of meeting her and looking into her eyes. He felt like a teenager trying to get his first date. What was wrong with him? He had bedded lots of women and some better looking than her so why was he so fascinated by this one woman? He didn't understand it, but he had to meet her.

Jerry sat watching Punky, "What's wrong with you?"

"I think I'm in love."

"Yeah right and who is the lucky girl?"

"The redhead over at the bar that is so beautiful."

"You aren't kidding are you?"

"No I've never felt like I do right now."

"What are you going to do about it?"

"Probably make a fool of myself."

Punky watched the redhead at the bar until he came up with an idea how to meet her. He turned to Jerry. "Old buddy, I need your help."

"Ok what kind of crazy scheme are you planning now?"

"Do you know the song, You Lost That Loving Feeling?"

"Yes I think so."

"Good you're going to be my backup."

"Now I know you are crazy."

Jerry finally went with him. Ma'am we have a request to sing you a song. She turned and stared at them. She wandered what they were up to. Then they started to sing. They weren't very good, but it made her smile. She had never had anyone sing to her.

She started laughing, "Enough, enough."

"But we were just getting warmed up," protested Punky. He sat down beside her.

"How long have you two been doing that?"

"It was the first time."

"I love that song, but you butchered it."

"Sorry."

"But I have to admit that's the first time I ever seen that pickup line."

"Did it work?" Punky asked.

"I'm afraid you wasted your time. I have a date for tonight."

"Just my luck we ship out tomorrow. Could you break it?"

"Here he is now." She turned around and Punky was gone. Something about the Lieutenant made her heart skip a beat. Her body temperature went up several degrees. When their eyes had locked for a few minutes sparks flew between them. She turned to Paul her date, He didn't have any effect on her body. It cooled off fast. She wandered if she would ever see him again. She wanted to explore the feeling she had when their eyes locked. Just thinking about him made her body hot.

When Punky came back over to table Jerry had two girls with him. "Well what happened?"

"I crashed and burned."

"I told you it was a crazy idea besides redheads have a bad temper and are nothing but trouble."

"You are probably right." He drank his beer and tried to enjoy the rest of the night with the pretty girl next to him, but he couldn't get the redhead out of his system. The girls turned out to be married and he didn't want to get involved with them. He didn't want a husband to hunt him down and kick his ass. They left the club at midnight and went home.

"She had green eyes."

"Who had green eyes?"

"The redhead had green eyes."

"Punky you have to forget that girl and get on with your life."

The next morning they went to the ready room until time to fly out to the carrier. Commander Owens approached Punky and Jerry. He told Punky that a factory representative for the helicopter would be coming on the cruise with the squadron and he would be responsible for the person.

His name was Charlie Crow. Punky wanted to know why he would have to babysit the guy. Commander Owens didn't know since he received the order from the Commander of the Air Group. Airframes put a jump seat in your helicopter. The jump seat was located between the pilot and copilot just behind them over the Doppler well.

Punky grumbled, "Just what we needed a back seat driver."

"Hey don't forget you get to babysit him all of this, cruise."

"Somebody up there hates me. I got to go back to clean living."

They had their backs to the door. "Gentlemen, could you tell me where I could find Lieutenant Punky Wilson?" Punky knew that voice. He turned and was face to face with the redhead. He stared at her and she stared back. You they both said at the same time.

"Who wants to know?"

"I do, I'm Charlie Crow and I have been assigned to him for the cruise."

"I'll take the assignment off your hands," whispered Jerry.

"Forget it I got it covered."

When Punky finally found his voice, he said, "I'm Lieutenant Punky Wilson,I thought you were a man."

"Well as you can see I'm not a man."

"Yes ma'am you are a woman, but where did you get the name Charlie? How many people call you crow?"

"Her temper started to show, "Where did you get the name Punky? I guess your mother thought you were a punk."

"Now kids we got to get along, we will be spending a lot of time together," said Jerry.

Punky stared at her and she stared back. "Truce," He held out his hand. She looked at it like it was a snake, but finally she took it, "Truce." Charlie was in a skirt and blouse and had to get flight gear. Punky took her and got her flight gear issued. She changed into the flight gear.

It was time to preflight their helicopter. Punky walked to the flight line followed by Charlie and his crew. Punky was the better pilot so he had taken over the flight crew. The crew was doing a preflight while Charlie with a clipboard took notes.

"Are we doing it right?" asked Punky.

"I'll let you know if you don't."

"How come you think you're so superior?"

"Probably because I have more flight time and pilot time than all of you put together. I test flight these helicopters all the time. I look for problems before they happen."

They were staring at each other and the sparks were flying. Punky became hot all over and it wasn't from arguing with Charlie, the more they were together the more she turned him on. Charlie turned her back and kept taking notes. Something was happening and she didn't know what. Every time she looked at Punky her body became hot. She was going to have to learn to control her body before she did something stupid. She was out here to do a job not have a love affair. She had more knowledge of the SH-3A helicopter than anyone here. She was sure of that.

"Punky, are you a good pilot?"

"I can hold my own."

"My company thinks you are one very good pilot or one lucky one. The helicopter you saved they couldn't figure out how you could have done it. I also know you crashed an aircraft to save a pilot."

"The navy isn't too happy with me right now for destroying two of their aircraft."

"The helicopter wasn't your fault and you crashed the other plane to save a life."

"But I disobeyed orders, I was ordered to take the flight home. I was his wingman and I passed the job off to Jerry."

"You don't like to take orders do you?"

"Not if I think it is the wrong order."

"You are a maverick, aren't you?"

"Some people call me one."

"It's time to turn and burn, let's do it."

They loaded on board and Jerry called the tower for liftoff. They lifted off and headed west toward the carrier. When they reached the carrier Commander Owens called Punky and told him to take plane guard. He came around to the starboard side and cruised with the carrier at sixty feet.

Charlie was smart about aircraft, but she didn't know anything about a ship. She decided to bite the bullet and tell Punky. "I have a problem."

"What kind of a problem?"

"I don't know beans about a ship. Will you teach me?"

It caught him off guard he didn't think she would admit anything. "Sure why not. Just ask when you want to know something."

"Why are we out here?" She didn't waste time.

"We are here in case of a crash on landing the Air group. We are on angel duty."

They held their position until the Air Group was aboard and then Punky eased them, down on the flight deck. Charlie was excited about everything since this was the first time she had ever been on a ship. She stared out the window while Punky folded the rotary wing and cut the engines. "Why do the men have different color shirts?"

"Each color shirt is responsible for a job. Yellow is for aircraft handling Officers, catapult and arresting gear Officers and Plane directors. Green is for catapult, arresting gear crews, air wing maintenance personnel, air wing quality control personnel, cargo handling personnel, ground support equipment troubleshooters, hook runners, photographer mates, and helicopter landing signal enlisted personnel. Brown is for plane handlers, aircraft elevator operators, tractor drivers, messengers and phone talkers."

"Are there many more?"

"Only a few more, purple is for aviation they fuel the aircraft. Red is for ordnance men, crash, salvage crews, and explosive ordnance deposit. White is for squadron plane inspectors, landing signal Officer, air transfer Officer, liquid oxygen crews, safety observers and medical personnel. That's all of them. You got it?"

"You got to be kidding. I only remember a few."

"In time it will come natural from watching them work the flight deck. Ok it's time to find you a bunk and room to yourself. It may be a problem since you are the only woman onboard."

"Don't you have two bunks in your quarters?"

"Yes."

"Well I can bunk in your quarters. I did coed in college."

"I don't think the Navy will buy it." They left their gear in the forward ready room.

"Punky was able to get two cabins at the front of the ship. She was across the hall from Punky and Jerry. Her door had a lock on it. Nobody knew there was a woman aboard yet. Punky and Jerry changed into their uniforms while Charlie changed into a Skirt and blouse.

He noticed she liked to wear skirts and blouses over a dress. He asked her and she told him they was more practical for her job. She wore pants and a blouse when working on an aircraft.

Jerry and Punky escorted her to the Officer Mess and Punky got them cups of coffee. It took a few minutes to register on the rest of the men that they had a woman in their mists. The men surrounded them wanting to know how she got onboard. They thought she was a stowaway. Punky was jealous of the men and couldn't help it. Charlie could see in it in his eyes and enjoyed it. She didn't understand why, but she liked to see him squirm in his seat.

She could see more than lust in his eyes and it scared the hell out of her. She became hot every time he was near her. He was very protective of her. Was he just doing his job by taking care of her? She didn't think so. It was more personnel.

She tried to talk with other men, but she kept looking back at him. Every time they locked eyes sparks flew. Her body became hot and she could see images of Punky and her together naked.

She had to get back in control. One of the men was talking to her and she didn't know a word he said. He asked her something twice before she came out of the fog she was in. Punky was grinning at her and she could kill him.

For some unknown reason Charlie was attracted to Punky. She didn't want to be, but she couldn't seem to shake off her feelings. She knew it couldn't be love could it? She didn't believe in the love at first sight so maybe it was lust for his body, it had to be it. He did have a great body. She could deal with that just keep her eyes off him.

Charlie felt cold, Punky had left the table. She realized she could sense when he came near her. Punky had left her to the wolves, but he couldn't baby sit all the time. He went to the ready room to check the flight schedule. He had a flight at eight the next day.

Punky went back to his room, but left the door open. Jerry was gone, probably to a movie. A short time later, Charlie came to her room escorted by two Officers. He stuck his head out and told her he had a flight and was she going on the flight? Yes she was going. Her two escorts left, Punky and Charlie were alone. He didn't want her to see he was jealous, but his voice was sharp and she picked up on it.

Charlie smiled as she went into her room. She liked the fact that Punky was jealous. She stripped and got ready for bed. Then she remembered she didn't know the flight time. She had on silk pajamas that showed all her curves and nipples. She started to put on a robe, but changed her mind. She knew she was playing with fire, but what did it hurt to tease a little.

She knocked on his door and he opened the door. Her breath caught in her throat. He didn't have anything on but shorts. He was just as shocked seeing her. He didn't expect to see her at his door. They stood staring at each other. Her nipples pushed at the material and Punky had an instant erection and turned away from her, but not before she seen what was happening. "What can I do for you?"

"I forgot to ask what time our flight takes off."

"Eight o'clock tomorrow morning. Be in the ready room at seven."

"Thanks." She started to leave, but couldn't help teasing him. Why do you have your back to me?"

"I have a big problem."

"You know what it is. Do you want to see what you do to me?"

Before she could think she blurted out, "Yes I would."

Punky turned around and stood with a big hard on. Yes he did have a big problem. She stared at the erection for a moment and fled back into her room.

CHAPTER FOUR

Charlie closed the door and leaned against it. She was embarrassed to death. She couldn't believe what she had said and stared at the results. What must he think of her? He probably thought she makes it with every man with pants on. She hadn't been with a man since she broke up with her boyfriend about a year ago. She didn't sleep to good she was still seeing images of Punky and her naked together. She realized she was wet down below. Dam that man.

After Charlie left Punky took a cold shower to cool off. It didn't help much, but he finally went to sleep dreaming about Charlie. It was a XXX dream.

The next morning she wouldn't look at him. They went on the flight deck and did a preflight. When the order came they lifted off. They took a screen position on the port side behind the carrier. McDaniel went active on sonar and searched for a submarine.

Punky explained what they were doing. Charlie knew the helicopter, but didn't know anything about sonar and how they used it. She asked questions and finally relaxed. If Punky didn't bring up last night she wouldn't either.

"Pilot sonar I have a target bearing 085 degrees, 500 yards, speed 10 knots and going away from us."

"Pilot sonar stay on him."

"Pilot sonar I lost him sir. Last contact 550 yards, 085 degrees, speed 15 knots."

"Sonar pilot he knows we know he is there, up sonar."

Another helicopter dipped his sonar close to the last contact. He got a contact. An S-2E aircraft flew over and got a positive mad contact. Another helicopter dipped close to the submarine. Punky was told to get ready for a drop on the submarine. McDaniel and Morgan went to the back to prepare for a bomb run. Charlie was excited watching them preform their chase.

Punky lined up on the submarine and made a run over him while another helicopter gave the coordinates.

"Sonar, pilot, drop, drop, drop."

"Pilot sonar drop away."

While they waited for the submarine to give the signal for a kill Punky explained the drop was a smoke, p. d. c. and smoke. The smokes were to mark the drop of the p. d. c. He told her the p. d. c. was a small bomb used for training.

"Well Charlie how did you like our submarine chase?" asked Punky.

"It was, exciding, reminding me of a foxhunt. The fox being the submarine and all your forces are the dogs."

"Sometimes we yell tally ho there goes the fox. Then the hunt is on."

The submarine finally gave the signal he was sunk. That made the crew happy for a job well done. The Bennington tower called and told Punky to remain with the submarine. It was going to surface and needed them to do a personal transfer.

The submarine came to the surface and cruised ahead at 10 knots. Punky circled around to the starboard side and to the rear of the submarine. He would approach at an angle and hover over the submarine while they both were moving.

"Sonar pilot what do you think?"

"Pilot sonar the seas are rough, let me talk you in." McDaniel and Morgan put on a gunner's belt and slid the back hatch open.

"Pilot sonar forward, forward, easy forward, easy right, hold steady, hold, hoist going down, steady, steady, hoist down, easy right, hold steady, man is in the sling, hoist is coming up, easy forward, easy forward, you are clear of the submarine, hoist up, man onboard, hatch closed."

"Sonar pilot job well done, Strap our guest in and let's go home."

"Pilot sonar guest strapping in."

McDaniel dropped the bench seat in the back and strapped the Sailor in. Punky turned the helicopter toward the carrier. Punky glanced around at Charlie did you enjoy your flight?"

"Yes very much, it was very exciting. I have flown a lot of hours, but I have never hovered over water or made a pickup from a moving ship. T would love to fly and do the things you do."

"No problem the next time we go out, I'll ride the jump seat and you can be the pilot."

"Good I would love it."

Punky was the last aircraft to land. He eased the helicopter down close to the island. The Plane gave him the signal for a hot refuel and the aircraft turning and burning.

They exited the helicopter and went into the island as another crew took control of the helicopter. Charlie asked, "What was that all about?"

"They are short on birds for the next launch so they fuel it and launch again."

Punky and crew went to the ready room for debriefing. They stored their gear and checked the flight schedule. They had a flight for the next day. They were scheduled to fly holy helicopter also pick up and deliver mail. It would be a full day.

"It's going to be a long day tomorrow," said Jerry.

"Punky glanced at Charlie, "You going with us?"

"You bet I am, I wouldn't miss it for the world. How many drops and pickups are there?"

"We drop and pick up the Chaplin from all the ships in the convoy. We do the mail at the same time."

"Well now we know our schedule let's get something to eat."

"I'm with you."

They went to the Officers mess for chow. As usual the wolves were out, but Charlie didn't say much to them. She liked being with

Punky. After they ate they went up in the island and watched flight operations. The catapults were busy launching aircraft. Two A-4B aircraft were launched first, followed by four S-2E aircraft. After the launch was complete it was time to recover the flights that were out. The arresting crew was busy now. Punky explained how the mirror landing system worked, also how the arresting cable caught the tail hook and stopped the aircraft. He also showed her the barrier system used if an aircraft had problems like a broken tail hook and the barrier would be used to stop the plane.

"Charlie, do you know what they call a carrier landing?"

"No I'll bite."

"They call it a controlled crash."

"Why?"

"You come in so fast and they stop you before you crash."

She laughed, "I think you are making it up."

"Honest would I lie to you?"

"To get what you want I think you would." Now where did that come from?

"And what do you think I want?"

She could lie, but for some reason she didn't. "You want to make love to me." She couldn't believe she said that.

"You are absolutely right I dream about us naked and making love."

Charlie stared at Punky and sparks flew. "So do I, I don't want to, but it happens."

"We will make love sooner or later, you know it will happen."

"It could get complicated."

Punky wanted to kiss her and make love to her, but this wasn't the place. He followed her to her quarters. At the door she turned, Punky opened his arms and she walked into them. She knew she shouldn't do it, but when she thought no her body said yes. After a long hot kiss she pushed at his chest. She turned around and opened the door. Glancing over her shoulder, "I'll see you later," she promised.

"This isn't over."

"It is for now I have some thinking to do."

She shut the door and leaned against the back of the door trembling. It was all Charlie could do to keep from dragging Punky in her room and having her way with him. She would have to take a cold shower to cool off. Wasn't that what men did to cool off? She giggled as she decided to take that shower.

She went to the head where the showers were located. Head is the name for bathroom in the Navy. When she reached for the door handle the door was locked. A moment later she startled when Punky came out the door with only a towel around his waist. "Well I see someone else is hot also."

"I was not hot I wanted a shower after our flight." she lied.

"Yeah I needed a shower to."

"You are a liar."

"Now Charlie you know I wouldn't lie to you."

She kept watching the towel, she liked his hard muscled body, but she was watching to see if the towel raised, up. It did and she giggled, she knew he had a hard on. "You had better take another cold shower."

"I will if you will take it with me."

"Not on your life," she giggled and shut the door in his face.

Punky went back to his room. He couldn't understand Charlie he knew she wanted him so what was the problem? Was she a virgin? No she had been around the block too many times. Maybe she didn't play around. She was probably the marrying kind. He would have to control his body because he wasn't the marrying kind. It was easy to say, but his body still wanted her in the worst way.

Charlie took her shower, but it didn't cool her off. She was a good one to give Punky advice, maybe she should take another shower, but she knew you only use enough water to soap up and rinse off or the ship would be on water hours. She heard the enlisted head didn't have a lock on it and the Master at Arms patrolled the showers to make sure too much water wasn't used. If they wrote someone up for using too much water they were sent to the bilge's to clean them. They were in the bottom of the hull. She finished her shower and went back to her room. She lay naked on the bed and touched her nipples. They were hard and she knew why, Punky. What to do about him, She didn't want to have an affair. Did she? Was she in love with him, yes, no, she didn't know. She knew she loved being around him. Was that love? She dozed off dreaming the same dream her and him naked making love.

They didn't have to go to briefing since they were the only one flying on Sunday. Punky and Jerry were doing a preflight when Charlie arrived at the helicopter. McDaniel and Morgan were loading mailbags marked by ship's names. The Chaplain stood by the steps waiting to launch. When they were loaded they took their places and prepared for liftoff. Charlie was in the pilot seat and Punky was in the jump seat. The Chaplain was strapped in the bench seat in the back.

Jerry called for liftoff, "Bennington tower holy helicopter request liftoff."

"Holly helicopter Bennington tower you are clear for liftoff. Have a nice day."

"Bennington tower holly helicopter roger."

Charlie lifted off smooth and headed for the first destroyer. It was located on the starboard side of the carrier way out in front. Charlie told McDaniel and Morgan to get ready for a transfer. McDaniel talked her in. Morgan lowered the Chaplain, lowered the mail and picked up the outgoing mail.

They flew around dropping and picking up mail while the Chaplain held services on the first destroyer. They flew back and picked the Chaplain up and dropped him on another destroyer. They flew back to the ship and unloaded mail. They went to the ready room and had coffee. They rested awhile until time to pick up the Chaplin and transfer him again. They repeated the pattern until the Chaplain had held services on all the ships in the convoy. Charlie was a pro by the time they finished the flight.

"You done great today, you are an excellent pilot," Punky praised her.

"Sugar and spice won't get you anything," she giggled.

"You can't blame a guy for trying."

They went to the ready room and stored their gear. A note on the bulletin board read all the flight crews to draw weapons from now on. Charlie wanted to know why. Punky told her it was for signal purposes, they loaded their 38 pistol with tracers. If they went down and got out of the plane they could fire tracers to signal for help.

It had become a habit for Charlie to follow Punky where he went except when they went to bed. She wanted to do that, but common sense told her she was a fool to get involved with Punky. She thought he was a find um, make um, leave um kind of guy. She knew he would break her heart. She was tired of the same dream every night her and Punky naked making love. She was about to let him do it then maybe she could get a good night's sleep.

They had the same routine every day, eat together and part company at their doors. Sometimes they went to the island and watched flight operations. Punky had finally quit trying to make out with her. She felt hurt that he gave up, but wasn't that what she wanted him to do. She missed his flirting with her. He may have quit flirting, but his eyes still had passion and she knew he still wanted her.

After eating, Punky walked her to her cabin. "You know we are pulling into Hawaii tomorrow."

"Yes I saw it on the bulletin board."

"How would you like to paint the town with me?"

"I would like it very much. Have you been here before?"

"No it's my first time over. We'll have to get pointers from McDaniel and Morgan. They have been here before and all the other countries that we are going to."

"I always wanted to come to Hawaii, but never could afford it. Now here I am."

"Well I guess I'll see you tomorrow." Punky turned and went into his cabin.

Charlie felt cold as she went into her own cabin. When she was with Punky she was on fire, but as soon as he was gone the fire went out. Was she bold enough to invite him to her cabin for coffee or a coke maybe more. A little voice said not to get involved, but her body wanted him to touch her. She went to the head and showered then put on her thin silk pajamas. She made up her mind she was going to live dangerously. She knocked on his door and he opened it. He only had his shorts on again.

"Would you like to come over for coffee or a coke? It's too early to go to bed."

"Like I'm dressed?"

Her face flushed, "That's up to you."

"Then I'll come as I am."

She turned and went back into her cabin with Punky right behind her. He locked the door behind him. She heard the door lock, but didn't say anything. She knew now she was living dangerous. She stood with her back to him trying to calm her nerves. Punky said, "Are you going to turn around?"

"I will when I get my nerve back. You don't have any clothes on."

"Those silk pajamas you are wearing don't leave much to the immigration. You have a cute rear end."

Shocked she turned around, big mistake she was staring at the front of his shorts. The shorts were poked way out in front. Punky had a big hard on. He grinned at her as he walked over and put his arms around her. She couldn't move like a deer caught in a high beam on a car. He covered her mouth with his pulling her tighter against him. She could feel his erection against her belly as he moved against her body. He touched her teeth with his tongue and she opened to him. He plunged his tongue deep in her mouth until he heard her moan. Punky placed her hand on the front of his shorts.

"Touch me I want to feel your hands on me, feel what you are doing to me."

Her face flushed as she pushed his shorts down and put both hands around his shaft. "Like this," she stroked him softly. Her heart hammered against her ribs.

"Oh yes," his face looked like she was hurting him.

She felt him throbbing in her hand and he moaned. "Am I hurting you?"

"Stop I can't take it any longer or I'll come all over you. I want to be inside you."

Charlie stared into his eyes as he unbuttoned her top. Punky put his hands on her hard nipples and gently pulled her toward him. He took one nipple in his mouth and sucked on it. Charlie put her hands in his hair and pulled him to her. She was on fire. She trembled against him and arched toward his erection. She could feel his aroused penis touching her folds through the silk. Little above a whisper she said, "Take me now I want you inside me. I'm burning up."

"Your wish is my command." He reached down and pulled her pajama bottom down to her feet. He teased her by touching his erection to her folds. "Tell me what you want."

A loud alarm went off, "General quarters, general quarters, man your battle stations. This is a drill, general quarters, general quarters, man your battle stations."

Punky screamed, "Dam, dam, not now."

"What's going on?"

"Put your clothes on and meet me outside. It's a drill and we have to go to the ready room."

Punky went to his cabin and jerked his clothes on then met Charlie outside. They rushed to the ready room and put on their flight gear. They had the ready helicopter and had to man it on the flight deck. The rest of the flight crews stayed in the ready room. If it was the real thing they would launch first and take plane guard position. They would launch the attack aircraft A-4B first. They would do anything to protect the carrier.

By the time the drill was over they were tired. They went back to the ready room, stored their gear and had coffee. It was late by the time Charlie and Punky got back to their cabins. "You were saved by the bell."

"Yeah I guess I was," She giggled.

"Wait until next time."

"I'll look forward to it," she smiled and shut the door.

Punky was mad, the mood had been broken just when he knew she as moist and ready for him, but duty comes before pleasure. He remembered how beautiful she was standing before him naked. He had that funny feeling again that sex wasn't the only thing he wanted from Charlie. He wanted more like waking up with her by his side every day. He didn't think she would like to hear that. She liked being single and he didn't think she would sleep around so where did that leave them? He didn't have a clue.

Charlie stripped off naked and lay in bed for a long time. She was more confused than ever. Would she have gone all the way with Punky? Was she in love with him? If she let him touch her she was lost. Her body was still passion heated. She touched her folds with her finger and moaned. She was wet and ready. She lay in bed and stared at the ceiling until exhaustion took her. Her last thought was Punky made her feel so good.

Punky knocked on her door. She came to the door to find him in dress whites. "Are you going to a party?" she teased.

"No party just flight deck parade going into Pearl Harbor."

"That sounds like fun."

"Believe me it's not fun. You are on your feet all the way in at attention most of the time. You can go up in the island and watch the scenery as we go in."

"I'll see you later."

Punky was in charge of a group of sailors and got them lined up facing the shore on the Pearl Harbor side. They steamed in past the Arizona Memorial with tugboats to escort them into the dock. A Harbormaster came out to direct them in. Two tugboats pushed the carrier up against the dock.

The carrier was secured to the dock. The carrier had a detachment of marines aboard and they were responsible for security of the carrier.

Charlie met Punky on the flight deck and they walked around sightseeing. The flight deck was around sixty feet off the water and you could see a long ways. The scenery was beautiful in all directions.

"The scenery is beautiful."

Punky hadn't noticed he was too busy watching Charlie. She had on a skirt and blouse. He could smell her perfume and woman scent. He wanted to finish what they had started, but he said, "Are you ready to paint the town?"

"When can we get off the ship?"

"As soon as they get the gangways up and security set."

"Are you going ashore in uniform?"

"No I'm going to change into civilian clothes. I'll meet you at the forward gangway." Charlie waited while Punky changed clothes and met her at the forward gangway. The Officers used the forward gangway. They exited the ship and there were hula girls to greet them with orchard lays to go around their necks. They walked around Pearl Harbor before catching a bus to downtown Waikiki.

They got off the bus a block from Waikiki beach. Charlie wanted to walk down to the beach before they went anyplace else. The sun was shining, the sand was white and the water was a deep blue. They sat on the beach watching people swimming, surfing and riding boats with outriggers not to mention the girls in skimpy swimsuits. Charlie punched him in the side, "Stop ogling all the girls."

"The way I figure it is if they are advertising you should check it out."

"If I was wearing one of those skimpy swim suits would you ogle me?"

"I would do a lot more if you let me."

Her body caught fire, "Would you?" she teased.

Punky reached over and pulled her onto his lap. She started to protest, but he covered her mouth with his and she melted against him. She shouldn't be doing this, but her arms went around his neck of their own accord and deepened the kiss.

Punky pulled back, "We better stop or I'll want to make love to you right here on the beach."

"We could pretend that we are the only ones on the beach," Charlie giggled.

"Somehow I don't think the Police or Shore Patrol will buy it."

"In that case let's go do some sightseeing."

They went back to the main street and walked up and down it. There were flowers and palm trees plus girls in swim suits everywhere. The people staying in the plush hotels walked to the beach in their swimsuits. It was warm and walking they worked up a thirst. They came to the International Marketplace and decided to go in a tearoom before the outdoor show started.

They came out just as the show started. The girls danced the Polynesian dance first. Then they danced telling a story with their body. A man with sharp knife's danced and put everyone on the edge of their seat. Then the clown act started. A man with a loincloth on started to take it off in front of the crowd. He worked it off to the music until he held it in front of him in front of the crowd. The women, including Charlie was on the edge of their seats waiting for him to drop the cloth. He made like he was losing it, but pulled it back in place. The women groaned they were disappointed they wanted to see it all.

"I saw you ogling that man."

"I was not I just wanted to see him drop the loincloth. It would be funny."

"And you would have turned your head if he dropped it?"

"Yes I would," she lied.

They did several more dances, fast dances with men and women telling a story. Most dances always told a story. The men and women showed a lot of skin when they danced. At the end of the show a man climbed a tree and dropped orchard lays on the crowd. The girl would put a flower above her ear. One side meant she was taken, the other ear meant she was available. Punky didn't know which ear was which so he put the lay around Charlie's neck and kissed her.

"That was fun, let's find something else to do," said Punky.

"I'm hungry, how about you?"

"Ok, but let's go to the Army Fort, it will be a lot cheaper."

They found the Officer's mess and ate a big dinner. They had steak, baked potatoes and a salad. They had tea to drink.

Charlie glanced at Punky, "I'm stuffed that was good."

"Anything free is always good."

"How come we don't have to pay?"

"I'm military and you are my guest."

"Good, now we have more money to spend on a club."

"Right, let's find a good club."

They found a club on down the beach and went inside. It was crowded, but they were lucky enough to get a table. They put on a big show with Polynesian dancers. Punky loved to watch them shake their hips to the music. Charlie was watching Punky while he was watching the dancers." You really like to watch the girls dance."

"I'm always fascinated at how fast they move their body, especially their hips."

"You're wandering, how it would feel to have her on top of you and moving those hips."

"No, I wasn't," he lied and she knew it.

"I wander if I could move that fast?" she teased.

"There's only one way to find out."

"I was just teasing."

"I'm not."

Charlie stared into his eyes seeing nothing but passion and looking at his fly she knew he had a big hard on. Was she the cause or was it the dancers? She was hot, but didn't want him to see the effect he had on her. "I'm sorry."

"Why are you?"

"For getting you turned on."

"You are hot too." He touched her knee and eased his hand under her skirt. Her skin was burning up. The show ended and a live band took to the stage. It had a big band sound and they didn't like it, but it changed to rock and roll. They played all kind of music. All you had to do was, wait until what you wanted played. Charlie wanted to dance to a rock and roll number so Punky went out on the floor and they kicked up their heels. Tired they set the next two out.

A flashy blonde came over to their table. She was a no brainer with lots of money and looked down her nose at Charlie. Her clothes probably cost more than Charlie made in three months. She asked if she could dance with her boyfriend. Charlie said he wasn't her boyfriend and he could do what he wanted. Punky didn't like the way the blonde treated Charlie. "Sure I would like to dance with a beautiful woman like you."

As he got up from the table she draped her arm on his. She turned and smiled back at Charlie. When they walked away, Charlie stuck her tongue out at their backs. She couldn't believe Punky was dancing with that rude woman. She was mad as a wet hen. She would get even with him if it was the last thing she did.

"You are a gorgeous man. You could do better than that."

"What did you have in mind?"

"You could come to my hotel room and we could get to know one another."

"I am responsible for her on this cruise and I can't leave her."

"You are a Navy Officer?"

"Oh goodie, bring her along and she can watch."

Punky could see him telling Charlie she could watch. He knew she was mad already. They were dancing a slow number and she was all over his body. She bumped and grinned into him smiling inviting further intimacies. Charlie was fit to be tied, if looks could kill Punky and the woman would be dead.

The song stopped, but she still hung onto him. She wanted to dance another number which turned out to be a fast one. Punky was swinging her and let her fingers slip through his hand. He smiled, "oops."

She went back across a table with her legs in the air and showing off her black panties. She had food and drink all over her when she finally got off the table.

"You did that on purpose."

"Now honey you know I wouldn't do a thing like that."

"Yes you would." She stormed out of the club.

Punky went back to the table to face the music. Charlie was laughing so hard she had tears in her eyes. She was mad, but couldn't stop laughing. She thought about what happened and remembered seeing the boys in school pull the same stunt.

"Punky you did that to that poor girl on purpose."

"Guilty as charged, after the way she was rude to you I couldn't help myself."

"What did you talk about?"

"Are you sure you want to know?"

"Yes I'm sure it has to be juicy."

"She offered me her body, but I told her I couldn't leave you so she said you could come and watch us while we made love."

"You're lying you wouldn't have turned that girl down."

"No I didn't, but after what happened she didn't like me anymore."

Charlie started laughing again, "Poor baby."

"Does that mean you will take her place?"

"Not on your life tonight, let's dance this slow number."

While they were dancing Charlie rubbed her body all over him until he groaned. She was having fun turning Punky on. She could feel his erection against her belly and arched against him. Punky moaned in her ear, "Stop that I can't take it anymore."

"You didn't tell the blonde to stop."

"She wasn't having the effect on me you are."

She smiled at that remark. She had to stop teasing because by teasing him her body was hot and she could feel her juices starting to flow. They went back to their table and had a couple more drinks. Drinks were very high and eat up your money fast.

They left the club and just walked around. It was pretty like being in paradise. They would have to find a place for the night or go back to the ship. Punky didn't want to go back to the ship. They were both starting to feel their drinks. They didn't want to spend all their money on a hotel room.

"I know what you are thinking we should have gone with the blonde to her hotel."

"No I'm not," he lied. It would have been fun with two women.

They finally decided to go to the Fort and get a room. She would have to sleep in a woman's dorm and him in a man's dorm, but it was real cheap. Both of them had slept in dorms in college so it wasn't too bad. Punky wanted to spend the night with Charlie. He wanted her real bad and he knew she wanted him just as bad, but hotels cost an arm and a leg. Punky kissed her and they went to their separate dorms. He was off tomorrow and he wanted them to see as much as possible. He had duty the following day.

The dorms weren't so bad if you could stand the snoring. Punky met Charlie in front of dorm ready to get breakfast. They ate a big breakfast at the Officer's mess and took off sightseeing. Punky rented a jeep and they headed out of Waikiki toward Mountain Diamond Head. They stopped at Blow Ho and watched the water spout coming up through the hole in the rocks. He drove around the edge of the island keeping the water in sight. He drove to the far side where big waves crashed upon the beach.

There were surfers trying to ride the huge waves. There were a few that could ride them all the way back to shore. This was one of the places used for surfing composition.

There was a mountain backdrop with small waterfalls running down the side of the mountain. Everything was green and flowers of every variety were everywhere. Punky drove the jeep up the mountain over-looking the ocean. They got out and looked at the view. Where he parked orchards grew wild everywhere. Charlie was thrilled as she watched the ocean wave's crash upon the beach. Punky liked to watch Charlie sometimes she was like a little kid.

"Isn't it beautiful?"

"Yes it is." Punky was looking at her rear end.

She turned and caught him watching her. She blushed as she realized what he was looking at. She looked at his fly and her face turned red. He had a big erection that was straining to get out of his pants. Punky didn't say a word as he opened his arms to her. She hesitated just a moment before she walked into his arms. He pulled her tight against his hard body. She ran her fingers through his hair. He picked her up and kissed her thoroughly before letting her slide down his body. His erection slid down the apex of her thighs and pushed at her belly.

"When are we going to make love?"

"Punky I don't know I still think it could be complicated."

"You know it will happen sooner or later so don't fight it."

"Have you ever ridden the waves?"

"Which wave?"

"The wave you have sex with."

"He decided to tell the truth, "Yes I have had sex with a few."

"And before you came in the Navy?"

"Yes I had sex a few times, but I have never wanted a woman as bad as I want you."

"That's nice to know."

"What is this, twenty questions? I have a few of my own."

"Are you a virgin?"

"No I lost my cherry in High School."

"Have you had sex lately?"

"Not in a long time."

Punky finally let her go before he took her right there on the ground with cars passing by to see them. They both were breathing hard and trembling. He led her back to the jeep and helped her get in. He pulled out on the highway which ran through the countryside.

When they got back to Waikiki Punky turned in the jeep. They found a place that had a lou-ow. They sat on the ground and enjoyed the feast while girls in grass skirts danced to a fast drum beat. Charlie punched Punky in the ribs. "You are ogling girls again."

"If you would dance for me like that I wouldn't have to watch the other girls."

"I think you are turning into a horny old man."

"Horney yes, old no."

They left the lou-ow and decided to go to Honolulu. They went by bus. They shopped and walked all over Honolulu. Last stop was a club which turned out to be a strip joint. Punky enjoyed the show, but Charlie was ready to go back to the ship. They were very tired by the time they got off the bus and walked the rest of way back to the ship.

They kissed and went to their own cabins. It had been a fun two days, but Punky still hadn't made love to Charlie. Hawaii was a beautiful place to visit, but who could afford to live there. Punky had seen most of the island and it was time to move on to the next liberty port. The next port on the list was the Philippine Islands. Since this was his first time over every port was an adventure. He was really looking forward to Japan and Hong Kong.

Punky had been watching the news and didn't like it. The United States had advisors in South Vietnam and it was heating up there. He was worried that we would end up at war. North Vietnam was coming over their border and going further and further into South Vietnam. Why did countries always have to start wars?

Punky lay awake staring at the ceiling. It was time to get his mind off of things that he didn't have any control over.

Punky had Shore Patrol the next day and it turned out to be real boring. He hated to mess with a bunch of drunks unless he was drunk himself. Charlie went sightseeing with Jerry. Punky was jealous, but he wouldn't let Charlie see it. They were in port one more day. Punky and Charlie went to the Arizona Memorial and along the banks where at one time was called Battleship row. They strolled around Pearl Harbor all day.

The carrier pulled out of Pearl Harbor the next day and headed for the open sea. Punky found Charlie in a jumpsuit checking a helicopter on the hanger deck. Even with oil and grease on her she still looked beautiful. She was standing on the right engine platform with a flashlight. She glanced down and saw Punky.

"What are you doing up there?"

"The pilot complained that the controls were stiff. I'm checking out the hydraulic system. I don't want another helicopter to crash on my watch." "What are you looking for?"

"I'm still not sure. I think it is a valve sticking and shutting off the flow of fluid."

"Did the company ever find out what caused my crash?"

"No, but they think it was a sticking valve. They could never prove it. That's the reason I'm on the cruise to find the answer to the problem."

"Good luck, I'm going to check our flight schedule. You are still part of my flight crew?"

"Yes you are stuck with me the whole cruise unless I find the problem."

"See you later."

Punky went to the ready room. They were going to start around the clock operations. HS-8 would have four helicopters in the air at all times. It would be another war exercise. It was their job to protect the carrier at all cost. Their next launch was zero eight hundred the next day.

Punky came back to the hanger deck where Charlie was still working. She was inside in the broom closet. He looked inside and stared at her rear end. She was shifting back and forth trying to see. He just stood there watching and Charlie's body heated up. She knew Punky had to be close by. She turned and caught him watching her. "What are you doing?"

"I am enjoying the view."

"Is that all you do, don't you ever work?"

"Not unless I have to," laughed Punky.

"Well I'm through inspecting this bird."

"Did you find anything?"

"No, but I wish I did. I got to find out why the birds go crazy before someone gets hurt."

"Don't be so hard on yourself, you'll find the problem."

"What did you want?"

What he wanted was to take her to her cabin and make love, "I thought you might like to watch refueling at sea."

Charlie followed him to the flight deck. Hoses were stretched from a tanker to the carrier. The carrier took on fuel for the aircraft, destroyers and the carrier. They had cables between the ships and were swapping movies. The ship's band played while the fuel was being transferred. It was a Navy custom to serenade the other ship. When the transfer was complete the tanker pulled all the hoses back aboard and the transfer lines. They saluted as they pulled away from the carrier. As the tanker pulled away a destroyer pulled alongside and fired a cable across. Charlie watched with interest. "Now what are they doing?"

"The cable they fired across is attached to a hose which they will pull over for fueling."

"Why doesn't the tanker refuel the destroyer?"

"If you look in the distance you will see the tanker refueling a destroyer. The carrier will help. They kill too much time with the tanker doing all the refueling."

"Punky how about some coffee, I need some?"

"Ok."

They went down to the Officer's mess. Charlie had her hair pulled up under a cap and nobody noticed she was a woman. Punky liked her dressed like that. He had her all to himself. He told her their first launch was at zero eight hundred tomorrow. They were starting a battle exercise around the clock. She was confused, "I don't know military time."

"Sorry, eight o'clock tomorrow morning."

"What would eight o'clock tomorrow night be?"

"Eighteen hundred at noon is twelve hundred so add one hundred for every hour after that. "Midnight would be twenty four hundred and then you start over."

"Sounds easy enough I think I got it."

Charlie went back to checking helicopters. Punky wanted to help her, but she declined. She couldn't keep her mind on the job with him around. He played like it hurt his feeling, but she knew he was putting on a show.

Punky went to the Electronics shop to see how work was going. He wanted to pass the word to McDaniel what to expect in the following days. They visited for a long time.

"How come you and Morgan didn't go ashore in Hawaii?"

"We saved our money for Japan."

"But Hawaii was so nice."

"Yes, but Japan is cheaper. We save our money and take leave. We find a couple of girls to take with us while we tour Japan."

"You mean like tour guides?"

"You might say that," laughed McDaniel.

"I get it I guess I'm stupid."

"With the girls they take care of you and your money. They get the best price on everything. Did you know there are three prices on everything in Japan?"

"No tell me."

"The cheapest price is paid by the Japanese, the sailor and tourist pays the next price, but the Merchant Marine pays the highest price. He makes a good salary so they hit him the hardest. Don't ever pay what is marked on an item. You would be a fish if you do. Jew them down, they like to play the game."

"It's nice to know somebody that has been there."

"Be careful in all the countries they think sailors are easy to part with their money."

Punky left and went back to the Officer's mess hoping to catch Charlie and eat some dinner. He missed her so he ate dinner and went back to his room. He met Charlie in the passageway on her way back from a shower. She had on a short nightgown and was beautiful. Punky was staring and couldn't help it. She blushed at his passion filled eyes and his raised fly. She knew he wanted her badly, but was she ready to cave in and let Punky have his way with her. He opened his arms and she couldn't resist any longer. She went into his arms placing her arms around his neck. He put his arms around her waist and pulled her tight against him. She smelled of shampoo and her woman scent. Her heat burned Punky through his clothes.

"Not here, Punky." She took his hand and led him into her cabin.

Once inside Punky reached down and pulled her nightgown over her head. She stood naked before him and he stood there enjoying the view. She reached for his shirt buttons and had his shirt open. Punky bent over and took a nipple in his mouth sucking on it then moved over to the other nipple. He thought tonight is the night.

The loud alarm went off. "Man your battle station, man your battle station, this is a drill, man your battle stations."

"Not again this can't be happening again."

"Saved by the bell," giggled Charlie.

Punky waited while she dressed and they ran to the ready room. They didn't have the ready bird so they had a cup of coffee and sat down to wait until the drill was over. The Air group manned their spaces and the aircraft. The ship's crew manned everything else. All hatches were locked down during a drill or the real thing. If they took a hit only the area they were hit would take on water with all hatches closed. They were watertight hatches. The drill took a long time as usual because of the training. Play like damage was everywhere and damage control teams had to take care of it. Gun crews manned their guns and got them ready for battle. Everybody aboard ship was assigned a job to do. Aircraft on the flight deck were ready to launch. When the drill was over it was late. Punky and Charlie went back to their cabins. Punky was kissing Charlie at her door called a hatch.

Jerry walked by, "Knock off that you two unless you're going to share."

"Sorry old buddy, but you'll have to find your own woman."

"It's not fair she is the only woman on the ship."

"Sorry life isn't always fair."

Punky kissed Charlie and they parted, "Maybe next time."

"Maybe," she teased.

Punky and crew was at the briefing at zero seven hundred and in their helicopter ready to lift off at zero eight hundred. Punky lifted off first and had plane guard for the launch. He assumed plane guard until the launch was over. The flight leader called Punky and instructed him to fly around until someone got a contact. He would be the attack aircraft.

"Sonar pilot McDaniel come up here and take pilot."

"Pilot sonar roger that."

McDaniel came forward and took the pilot. Morgan moved over under the sonar console and Punky took his seat behind Charlie in the jump seat. He liked being behind her where he could watch her without her knowing g it. She glanced back at him. "I didn't know enlisted men could pilot an aircraft."

"They can't by Navy regulations, but you know me I'm a maverick."

"Then why do you do it?"

"Very simple, if I get hurt or Jerry gets hurt I have two pilots onboard to take the aircraft home."

"Doesn't anyone know you do it?"

"Some of the other pilots let their crewmen fly, but we keep it to ourselves."

"How long have you been doing this?"

"Awhile now, long enough that McDaniel or Morgan could bring us home if they had to."

"Why is the Navy set against it?"

"I don't know for sure and I don't care. I just care about my crew being safe."

After an hour, McDaniel and Morgan swapped places. Morgan flew pilot for an hour before Punky asked Charlie if she would like to finish the hop as pilot. She was all for it and wanted the practice. So far none of the choppers had any trouble, but Charlie kept inspecting them. She wanted to find out why the others crashed and wouldn't give up until she found the problem.

Their next flight was zero four hundred. The flight deck was dark and dangerous. You could be blown off the flight deck by aircraft, sucked into an engine or walk into a propeller. The insurance companies rated the flight deck as the most dangerous place in the military except combat. Punky took the lead out of the island with the rest of the crew following him. The only lights on the flight deck were the flight deck running lights. They performed a preflight with flashlights the best they could. Once they were turning and burning they had running and cockpit lights so it wasn't so bad.

Punky lifted off and followed the flight leader waiting for instructions. He was stationed on the starboard side forward of the carrier. They dropped their sonar for screening.

"It sure is dark out tonight," remarked Charlie.

"Yes it is," replied Punky, "I'm flying on instruments."

"Jerry, keep track of everyone we don't want to run over anybody."

"I am trying to mark them on the plotting board."

The weather turned bad and they flew into a rainstorm. The helicopter pitched and rolled. Punky had a hard time controlling the aircraft. When the flight was over the storm was still raging. He had a hard time landing, but his Plane Captain braved the weather to guide him in with lighted wands. Plane handlers on the flight deck did a fantastic job in any kind of weather.

Punky and crew made it to the ready room, but were like drowned rats. They got rid of their flight gear and made for the coffeepot. They were told during the storm a submarine got a hit on the carrier before being chased off. The submarine was hard to detect in bad weather.

A destroyer picked him up as he fired his first torpedo solution and was hot on his trail, but lost him in the nasty weather. Well he waited until the right moment to strike. Guess you couldn't win them all. It just showed no mater, how hard they tried to protect the carrier sometimes the bad guy got through the screen.

For the next four days they flew day or night and sometimes not much time in between flights. Punky and crew was getting exhausted and were sure glad when the training exercise was over. They finally got a good night's sleep. Now that all the hard work was over Punky had Charlie on his mind and back in his dreams. When he closed his eyes he saw Charlie and him naked and making love. He couldn't place where they were at while doing it.

Charlie was having the same dream and moaned in her sleep. She woke up hot and bothered. She still didn't want to get involved with Punky, but her body betrayed her every time she was near him. It would be fun to let go and do something crazy, but she was out here to do a job not have a love affair. Her body couldn't get the idea it wanted attention only Punky could give it. Charlie never felt anything around all the other men so why Punky? He was waiting to walk her to breakfast when she opened the door. There weren't any flight operations today. The ship was steaming toward their next liberty port. They were on their way to the Philippine Islands and would put in at Manila Bay.

The air raft carrier U.S.S. Bennington cruised onto Manila Bay with a full flight deck parade. The ship anchored out and everybody used a liberty launch to and from land. They were going to be there about three days. Punky decided to save his money for Japan and not go ashore. After Hawaii it wouldn't be much to see like going to Disney Land and then going to Six Flags. Punky told Charlie to go with Jerry if she wanted to go ashore, but she elected to stay onboard with him. He wanted her to stay, but he didn't want to hold her back if she wanted to go.

The Admiral and Captain wanted someone to fly them to Manila airport to meet their wife's, which had flown over to be with them. They were looking for a pilot and crew so Punky volunteered to be the pilot and Charlie said she would fly copilot. Punky went to the Electronic Shop and found a crewman that had duty. The Plane Captain prepared the plane for a special flight with the Admiral stars on the side. Slipcovers were put on the seats and curtains hung on the windows. Punky and Charlie pulled a preflight on the helicopter and sent the crewman to fetch the Admiral and Captain.

When the Admiral and Captain were onboard the crewman helped them get strapped in. The Plane Captain pulled the chocks and tie down chains. He held up the chains for Punky to count. He gave him the signal to lift off. Punky lifted off the port side and climbed to five hundred feet. He picked up a heading to the airport. It was a short flight. Punky called for clearance to land and was granted it. He sat down not far from the airliner the wife's were on. The crewman dropped the front hatch for the Admiral and Captain. A car was there immediately to pick them up. The crewman closed the hatch and strapped in. Punky lifted off and headed back to the carrier.

"Well that didn't take long," said Charlie.

"It gave us something to do and we can look things over from up here." They did some sightseeing on the way back. The Plane Captain was waiting on the flight deck to guide Punky in. He landed, folded the blades and shut down the engines. The Plane Captain took over from there. They went to the ready room and stored their flight gear.

Charlie glanced at Punky, "Are you hungry?"

"Starved let's get some lunch." They went to the Officer's mess.

They had fried chicken, mashed potatoes and gravy, corn-on-the-cob, plus too much more to mention. Punky said, "Good food and good sex go together."

"Sex wasn't on the menu."

"It should have been I would have had a double helping."

"You want to come to my cabin and see my etchings? Jerry went on liberty."

"Punky you don't even know what an itching is."

"No, but isn't that the line that gets the chick to come to his room?"

Charlie was nervous and having a hard time breathing. She was trying to play it cool and put Punky off, but her body wanted to be touched plus more. She knew she should put an end to things right now, but when their eyes locked she could see the heated passion in his eyes and her body melted. She couldn't move or talk. Punky got up from the table and held out his hand. She took his hand like she was in a trance and followed him to his cabin.

Punky pulled her into his arms and covered her mouth with his. He unbuttoned her blouse, letting it fall to the floor, unsnapped her bra and let it fall to the floor. He unbuttoned her skirt and let it fall to the floor. He picked her up and carried her over to his bunk easing her down on the bunk as he reached for her panties. She raised her hips so he could slide them off. Punky stood back and admired his handy work. Charlie blushed under the scrutiny and put her hand over the triangle of hair at the apex of her thighs. He got down on his knees, moved her hand over and touched her folds. She arched her hips toward his hand as he slid two fingers into her throbbing passion. She tightened her inner muscles around his fingers and arched her back. She thrashed her head from side to side.

"I want you in me now."

"The first time is for you. I want to touch you, taste you and watch your eyes as you climax."

Punky slid upon the bunk beside her, stroking her with his fingers, he put his mouth over a nipple and sucked on it. She was burning up, "I'm coming, I'm coming, I'm coming," and she came. Punky kept stroking her and she thought she would die of pure pleasure.

She was throbbing and trembling as Punky stood up and started taking off his clothes. He was down to his shorts when someone started banging on the hatch.

"Now what," this couldn't be happening again.

Charlie rolled off the bunk naked and hid behind the hatch as Punky cracked the hatch.

"What do you want?"

"Sir there's been an accident in the Electronics shop."

"What happened?"

"I don't know, I was told to get you since you are the Division Officer."

"I'll be right there."

Punky shut the hatch and turned to see Charlie putting on her skirt. He knew he could forget it for now. "I was going to say hold that pose, but I see it isn't going to happen."

"Sorry, but we almost got caught having sex."

"Was that what it was to you? I thought we were making love."

"Isn't it the same?"

"No I'll explain it later I got to go."

Punky arrived at the shop where two people from medical were working on the crewman that had gone with him on the flight. They said he was working on a transmitter and dropped a tool in the unit. He grabbed it trying to remove it, before it blew the transmitter. He got a bad shock and they were trying to revive him. Finally he moaned and opened his eyes. Punky was glad he was going to be ok so he could kill him for messing up his love life. They took the sailor to sick bay for observation for the rest of the day and night. Punky filled out a report for the accident. He left it on a clipboard so McDaniel could find it. He went to Officer's mess for coffee. He was very frustrated when he remembered what didn't happen. He should have jumped her bones as soon as they were in the cabin, but he wanted to make it a night she would never forget. Well she would never forget it they should have went to her cabin where she had a lock. Now she was really gun shy. He would have to work at it to get her back in his bed. Why was he so set on making love to Charlie?

He could get a woman as soon as he got to Japan so why was he so down in the mouth? Was he in love? Where did that thought come from? He had never felt like this before not even when he walked away from his girlfriend at home and joined the Navy.

Charlie flashed before his eyes and caused him to have a hard on. Was it a big case of lust or was there more to it. When he got to Japan he would find him a nice young girl, make love to her and find out about his feelings. If he were content after he would know it was a case of lust. His mind made up he went back to his cabin and tried to read a book. Charlie lay naked in her bed reliving what happened. How could she have been so foolish to let Punky take her to his room? It didn't have a lock on the door. Well they almost got caught and it wouldn't happen again. Her mind said it wouldn't happen again, but her body would do it anytime and anyplace. She was hot just thinking about Punky. Was she in love? Was it a case of lust? Maybe it was both. She was totally confused. She drifted off to sleep dreaming the same dream Punky and her naked making love.

The next day Punky decided to go to the beach to a ship's party. It would be a cheap day out. He asked Charlie to go with him and she accepted. They wore their swimsuits under their clothes and took a blanket to lie on. The liberty launch docked at a small pier. They walked along the beach for s short distance and joined the crowd. The ship had furnished the food and plenty of beer. The cook had a whole pig on a sip and was turning it over and over. Where had they got the pig? Knowing the sailors he wouldn't ask, just enjoy the meat.

Punky filled two plates with food while Charlie found a place to spread the blanket. He grabbed a couple of beers and returned to the blanket. Charlie had her hair pulled up under a cap and nobody had realized she was a girl. There were lots of Filipino girls that were invited to the party and the sailors were flirting with them.

Charlie glanced at Punky, "Why aren't you watching the girls?"

"I'm watching, but only one girl."

"Which one are you watching?" She knew he was watching her, but she wanted to hear him say it.

"You are the one I'm watching."

She blushed and felt her body heat up. Well so much for playing it cool. They had been here ten minutes and her body betrayed her already. She knew Punky could see her nipples straining at the material of her jumpsuit. She shifted sideways, but that gave him a better view. Punky teased, "If it makes you feel better look at the effect you are having on me."

She shyly looked at his fly and it was standing out. "Oh my, what have I done?" she giggled.

"You will pay for it if I can ever get you alone where we won't be disturbed."

"Promises, Promises."

"It would be fun to make love to you right now if we weren't in the middle of a crowd."

"I'm game if you are."

"Yeah right I can see us now and the Shore Patrol arresting us."

"Well we can go swimming," she pulled off her jumpsuit and cap.

Punky stared at the beautiful body before him. She had on a skimpy pink two piece swimsuit. He didn't like the looks the sailors were giving her, but it wasn't much he could do about it so he pulled off his clothes and joined her. They dove into a wave as they hit the water side by side. They were both good swimmers and swam out to deep water before turning back toward shore. When their feet touched bottom they stood up and Charlie walked into his arms. The water was cool, but when their bodies touched they were hot. Punky couldn't keep from kissing her if he wanted too, her body had melted against him. They were in the water up to their necks so Punky could play with her body. He slid a hand under her top and played with a nipple until she moaned in his ear. She had her arms around his neck and clung to him. She jumped up and clamped her legs around his waist. Punky with his other hand reached down and slid his hand in her swimsuit and touched her folds. She arched toward his hand so he slid a couple of fingers onto her heated body.

Punky looked into her eyes as he brought her to an orgasm. She clung to him until all after effects wore off. She was as contented as a cat with a bowl of milk. She nibbled on his lips before kissing him hard.

"You can enter me if you want to."

"Are you sure?"

"Yes you are always making me feel good it's your turn." She slid down his body.

She slid his swimsuit down to his knees. She took the length of him in her hand and began stroking him softly. When he had a rip roaring hard on Charlie jumped back up and locked her legs around his waist. She had her arms locked around his neck.

"Now slide my suit over a little and as I lower myself guide yourself in."

"Like this," he entered her as she lowered herself on his erection.

"Yes, yes, yes," she took all of him.

"You are so tight and it feels so good." She was not moving giving herself time to adjust to his size.

"It's been a long time since I've love so take it slow until I stretch to accommodate you. You are so big, but it feels good."

Punky took it slow, but it was killing him. His erection was throbbing and he knew he couldn't hold back much longer. Charlie started to move up and down on him. She had finally adjusted to his size. He bit his tongue to keep from yelling how good it was.

She moved higher up his body and slammed down hard taking him deeper each time. She had a death grip around his waist with her locked legs. Suddenly she could feel a spasm coming and squeezed his manhood until Punky groaned in her ear.

"You're killing me."

"Good at least you should die happy."

"I'm coming, I can't hold back any longer."

"Do it I'm coming along with you." She felt him throbbing deep in her body.

Punky kissed her and ran his tongue deep into her warm mouth while he came. Charlie clung to him trembling from her climax. They stood there locked together for a long time before Punky pulled out and let her feet touch the ground. He pulled his pants back up.

"Punky that was fantastic I've never enjoyed making love as much as this time."

"We were good together and practice makes perfect," he grinned at her.

"Well don't get your hopes up. You know how hard it is for us to have time alone."

"Yeah right, I can't believe we made love our first time neck deep in the ocean."

"I'm hungry after all that exercise."

They swam back to shore and dried off. They both ate a big plate of food to get their strength back. The beach party lasted into the night. Fires were built and Punky brought more beer for them as they sat on their beach towel. Punky noticed couples leaving and going off into the darkness.

"I see some of the Sailors are getting lucky," giggled Charlie.

"I guess we should have waited until dark before making love."

"You can forget it if you are thinking what, I think you are thinking."

"You want to sneak off into the darkness and make love again?"

"No I can't."

"Can't or won't do it."

"Can't you were big and now I'm too sore to move must less make love."

"Then I'll take a rain check."

"You are cocky and sure of yourself."

CHAPTER FIVE

The Aircraft Carrier U.S.S. Bennington cruised out of Manila Bay and set a course in the direction of Japan. It would start round the clock operations again on the way to Japan. They had to contend with Russian submarines and planes trying invade the convoy. Punky and crew had a flight at zero eight hundred the next morning.

Punky's flight lifted off and they were assigned screen starboard and forward of the carrier. The next three days were quiet and routine flights. Punky missed taking Charlie into his arms and making love, but it was work time now. Playtime would come later. Sailors worked hard and then played hard.

"Jerry what kind of ship is that?" asked Punky.

"Let me look it up."

"Did you find it?"

"No, but I think it is a Russian intelligence gathering ship. See all the antennas on the main part of the ship."

The ship was smaller than a destroyer with a shiny wood deck and was fast. Punky flew in for a better look. They were in the middle of the fleet. Jerry called the carrier to report the ship.

"Bennington tower 05 we have an unknown ship in the middle of our fleet. They are not flying a flag, but we think it is a Russian spy ship."

"05 Bennington tower roger your message."

"This is the Admiral get that son of a bitch out of my fleet now."

Jerry glanced at Punky, "You heard what the man said, but he didn't say how."

"Then let's have some fun." Punky turned the helicopter on a collision course with the ship.

"What are you doing?"

Punky glanced at Jerry and Charlie, "Did you ever play chicken?"

"Yes but the ship is so much bigger than us."

Punky stayed on collision course until the last second before he turned off to the right. He came around for another run, but hung back. A destroyer had turned and was on a collision course with the Russian ship. The Russian ship saw the destroyer coming and turned tail and ran. Punky and the destroyer chased the Russian ship until he was far away from the fleet.

"This is the Admiral, I like the quick way you think, the pilot of the helicopter and the destroyer skipper thanks for a job well done."

"Well guys, wasn't that fun?" asked Punky.

"Pilot sonar did you see the gun mount on the rear of the ship that was trained on us as we flew away from the ship?"

"Punky stared at Jerry as a matter of fact we didn't see any guns." That ruined their fun.

They were glad the ship didn't open fire on them. The game they played could have got sticky. The Russian ship could have said they were under attack and was defending themselves. It could have turned into a national incident. The cold war got sticky at times.

"Pilot crew watch out for more Russian ships or planes. Sonar, keep a close watch for sonar contacts. We won't know if we have a Russian submarine or American. We will treat all contacts as unknown until we can identify them. We will make attacks on all contacts."

They made three attacks on contacts that day, but not one gave the signal they were sunk which led them to believe they were Russian and didn't know how to play the game. They took off when they were bombed.

A Russian Bear flew close to the fleet and three A-4 aircraft met them and turned the Bear away from the fleet. They finished the training round the clock exercise and set a course for Yokosuka Japan.

Punky and crew caught mail duty again. It took a while to deliver to all the ships in the fleet. They dropped a bag of mail and picked up a bag of mail. Mail was slow coming, but everyone was happy when they finally received mail. The cod had come in with a load of mail that morning.

Punky let Charlie pilot the last of the deliveries. She was glad to get the practice. They finally finished the mail delivery and headed back to the carrier. Punky sat behind Charlie and watched her. He liked to watch her movements. Everything about her was sexy even if she was in flight gear. He couldn't get enough of her.

Punky turned to Morgan, "Are you and McDaniel still taking leave when we pull in?"

"Yes sir we worked hard all the way over and now we have fun."

"Do you know where you are going?"

"No we'll let the girls take us where they want to go. They are good at planning a trip. They also handle the money and get our money's worth."

"Sounds like a good plan to me."

McDaniel and I have done it before. Would you like to come I'm sure we could find a girl for you."

"I guess I'll pass this time. I'll probably go on a sightseeing tour."

"Don't forget about the money difference. The rate is about thirty six hundred yen to ten American dollars."

"Wow that is a big difference."

McDaniel said, "I was a fool the last time I was over here. This beautiful girl asked me to come home with her and spend the night, but she asked me for four thousand yen so I turned her down. Do you realize that is only a little over ten dollars? A hotel cost more than that. I would have had a place to stay, food, and sex all night. I still want to kick my ass for being stupid."

Charlie was listening to them over the intercom. Her heart almost stopped when McDaniel ask Punky to go with them. When he turned them down she took a deep breath that she had been holding. She realized she must be in love. It shouldn't have mattered to her what Punky did, but it did. She knew when the cruise was over she may never see him again. Charlie decided she would live for the moment and enjoy their time together. She wanted the next time they made love to be in a bed.

Charlie pulled up beside the carrier on the port side and Jerry called for permission to land. She set the helicopter down nice and easy. She was a natural pilot and could fly with the best.

They had a long flight and were tired. Punky, Charlie, and Jerry went to the Officer's mess for food and plenty of coffee. Jerry said, "What are you two going to do when we hit port?"

"Probably go on a tour bus." Charlie grinned at Punky.

He knew now that she had been listening and grinned back at her. "Probably go on a tour."

They finished their food and decided to take in a movie. For some unknown reason the movies were always war movies. Tonight's movie was Run Silent Run Deep a submarine movie. They laughed as they got a cup of coffee and sat down to watch the movie. They had seen it before it was the only movie in town, besides Punky liked war movies. He liked John Wayne movies best. He was his hero growing up and still was. He could watch John Wayne movies and never get tired of watching them.

The next morning Punky and Charlie were in the ready room drinking coffee when a call from Flight Operations came down. There was a small, Japanese fishing vessel in trouble of sinking and called an S.O.S. They wanted a helicopter in the air as soon as possible. Punky told them he would take the flight.

Word was put out over the PA system for Jerry, Morgan and McDaniel to report to the flight deck immediately for an angel flight.

Punky and Charlie had a preflight done by the time they arrived. They piled into the helicopter and were turning and burning in a short time. Jerry called for permission to lift off and they were on their way. The tower gave them bearing and distance to the fishing vessel. The carrier Command Center was tracking them on Radar. When they arrived at the scene the fishing vessel was slowly sinking. They counted five fishermen on the deck standing in two to three feet of water. Charlie went to the back to help out. They put on gunner belts and slid open the back hatch. Charlie talked to Punky to keep him over the vessel. McDaniel operated the hoist as Morgan went down on the hoist cable to make a rescue. One fisherman was hurt and was brought up first. The fishing vessel sank and the last two fishermen were rescued out of the water.

When all the fishermen were safely onboard jerry called the carrier and gave them the good news. None of the fishermen spoke American, but you could tell by their actions they were happy to be alive. They were given food, dry clothing and a place to rest until the carrier pulled into port.

Commander Owens gave Punky and his crew a well done. "Punky how is it that you and your crew are always around for the action?"

"Just lucky I guess."

"Well keep up the good work. I understand Charlie helped on the rescue also."

"Yes sir she did."

"You seem to have a well, trained crew."

"Yes sir we do."

The carrier pulled into Yokosuka that evening and it was almost dark before the ship was tied down. The Marines set up security and the gangways secured in place. Thirty minutes later liberty was sounded. Sailors made a wild dash to get off the back gangway. Punky decided to wait until the next day to go on liberty. Maybe Charlie and Punky could made love tonight.

Punky found Charlie on the flight deck looking at the sights. From sixty feet in the air you could see a big part of the city. The city was lit up and pretty to watch at night. Charlie had changed into a skirt and blouse. She was beautiful to watch. He would never get tired of watching her. He put his arm around her shoulders while they stood watching the city lights.

"Who would believe we could be here after the terrible war with Japan," said Punky.

"McDaniel and Morgan say the people are real friendly except maybe a few of the old ones that will never forget the war."

"Charlie how would like to take some tours while we are in Japan?"

"I thought you would never ask."

"But right now how would you like to go to your cabin and make love?"

"Yes, Yes, Yes."

"Then let's not waste time." Punky grabbed her hand and led the way to her cabin. Inside her cabin and the door locked, Punky and Charlie shed their clothes as fast as possible. They made love like two animals in heat. After they both climaxed they lay curled together while their breathing returned to normal.

"We did it without an interruption now let's take it real slow," Punky whispered.

"Sounds like a plan to me, but I want to control the action."

Charlie rolled over and straddled Punky's thighs. As she raised up, Punky guided his erection into her hot folds. She lowered herself slowly until she sheathed all of him. She rocked and grinded as she, went up and down. She was taking it slow wanting it to last as long as she could. Charlie felt Punky throbbing inside her so she picked up the pace and went over the edge with him. She collapsed on his chest and soon fell asleep with them still hooked together.

They slept that way for a long time before Punky's shaft became hard and woke Charlie up. Punky hadn't woken up yet so Charlie lay still as she could and let his erection fill her. Finally she couldn't control her body any longer her inner muscles squeezed his erection waking Punky up. She was looking down at him, "I thought you would never wake up."

"What a nice way to wake up."

"Well now that you are awake do your part and sock it to me, oh yes, faster, faster."

They rocked off into space and exploded into a thousand pieces. When they finally returned to earth they were tired, cuddled together and went back to sleep. This will be a night neither one would ever forget. Charlie tried to remember if she had told Punky she loved him in the heat of passion, but in his arms making love she didn't even know her own name. Everything was lost except Punky slamming into her body. It was like being in a different world. She had never felt like this before, it was totally new to her. She had sex before bur never like this, but she loved every minute of it and wanted more. She couldn't get enough of Punky touching her and being inside her. She wandered if he felt the same way. She realized she was naked in bed by herself. She looked around the cabin, but no Punky. Surely he didn't leave after the fantastic night they had spent together.

The hatch opened, "Well sleepy head I see you finally woke up."

"Where have you been?"

"Steeling coffee and food from the mess hall." He held up a paper bag.

"I would kill for a cup of coffee."

"Here have a cup." He handed her a large cup of steaming coffee.

"I love you." It slipped out before she knew what she was saying.

"I love you to," Punky said without thinking.

They sat and stared at each other finally realizing what they both had said. They knew when the cruise was over they would probably never see each other again. Charlie knew that would break her heart. She realized that she wanted to wake up every morning beside him. Punky was wandering how he would make it with Charlie gone. She had become so important in his life. She was fun to be with smart, beautiful and made love like there was no tomorrow. Maybe there wasn't a tomorrow for them.

"Charlie drank your coffee before it gets cold." He put two paper plates filled with eggs, bacon and toast on the desk. "This should fill us up."

"We have to talk."

"Ok, but let's eat first."

They ate in salience and stared at each other. They finished their food and coffee before they started their talk. "Charlie you be first."

"I didn't mean to fall in love with you, but it just happened."

"The same thing happened to me."

"Punky what happens now?"

"We enjoy our time together and try to work something out when the cruise is over."

"But how can we make it work? You are in the Navy and I work for a large company."

"I don't have an answer now, but we can work on it."

Charlie had been so caught up in the discussion that she forgot she was naked. She glanced down at her body and blushed. Her cheeks had turned a bright shade of red. She grabbed a sheet and tucked it around her.

"Too late now, I have seen everything."

"I don't know what came over me I forgot I was naked. You make me crazy."

"Good maybe you will run around naked all the time when we are together."

"Not likely."

"But think how easy it would be to jump in bed and make love. We wouldn't have to lose time taking off our clothes."

Charlie was getting hot all over at them talking about making love. "Time to change the subject, what are we going to do today?"

"I thought we would see the sights and do some shopping."

Charlie threw the sheet on the bed as she stood there naked, "Let's get dressed."

Punky stared at her naked he wanted to get undressed, but she had her panties on and was working on her pajamas. She got a towel, fresh clothes and left to get a shower. She could smell Punky and her sex from last night, time for a shower.

Punky had already took a shower and shaved. He was in dress pants and a polo shirt. He sat and thought about their talk while he waited for Charlie to get ready. He hadn't planned on falling in love with Charlie. When had it happened? He didn't even pause when he said it so it had to be true, but he had never been in love. How did he know what love was?

Charlie came back dressed in a blue skirt and white blouse with a small amount of makeup. Her skin was soft and flawless. He cupped her face and brushed a light kiss on her mouth. "What was that for?"

"I just needed a kiss let's hit the town."

They left the ship and headed to downtown Yokosuka. Most of the Japanese people that ran a business spoke American. Charlie bought some clothes. Punky liked the two piece swimsuit she bought, but had to buy it two sizes larger than American sizes. Japanese women were small so they were sized smaller. Punky bought a smoking jacket, why he didn't know because he didn't smoke. They decided to go eat.

When they were seated and ready to order they had a problem. They couldn't read the menu and tried to figure out what to order. The waiter didn't speak American so they finally pointed to some items on the menu.

Punky, do you have any idea what we ordered?"

"I don't have a clue I guess it's like pot luck."

When the food arrived they knew what rice was, but that was all. They didn't know what the meat was or the vegetables. They did figure out they had ordered fish head and rice. The fish's eyes were staring at them from the rice. They did get the beer right.

"Punky what do you think the meat is?"

"Probably monkey or dog," he laughed.

"That wasn't funny."

"You don't see any stray dogs or cats running loose around here."

"No," She decided to eat the fish head and rice at least she knew what she was eating.

Punky ate the meat and loved it, "Who cares what it is it tasted good."

"Charlie ordered some egg soup, "I'm only eating what I know I'm eating."

"Spoiled sport you don't know what you are missing."

They finished their meal and continued with their shopping.

"Punky, look at that girl in the alley. She dropped her panties and is taking a leak."

"That's normal over here, the only people that look at the girl is some sailor."

"Well I'm not going I'll wait until we get back to the ship."

Before the day was over they saw men whip it out and relieve themselves. Punky couldn't hold it until they got back to the ship. He went into an alley and relieved himself with Charlie watching him. He noticed a couple of girls ogling him and giggling.

"I thought you said nobody would pay any attention to you."

"The girls saw something they liked," teased Punky.

"Then maybe I should try it and see how many men look."

"Forget it we're almost back to the ship." He didn't want anyone looking at Charlie.

Charlie could tell Punky was jealous and she liked it, but he tried to hide it. They tried not to fall in love, but anyone could look at them and know they were in love. He couldn't get enough of her and she couldn't get enough of him. They went back to the ship after a long day. They ate dinner in the Officer's mess before locking themselves in Charlie's cabin. With her cabin at the end of the passageway it was real private. They planned to make slow passionate love and sleep in the next day.

"I wander how McDaniel and Morgan made out on their leave?"

"Punky you wanted to go with them didn't you?"

"No I got all I want right here," he reached for Charlie and started to undress her.

"Then you had better show me," and he did.

McDaniel and Morgan made their way down one of the main streets of Yokosuka until they came to a small restaurant. It was the place where Linn Sue Lang worked. She went with McDaniel the last time he was over. She was happy to see him. She knew he would want to take a trip and sightsee and she could plan the trip. He wanted to know if she could find another girl to go with Morgan. The girl Morgan went with last time lived in Sasebo. Lin Sue took them to the back of the restaurant through a patio with a fountain, bamboo chairs and beautiful flowers around it. They entered into the living quarters. They were divided into small box like cubicles having a sliding bamboo door on each wall. The living area consisted of a small table with short legs, pillars on the floor to sit on and a stone cooking place used like an American grill. Linn Sue's room had a hand weave mat to sleep on in one corner and pillars scattered around to sit on. Her clothes hung on a rod in the other corner. There was no running water or electric in the living quarters. They used candles for light and carried water from the restaurant. She had few private items, but not many. If you had to use the bathroom you went inside the restaurant and used it there which consisted of a hole in the floor with a crock like fixture to do everything in.

Linn Sue returned with a girlfriend for Morgan. Her name was Min Lou Son. She brought food for Dinner chow main, salad and Hot Sokki to drink. Neither girl spoke good English, but Linn Sue had everything planned out. They would start their trip tomorrow. Both girls were short and slim. They had shoulder length black hair, a round face with slant eyes and off white skin. They both wore short dresses, no bra and lacy panties. They both wore sandals which they remove inside.

McDaniel and Morgan removed their shoes when they entered the house as was the Japanese custom. After they finished their food they sat awhile letting their food settle. The girls told them to remove their clothes which they did. McDaniel lay on his stomach. Linn Sue straddled him and started a slow massage, rubbing and kneading to stimulate circulation which he didn't need. He had a hard on and her on top was pressing it into the floor. She stood up and walked on his back kneading as she walked back and forth. Morgan and Min Lou watched as Linn sue worked her magic. After Linn Sue finished with McDaniel Min Lou started on Morgan while Linn Sue pulled McDaniel's head into her lap to watch the show.

When Min Lou finished with Morgan he turned over his manhood standing at attention. Min Lou took his shaft in her hand and slowly massaged it until it was hard as a rock. "I think you have a problem," she giggled.

"Can you fix the problem?"

"Yes I fix." She pulled off her dress and panties.

She raised, up and guided him into her and lowered her body taking all of him. She didn't move for a moment adjusting to his size. She was a small woman and he had a huge shaft. McDaniel had heard all black men were hung like a stud horse, now he believed it.

The girls weren't shy and it didn't bother them to have sex in the same room. Sometimes whole family's lived in one small room. Sex wasn't anything to be ashamed of in Japan. Linn Sue watched them have sex and couldn't believe how big Morgan was. It made her hot watching them.

"Turn over and give it to me now I hot." She pulled off her dress and panties.

"Glad to hear it I have a problem also."

McDaniel slid between her legs and slammed into her folds. She cried out and he set a fast pace. Min Lou moaned and screamed as Morgan took her over the edge. She fell forward on his chest exhausted, but contented. He was still inside her. McDaniel put his arms around Linn Sue's legs and raised them straight up slamming into her faster and harder.

"Oh yes, oh yes you make me come."

"Linn Sue you make me come to."

McDaniel rolled over with Linn Sue on top and still inside her. He knew the girls liked to sleep on top. They weren't heavy only weighing less than a hundred pounds. That way later on if they were filled with a hard on, they would take care of it sometimes so gently they didn't wake the guys.

"Linn Sue if I get as hard on while sleeping be sure to wake me, I don't want to miss out on you making love to me."

"But you tired, I make you relax. Make love slow, easy until come not wake you."

"I'm not too tired to make love."

"Ok poky I wake you make feel good."

A couple hours later Linn Sue kissed him waking him from his dream. It wasn't a dream. He had a big hard on and she was moving slowly up and down on it. He thought he would die from pleasure. He glanced at Morgan who was still sleeping and Min Lou was very slowly up and down on him trying not to wake him. He was smiling and McDaniel knew he was dreaming.

"You like feel good," whispered Linn Sue.

"Yes joy son it feels good." Joy son was a name used for young women who gave pleasure and boy did she give pleasure.

They had a climax together, cuddled together and went to sleep. Min Lou was still slowly making love to Morgan and would until she felt him throbbing inside her. She would squeeze his manhood with her inner muscles until he went limp.

Then she would cuddle with him and go to sleep.

The next morning Punky woke up first. He went to the mess hall and got donuts and coffee. Charlie woke up as he shut the hatch.

"Good morning sleepy head."

"You wore me out last night."

"Good I intend to as often as you let me."

"I'm hungry bring on the food."

Punky gave her coffee and donuts which she wolfed down. He ate slow and sipped his coffee. "What do you want to do today?"

"I don't know Punky. Why don't you pick it?"

"Are you sure?" I might pick something you won't like."

"I'm game for anything."

"You said anything." She was still in bed naked.

Punky quickly undressed and joined her on the bed. He lay on his back with a big erection standing straight up. They looked in each other's eyes. Punky stared at her mouth and then his erection. She got the drift and smiled at him. "You dirty rat."

"You said anything, are you backing down?"

"No, but I will make you scream for me to stop."

Charlie took his shaft in both hands and squeezed the base, lowered her mouth and teased him with the tip of her tongue. He reached for her head and pulled it down filling her mouth. She gently nipped him with her teeth and he pulled back. She curled her tongue around him and continued to tease him. Now he knew what she was going to do to him trying to make him scream. He gritted his teeth and took everything she gave. There was only one thing wrong with her plan she was so hot and was trembling. She couldn't take it any longer and changed her plan. Taking all of him in her mouth she straddled him with her folds only a couple inches in front of his face. He didn't hesitate pulling her to him and plunging his tongue into her hot core. Charlie was going to stop before he came, but she had never had the experience before and wandered what he would taste like so she sucked him until he came. It tasted a little salty, but didn't taste bad and she loved him and wanted him to enjoy it. She sucked on him until his shaft went limp. Punky slammed his tongue deep into her and she screamed as she climaxed. He smelled and tasted the scent of his woman. He had put his brand on her.

"Well sweetheart nobody won."

"No, but didn't we have fun trying?"

"That we did we'll have to try this more often."

"Punky that was the first time I done, you know, tasted, I never—."

"I knew that when you hesitated when I was throbbing for release."

"Punky I love to make love to you. I can't get enough of you."

"I feel the same way about you. What are we going to do when the cruise is over?"

"I don't know you have your career and I have mine."

"Charlie let's live a day at a time and enjoy each other."

"Now are we going on the beach?"

"Yes let's get a shower and hit the beach. Bet I'm ready before you."

"No fair it takes a girl longer because she has more to do to look good."

"Honey you look beautiful naked."

"Well I'm not going on the beach naked," throwing a pillar at him as he closed the hatch. Charlie smiled at the thought of walking off the gangway naked. That sure would get everybody's attention and Punky naked with a big hard on walking beside her. She giggled and started to get ready to hit the beach.

After leaving the ship they strolled down a main street in Yokosuka going in and out of the many shops. They found a Pichinco Parlor and decided to gamble for a while. Charlie was lucky and won continuous, but Punky lost as fast as she won.

"Punky can't you win just one time."

"I never was lucky at gambling. When I was in high school my buddies and I would go to a friend's cabin in the woods and gamble. I always lost my shirt."

"Then quit playing and watch me."

Punky quit playing the game and watched Charlie win several big pots. She had on a shirt and blouse that clung to her curves. He stared at her and enjoyed watching her play the game. Finally she cashed in her winnings and they continued on their way. "I'm sorry you couldn't win."

"I'm not I enjoyed watching you more than playing the games."

"You did?" Charlie blushed.

"I was thinking about last night when we made love."

"It was great wasn't it?"

"Yes it was"

"Punky look over there it's a sauna bathhouse. Have you ever been in one?"

"No but I'm game if you are."

They didn't know what to expect. Two young women escorted them into a large room. They were told to remove their clothes. Punky looked at Charlie, "Are you sure you want to do this?"

"Why not, it could be fun."

Charlie undressed and handed her clothes to one girl. The other girl looked at Punky waiting for his clothes. "What the heck nothing ventured, nothing gained."

Punky undressed and handed her his clothes. The girls left to put their clothes away. Charlie and Punky both naked stood, staring at each other. "What if they don't come back?" giggled Charlie.

"No one would pay any attention to us on the way back to the ship, but it might prove interesting to convince the Officer of the Deck to let us come onboard naked."

The girls came back stripped to the waist with only a loincloth below. They smiled at Charlie and pointed to the mats on the floor. "Please for you to lie face down."

Punky and Charlie lay down and waited. A young man came in carrying hot rocks and put them in a container. He poured water over the rocks creating steam. When the room was nice and hot the girls got down on their knees beside Punky and Charlie. They put oil on their hands and messaged them from head to toe. It felt like heaven. Punky couldn't help it, but he had a hard on. It was a good thing he was on his stomach. They wiped the oil off and stepped on their backs walking up and down their backs wiggling their toes. It felt so good. The girls weighed less than a hundred pounds each. They stepped off and got down on their knees. "Please to turn over."

Charlie turned over, but Punky didn't. "What's wrong?" asked Charlie.

"I got a hard on."

"Chicken turn over," giggled Charlie.

Punky turned over and everyone stared at him. His manhood was standing tall and hard. It was large.

"Oh so man have problem I fix."

The girl put oil on her hands and stroked his manhood. The other girl put oil on her hands and massaged Charlie all over including her breasts and nipples as they turned hard as marbles. She had a hard time trying not to moan, it felt so good. She glanced over at Punky. He had his eyes closed while the girl stroked him faster. It made Charlie hot watching.

"Him almost ready, him come any minute. Me take him inside me if you no care."

As if on cue the other girl slipped two fingers into Charlie's folds. "Go ahead and do it to him." She had lost her ability to think.

The girl straddled Punky and lowered herself on his shaft. "I make it good."

She took all of him and bounced up and down on his erection. She lay forward and her nipples brushed Punky's chest. "It feel good yes?"

"Yes it feels good, but slow down and make it last."

She slowed her pace and stopped for a moment. She was starting to get hot. The girls tried to stay cool as they worked on customers, but Punky was big and filled her completely. She started again and moaned when Punky arched and slammed up deep into her small body. "Oh you make so good I think I come now."

"I think I'll come with you."

She screamed as they came together. She was exhausted and collapsed on his chest. Her hard nipples dug into his chest. Finally she slid off and sat beside him "You boyfriend very good make me feel good."

Charlie didn't know what to say. The girls washed them and dried them. They brought their clothes to them and they dressed. Punky paid the girls for their service and they left feeling like a wet noodle.

"Well that was an experience. Did you enjoy yourself?"

"Yes except when the girl made love to you. Don't let that happen again."

"I won't." Punky liked the fact that Charlie was jealous.

They strolled down one street and then another. Punky liked to the watch the people and their dress. The old dressed in their old custom, but the young people dressed like young people in America. Short skirts were in at the time.

"Stop looking at every young girl that walks by." Charlie didn't like the way they looked at Punky.

"If I shut my eyes I can't see where I'm going."

Charlie put her arm around his waist. "Shut your eyes when a girl walks by and I will lead you," she laughed.

They strolled around for a while and spotted a movie theatre with John Wayne staring in it. "Hey let's take in a movie," said Punky.

"But it will be in Japanese."

"We can read lips."

Punky bought tickets and they went to the movies. It was another fun experience. Punky couldn't keep from laughing at John Wayne speaking Japanese. They did have fun lip reading. After the movie was over they got something to eat and went back to the ship. Charlie came to Punky's cabin, but they were too tired to make love. Charlie curled up naked beside Punky and was fast asleep in just a few minutes.

The next day Punky had Shore Patrol. Charlie went back to her cabin and slept all day. She was still tired from the day before. Punky knew he would be dead by the time he got off Shore Patrol. He had a First Class for a partner. The day went by slow. They checked all the bars and clubs to watch out for Sailors in trouble.

"Sir I want to show you the beautiful girl I was with last night."

"Sure where does she work?"

They entered the bar, "There she is."

Punky wanted to laugh at the expression on his face. He knew the old saying, they all look better at closing time. She didn't look bad, but she wasn't a ten, five maybe. He looked at Punky and didn't know what to say. "I guess I was a little drunk last night."

"Yes I would think you were, but it happens to all of us sometime."

They left the bar and continued their patrol. All and all they had an easy night, but they were both tired when they got off Shore Patrol.

They passed a bar and the First Class motioned to the bar. "How about a drink before we go back to the ship. It has been a hard day and I could use one."

Punky was never one to follow rules. "Pull off your Shore Patrol gear."

They pulled off their Shore Patrol gear and Punky gave it to the bartender. He put the gear under the bar. The First Class ordered two setups. The bartender reached under the bar and got a bottle. Punky noticed a name on the bottle.

"I like to keep a bottle in several bars. I can get good liquor when I want it. Nobody will ever drink out of my bottles unless I say so. The Japanese are real honest people."

Two young girls sat down on either side of them, "We show good time."

"Sorry honey we are on duty tonight, but we'll buy you a drink."

Punky and the First Class finished their drinks and picked up their gear from the bartender. They exited the club and headed back to the ship. Punky went to the Officer gangplank and the First Class went up the enlisted gangplank, Punky felt his stomach grumble. He went to the Officer's mess for food and coffee.

He took a shower and went to bed. He thought about Charlie for a minute before sleep overtook him. He was dead tired. Charlie heard the hatch slam when Punky came back from Shore Patrol. She started to get up and go to his bed, but decided to let him rest. He would be too tired to fool around so she would let him sleep.

Punky knocked on her door and peaked in. She was still in bed.

"What are you doing up so early?"

"I have visitor duty today. They let all the local people onboard for a tour of the ship. I caught tour guide. You know Officer and a gentleman."

Charlie giggled, "I question the gentleman part."

"If I had time I would show you a thing or two."

Charlie sat up in bed and let the sheet drop to her waist. She was naked. "Promises, promises, promises." She teased.

"If only I had got up earlier."

"Sorry about that."

Punky shut the hatch and went to his assigned post. They started letting the public onboard. There were so many people onboard he thought the ship would sink. He gave tour after tour answering questions. The people came up the Officer gangplank and were shown the first half of the hanger deck. Then they went up the number one elevator to the flight deck. They were shown the flight deck before they went back down elevator number three to the hanger. They were shown the rest of the hanger bay and then they were given hot dogs, hamburgers, chips and a drink. After they finished eating they left by the enlisted gangplank. By the end of the day Punky was dead on his feet.

He took a shower and lay down naked with a sheet pulled up to his waist. Charlie heard Punky close his hatch, but he didn't come to her cabin. She wasn't going to let him off that easy tonight. This was their last night in port. They would get underway the next morning and they wouldn't have any time to themselves. They would start round the clock operations again.

Charlie opened the hatch and peaked in, "Do you want some company?"

"Yes close the hatch and join me."

Charlie removed her robe and stood naked before him. She raised the sheet and slid in beside Punky. He opened his arms and she came to him. She put her leg across his legs and put her head on his shoulder. "What's the matter? Is the baby tired?"

"I'm very tired."

"Ok we sleep and make love later."

About three hours later Charlie woke up. She sat up and watched Punky sleep. She didn't realize it, but Punky was a thief, he had stolen her heart. How was she going to live without him when the cruise was over? She didn't mean to fall in love, but it just happened. Her life had become messed up and she didn't know how to fix it. She knew she didn't want to leave Punky, but she loved her job.

She eased over and straddled Punky. She took his shaft in her hand and slowly stroked it while it came to life. She eased up and guided his shaft into her folds. She eased down and sheathed all of him. She waited to see if he woke up and he didn't. She tightened her inner muscles and eased up and down. Punky dreamed he was making love to Charlie. He smiled, but didn't wake up.

Charlie slowly kept moving up and down. It felt so good taking it nice and slow. She would go for a while and stop. She would stay still until she calmed down before starting again. She managed to come to the point several times before she couldn't take it any longer. She tightened her muscles and Punky's shaft throbbed inside her. She knew he was coming inside her and she came along with him. She slid off him and curled up next to his body. She was back asleep in a couple minutes. She was contented and would sleep well the rest of the night. Punky finished his dream. He dreamed he climaxed in Charlie. The dream was so real.

The next morning Punky woke up first and nibbled on a nipple until Charlie opened her eyes. "Good morning sunshine."

"Good morning."

"I'm sorry I was so tired and we didn't make love last night."

"You sure are a sound sleeper."

"Why is that?"

"I made love to you last night and you didn't wake up."

"No way, I would have slept through it."

"You did and I abused your body."

"Now I do remember dreaming that we made love."

"It wasn't a dream we did it for real."

"You took advantage of me while I was sleeping. Wait until I get even with you."

""You should have woke up, but you slept through all of it even when we came."

"Never turn your back on me," teased Punky.

"I won't."

They got up. Charlie went back to her cabin and got ready for the day. They ate a good breakfast of eggs, toast, bacon, fruit, and coffee. They loaded the ship with fresh stores while in port. After a while they would be back to powdered eggs and powdered everything. The crew hated it when they ran out of fresh stores.

Ten Hundred sharp the ship prepared to get underway. The gangways were removed, the lines to the ship removed and the ship slowly moved away from the dock. Punky was on the flight deck for flight deck parade. As soon as they headed out to sea flight deck parade was dismissed and everyone went to his assigned duty.

Punky changed uniform and met Charlie in the ready room. They were briefed on the upcoming operations. The next day they would go to around the clock operations. It was hard to get back in the swing of things after several days in port. It was all business while out at sea. Punky thought the Navy motto, work hard and play hard.

The Flight Operation Officer called Punky over and informed him the Admiral ask for His crew to transport him over to the cruiser. Punky had to pick a new crew because McDaniel and Morgan were still on leave. He didn't like going with a crew he didn't know, but it couldn't be helped. Well he still had Jerry and Charlie. The Plane Captain prepared the plane for V.I.P. duty with stars on the side, curtains and seat covers. Jerry and Charlie did a preflight on the helicopter while Punky greeted the Admiral.

"So you were the pilot that helped chase off the Russian ship. That was fast thinking. I like men who can think on their own, well done."

Charlie escorted the Admiral and his aid to their seats. They sat at the sonar stations while the crew would sit in the back.

After the Admiral and his aid were seated Charlie said, "I will be your flight attendant for this flight and anything I can get you just ask."

The Admiral was impressed, "Thank you young lady."

"Admiral I bought drinks and sandwiches in case you get hungry."

With the crew onboard and strapped in Jerry called the tower for lift off instructions. It was a short flight to the cruiser. Punky made an approach on the cruiser and hovered over the fantail. The Admiral and his aid went to the back hatch. They were lowered by hoist to the cruiser.

Punky pulled away from the cruiser and flew beside the ship. They would wait until the Admiral was ready to return to the carrier. Two hours later Punky received the signal to pick up the Admiral. The Admiral was picked up and returned to the carrier. After the Admiral and his aid left the helicopter Punky thanked the crew for a job well done.

"Charlie, are you starting a new career."

"No I just thought I would put a good touch to the flight. It was fun and I think the Admiral liked it."

They went to the ready room and got out of their flight gear. "How about I buy you a cup of coffee?" asked Punky.

"I would like that," replied Charlie.

Punky and Charlie read the flight schedule and went to the Officer's mess for coffee. They had a flight at eight hundred in the morning. They caught plane guard for the morning launch. Punky and Charlie sat at a table and had coffee. Some of the other Officers kind of invited themselves to the table. They just wanted to talk to a woman for a change.

Charlie and Punky kissed in the passageway and went to their cabins. Punky lay in bed thinking about Charlie. The same thoughts hung with him. What would they do when the cruise was over? He knew he loved her and wanted to spend the rest of his life with her. He liked the Navy, but the Navy was hell on married couples. He saw too many couples break up. The women got lonely while her man was gone and found love in the arms of someone else. The men did the same thing. They loved their mates, but they were lonely and needed sex.

Charlie lay in bed thinking about Punky and what they would do when the cruise was over. She didn't have any answers just questions.

"Are we ready crew?"

"Sonar ready, sir."

"Observer ready, sir."

"Jerry, call the tower and get us airborne."

"Bennington tower 05, request liftoff."

"05 Bennington tower, you are clear to launch."

"Bennington tower 05, roger."

Punky lifted them off on the port side and circled around to the starboard side to assume plane guard position. The fixed wing aircraft launched first. After that the UH-2A launched and came around to relieve them of plane guard.

"05 Angel 01, relieving you from plane guard, Sorry we had plane problems again.

"01 Angel 05, you have plane guard."

Punky pulled forward and starboard to the carrier to assume screen duty. Punky flew the helicopter into a fifty foot hover.

"Sonar pilot set your dome at one hundred feet and do a standard search"

"Pilot sonar dome at one hundred feet and active."

After several dips they settled into a routine, dip and move, dip again. It looked like an easy day ahead. So far they hadn't had a target.

Suddenly a distress call came over the airwaves. "Bennington tower 01 Angel mayday, mayday I'm going down."

"Sonar pilot up dome and secure it."

"Pilot dome up and secured."

They were off the starboard side of the carrier about fifty yards out when their engine quit. Punky turned the helicopter around and headed for them. They hit the water and parts flew off the aircraft. They had a lot of trouble with the Angel helicopter since the cruise had begun. They were the rescue team and now they would have to be rescued. They didn't like that at all. The crew bailed out of the downed helicopter and swam away from it as it started sinking. Punky flew into a fifty feet hover over the crew. Both sonar and Charlie went to the back. Charlie took command of the joystick to guide the helicopter. Charlie and the two crewmen put on gunner belts and slid the back hatch open.

"Charlie you now have control."

"Roger I have control."

Charlie eased the helicopter over the first crewman to be picked up.

Charlie did the talking and flying while the two crewmen worked the hoist. The pilot and copilot had to rely on the crew because they couldn't see what was happening. The crewman lowered the hoist.

"Hoist going down, sir."

"Survivor is in the sling."

"Hoist is coming up"

"First survivor is in the helicopter."

The second survivor was brought up into the helicopter. Charlie eased the helicopter over the last survivor. They had a problem the last pickup was too tired to get in the sling or were hurt.

"The crewman looked at Charlie, "I'll get him."

He dropped into the water close to the man and swam over to him. He put him in the sling and gave the thumbs up.

"Hoist is coming up."

"Survivor is in the helicopter."

"Hoist is going down."

"Crewman is in the sling."

"Hoist is coming up."

"Crewman is in the helicopter and hatch is closed."

"Sir you now have control."

"I have control, thank you crew for a job well done."

Jerry called the tower for permission to land and gave the report that the Angel crew was onboard and safe. Punky landed close to the island. The Angel crew exited the aircraft while they were still turning and burning. Jerry called for permission to launch.

"05 Bennington tower you are clear to launch."

"Bennington tower 05 roger."

Punky lifted the helicopter off and returned to their assigned screen position. They started their same routine over again.

"Wasn't that fun doing the rescue and nobody got hurt?' said Punky.

"Yes, but they got their pride hurt," replied Jerry. "Well it's not their fault they have to fly that helicopter. I wouldn't like to fly it myself. It has too many problems.

"Hey guys remember me I'm on this cruise because this bird has a problem that we haven't solved yet. Maybe none of these helicopters have the problem, but we don't know for sure. I want to find the problem before the cruise is over."

"One bad thing about losing the Angel helicopter is our squadron will be flying plane guard for the rest of the cruise if we don't get a replacement helicopter."

"Good point Punky," murmured Jerry.

"Time to call it a day they are launching our relief."

As soon as the launch was airborne Punky flew into position for plane guard for the recovery of their launch. All planes landed without incident. Punky came in and set their bird down easy. They went to the ready room for debrief. Commander Owens came over to them.

"Punky, tell me one thing, how is it that you are always in the middle of everything?"

"Just lucky I guess."

"Something tells me before the cruise is over you will be into something big. I don't know what, but I feel it in my bones and they don't lie."

"Sir I'll try to keep it cool."

"Please do."

"Yes sir."

"By the way you did an excellent job on the rescue."

"Sir I have a good crew that's works well together."

"Charlie, how is the problem coming along on our aircraft?"

"Sir, we haven't found anything so far."

"Well keep looking I don't want to lose any planes or lives."

Charlie and Punky went to the Officer mess for coffee and some lunch. Jerry tagged alone with them.

Punky and Charlie sat staring at each other. Jerry glanced back and forth between them. He knew they had something going on between them, but didn't know they were in love.

"Punky I was going to ask you to go on liberty in Sasebo with me, but I guess that is out from the looks of things."

"What did you say?"

"Never mind, it was nothing. You two get a room."

At times they couldn't keep their eyes off of one another. They sat and stared at each other remembering when they made love. Jerry gave up.

"I'll see you two later when you come out of your trance."

Jerry left them still staring at each other. Finally they broke the trance. "Where is Jerry? I thought he was sitting with us."

"He was, but I think he got bored with us and left."

They went back to the ready room and took a couple of seats in the back. They talked for a while before they dozed off to sleep. They both woke up when the first plane hit the deck from the flight that was coming in for recovery.

"Charlie how would you like to get a bird's eye view of the recovery?"

"Sounds good to me, where do we go?"

Punky got up, "Follow me."

Punky led the way on the catwalk under the flight deck until they reached the arresting gear. He led her to the outer catwalk beside the arresting gear operators. They watched as the planes landed one by one. Just before the last plane landed Punky and Charlie stepped back in the catwalk under the flight deck.

As luck would have it or someone up above was watching over them, the arresting cable broke on the last landing. They looked back to see the two operators wrapped up in the cable. They hurried back to give aid to the downed men. One man had an arm missing half way up. "Charlie check the other man, I'll help this one."

Punky took his belt off and used it as a tourniquet to stop the bleeding until help arrived. The man was out cold. The cable had caught the other man in his mid-section.

"Punky I think he is dead or hurt real bad, I can't find a pulse."

"Hold on I'll be with you in a minute."

Punky came over and checked the other man. "He is still alive, I feel a weak pulse."

Medical personal poured onto the catwalk including a Doctor. Punky and Charlie backed up out of the way and let them do their job.

"Come on Charlie let's get out of here."

"Do you think they will live?"

"I don't know, but one man is out of the Navy. He lost an arm."

"That was horrible. Did they find the arm?"

"I think it went over the catwalk into the water." The flight deck is a very dangerous place. If you don't get cut up, you can get blown off the flight deck.

"Are we in trouble?"

"Yes if Commander Owens finds out."

"We weren't allowed in the catwalk while planes were landing, were we?"

"As a matter of fact we weren't."

"Punky, do you ever follow rules?"

"Sometimes I do."

They went back to the ready room. They had just sat down when a young seaman came in the ready room. "Is there a Lieutenant Wilson in the ready room?"

"Over here."

The seaman handed Punky his belt. "Sir with your fast thinking you probably saved the man's life." The belt had his name on it.

Commander Owens heard the conversation and came over. "What were you doing back at the arresting gear?"

Punky knew the fat was in the fire. "Watching the planes land sir."

"You know better than that. I don't want to lose a pilot to a broke cable."

"Sir I was under the flight deck when the cable broke."

"You shouldn't have been there in the first place."

"Yes sir."

After the Commander left Charlie said, "Why didn't you tell him why you were up there?"

"Why get both of us in trouble?"

"Ok I owe you one."

"Punky grinned at Charlie, "Good because I keep track of what you owe me and I will collect some-day."

Charlie blushed red, "You are crazy, but I will pay up."

They stared at each other. They were both thinking the same thing. "Charlie I believe you have your mind in the gutter."

"I think your mind is in the gutter also."

"Not me, "I am a good kid without bad thoughts."

"Liar and it's going to snow tonight."

Punky checked the flight schedule and was not happy. "I have a midnight launch tonight. Do you want to skip the flight? You can if you want to."

"No you don't get rid of me that easy."

"Well we had better get some sleep. It is going to be a long night."

They went back to their cabins to get some sleep. Punky wasn't sleepy, but he went to bed anyway.

Charlie met him in the ready room for the brief before they went to preflight the aircraft. It started to rain just as they finished the preflight. It started raining cats and dogs. "I don't like to launch in a storm, but this is suppose, to be an all-weather bird."

"Punky, do they always launch?"

"Yes."

"It looks like they could wait until the storm is over."

"Jerry, call the tower and get us airborne. Maybe it will be better higher up."

"Bennington tower 05, request permission to lift off."

"05 Bennington tower, you are clear to launch and take up plane guard position."

"Bennington tower 05, good luck it's real bad out tonight."

Punky eased the helicopter off the flight deck and took up plane guard position. It was raining so hard they had a hard time seeing the planes as they launched. Believe it or not all the flight got off the carrier safe and sound. "Well they all got off the carrier let's hope it lets up before we land."

Punky pulled up to two hundred feet, but he still had to fly on instruments. It was going to be a rough night. "Well crew we will earn our paycheck tonight."

It was pitch black out and Punky didn't like to fly on instruments. He liked to be able to at least see the water. You couldn't see anything. He had to rely on his instruments completely. "Standby crew, I'll try to get us in a fifty foot hover so we can dip sonar."

Punky put the helicopter in automatic approach set for fifty feet. He put one hand around the stick and the other one around the collective, but held them loosely. He had his feet on the rudder controls, but didn't apply any pressure. He let the automatic approach do the work and he was the backup in case something happened. The helicopter came down into a perfect fifty foot hover.

"Sonar pilot down dome and do a standard search."

"Pilot sonar dome at fifty feet and active."

The automatic pilot had a hard time maintaining a fifty foot hover. The wind was blowing hard and it was raining so hard they couldn't see the water below them. It was real scary.

"Pilot sonar the search is complete."

"Sonar pilot raise the dome."

The next three hours they were at the mercy of the storm. The wind blew and the rain came. "Well we only got three more days at sea before we pull into Sasebo. "I hear the liberty is good," said Jerry.

"I want to go to Nagasaki and see where the bomb hit," said Charlie.

"Just don't ask the people where the bomb hit," replied Punky.

"I'm not that stupid."

It had almost quit raining by the time their flight was over. Another helicopter took plane guard and Punky was the second helicopter to land. The crew was exhausted from putting up with the weather. They went to the ready room for debrief. It was five o'clock in the morning by the time it was over.

"Charlie, do you want to get some breakfast?"

"Sure I'm starved."

The next three days went by without any problems. The carrier pulled into Sasebo the next day. The ship's crew was ready for some liberty.

CHAPTER SIX

Charlie and Punky stood on the flight deck looking over the town. At sixty feet in the air they could see most of the town.

"It looks like a big city," said Charlie.

"The streets are small and there are so many people per square foot. Everything is so close together. The cars are small to be able to go down the streets. The trucks are small and a lot of them have only three wheels like that one unloading stores for the carrier."

"What are we going to do today?"

"I thought we would look over the town today. Maybe tonight we could hit the bars and get drunk."

"Yeah right, have some drinks yes, but to get drunk no thank you."

"Charlie, have you ever been drunk?"

"I have a few times in college."

"Well I think it's time to hit the beach. I'll knock on your door when I'm ready."

"Girls never get ready first."

"We'll see about that."

Punky got ready first and stood outside her cabin. He didn't knock. Charlie came rushing out to knock on his door. "Ok so girls are slow, but we have so much to do to look nice."

"You are beautiful and smell so good."

"You look pretty good yourself."

Charlie had on a skirt and blouse while Punky had on slacks with a pullover sweater. He looked like a dream come true to Charlie. She had butterflies in her stomach and hot pants just looking at him. Maybe they should stay aboard ship and make love. She thought about making love, but said, "Are you ready to go?"

They left the ship and took a cab downtown. They decided to eat first. Charlie pointed to a small quiet little restaurant. There was a sign, but it was in Japanese.

"Charlie what do you think, is it a place to eat?"

"If this isn't a place to eat we will make a fool of ourselves."

They were shown to a table. It had short legs and they sat on pillows on the floor. Punky looked around the room. It was full and people were all around them. He scanned the tables until he saw something that looked good.

"What are you doing?"

"We can't read a menu so look around until you see something you like."

"This is stupid," but she looked anyway.

The young joy son asked in Japanese what they wanted. Punky pointed to a dish on the table to his right. "I'll take what they are eating."

"I'll take the same," said Charlie.

The joy son brought a bottle of red wine and two dishes loaded with meat. It was fish, shrimp and squid. She brought two more dishes of vegetables and fruit. "Now that's more like it."

"Punky I don't think I can eat all this food," but she did eat all her food.

"For eating all your food you can have desert."

The joy son brought desert. It was like hot pocket with fruit in it. When they finished Punky paid the girl eighteen hundred yen. It sounded like a lot of money, but it was only five dollars American money.

"I'm full as a tick," said Charlie.

"Come on we'll walk it off."

The main shopping district had real narrow streets that were sealed off to traffic. The streets were crowded with shoppers and tourists. A man crossed their path on the way to the bathhouse. He had a bar of soap in one hand, a towel across his other arm and sandals on his feet.

"Did you see that? Can you believe it?"

"Charlie it's just a guy on the way to the bathhouse."

"Could you see someone in America doing that?" giggled Charlie.

"Sure, but he would be arrested."

Everyone takes a bath together at the same time. Men, women, and children take a bath at the same time. Punky and Charlie watched as people went in and out of the bathhouse. "Are you ready for your bath," asked Punky.

"It would be another experience to tell about. What do you think?"

"Let's take a bath and I'll even wash your back."

They entered the bathhouse and an old woman referred to as Mommy Son led them into a small room to undress. "You leave clothes here." She handed them a bar of soap and two towels.

"Thank you," said Charlie.

"Ok, are you ready to do this?"

"Punky you are crazy. I don't know why I let you talk me into these things."

"Because you are like me, you like adventure just like I do."

They undressed and hung their clothes on pegs on the wall. Punky led Charlie into the next room where a huge tub or maybe it should be called a tank was full of water. It was also full of people, men women and children. The children played in the water while adults talked and laughed. They hoped the people weren't laughing at them. The people were all speaking Japanese. Punky and Charlie didn't understand a word they said. They climbed in the tub and moved to one end where a family was washing each other.

"You join us," said the father.

"Thank you," replied Charlie.

"This is my wife and our two daughters."

"I'm Punky and this is Charlie."

The bowed to them and they bowed back. "Here in Japan my wife called Mommy Son, daughters call Joy Son's."

"How you like Japan so far?"

"We love it," they said in unison.

Punky took the soap and started washing Charlie's back. Mommy Son stared at them and said, "That Joy Son job."

The two girls about sixteen moved over behind Punky and Charlie. One took the soap from Punky and started to wash Charlie. The other one had a bar of soap and started washing Punky.

"We wash clean yes."

"Thank you," said Charlie.

After they finished their backs they moved around in front of them. Punky couldn't keep from staring at the firm breasts and nipples of the young girls. They didn't seem to mind.

"We wash front."

Punky and Charlie glanced at each other as the Joy Sons started washing their fronts. They started at the top and worked down. Charlie watched as Joy Son washed Punky's chest and worked her way down his body. He jumped when her hand closed around his manhood. She washed his whole body all the way to his toes. Punky watched as Joy Son washed Charlie's breasts and nipples and worked her way down her body. Punky grinned when he saw her nipples turn hard. Charlie vowed she would kill Punky when this was over. It was all she could do to keep from moaning when Joy Son touched her below. After they finished they sat beside Punky and Charlie. They seemed to enjoy being with them.

"You feel good now?"

"We feel great," they said in unison.

"You off the, American ship?"

"Yes we are," replied Punky.

"Papa Son, work in machine shop, Mommy Son wash clothes and we work where we find it. What you do?"

"I'm a pilot and Charlie works for a large helicopter company."

"Mommy Son is real quiet," said Charlie.

"She, no speak American. We try to speak. Get better job if speak American."

"You, Joy Sons are doing real good," said Charlie.

"Thank—thank—you, need—need more practice."

They had been in the tank a long time and enjoyed talking to the family. They decided it was time to leave.

"You have to go back to the ship?" asked Papa Son.

"No we don't," replied Punky.

"You home with us."

Punky looked at Charlie, "You want to go home with them for the night?"

"We couldn't impose on them."

"No imp—impose, you teach us American."

Charlie looked at Punky, "I guess you have house guest."

"We go now."

They all got out of the bath and got dressed. Punky and Charlie followed them as they led the way home. They didn't live far from the bathhouse. They entered a small house with two rooms. It didn't have a lot of furniture. They had a couple of wicker chairs, a small table with short legs and pillows on the floor around the table.

"Mommy Son, fix food for guests."

She walked over to a small table and started to fix some food. Charlie stood by her and offered her help while trying to teach her English.

"What can I do?" asked Punky.

Papa Son handed him a large bucket, "Go with Joy Son and get water."

Charlie smiled as the girls left with Punky, one on each side of him. They were having the time of their young lives with a tall fine looking man between them. They were asking questions a mile a minute.

"Joy Sons like young man. Is he your man?" asked Papa Son.

"Yes," she said without hesitation, "He is my man."

"You are lucky I can sense things like that. He is fine man."

Punky and the girls returned and they were giggling like young girls. Punky placed the bucket of water beside the table.

Mommy Son made rice, egg soup and fish. Charlie placed the bolds of food on the table. It was a simple meal, but it smelled good. They had water to drink. Punky sat on the floor with a young girl on each side giving a lesson in English. They were eager to learn as much English as they could while they had a teacher.

"Time, eat," said Papa Son.

They gathered around the table on pillows. Mommy Son dished out food in small dishes. Charlie looked around for silverware. Mommy Son handed her chopsticks.

"I'll starve to death I never could get the hang of using chopsticks."

One of the girls helped her get used to using them. Finally Charlie could get some food in her mouth. "Thank you."

"You welcome," she giggled. They were learning to speak English fast.

After they finished their meal they talked a long time into the night. Finally Papa Son looked at them. "Time go to bed." He got up and motioned for everybody to follow him. The bedroom consisted of mats on the floor. There were two mats on one side of the room and two more on the other.

"You take mats on that side," said Papa Son.

"We can't do that those are the girl's mats."

"They get more mats."

Papa Son pulled off all his clothes except his shorts. Mommy Son took everything off except her panties. She wasn't wearing a bra just a simple dress. They lay down on their mats close together.

"You take clothes off," said Papa Son.

Punky looked at Charlie, "When in Rome."

"Yeah I know do as they do."

Punky undressed down to his shorts and lay on his mat. He smiled at Charlie, "Your turn sweetheart."

She glared at him, but removed her clothes down to her panties and bra. She hesitated for a moment as Punky watched her. "What the heck," she pulled off her bra and lay down beside Punky.

He put his arms around her and pulled her close. It was warm and they didn't have any covers. Her breasts were crushed against his chest. Her nipples became hard and dug into his chest. She could feel something hard against her belly and knew Punky had a hard on. She was burning up with passion and couldn't do anything about it. It was pure torture lying next to Punky.

The Joy Sons returned with their mats and put them one on either side of her and Punky. They undressed down to their panties and lay down close beside them. Punky scanned Papa Son and Mommy Son they were asleep already.

The Joy Son next to Charlie said, "You up tight me fix."

She massaged Charlie's back until Charlie let out a moan. The other Joy Son eased her body close to Punky and massaged his back. They massaged until they could feel Punky and Charlie relax. She cuddled up against his back with her nipples digging into his back. She put her arm across his waist.

The other Joy Son did the same to Charlie. Punky felt like he was in a torture chamber, but it felt so good. A few minutes later he could tell the Joy son was asleep.

"Charlie, are you asleep?" he whispered.

"You got to be kidding I'm burning up with passion."

"I'll fix that."

He eased his arm down between them and pushed her panties to one side. He eased his erection into her folds as far as he could with her facing him. She almost moaned as she took him inside her. "That's the best I can do now go to sleep," whispered Punky.

Charlie couldn't sleep and knew she couldn't move. She squeezed him with her inner muscles until she felt him throbbing inside her and knew he was coming. She kept on squeezing until she had a climax. They dozed off still coupled together. She was as content as a cat with a full bowl of milk. With Punky inside her and a hot body against her back she had never felt so contented and slept like a log.

Punky thought the Joy Son next to him was asleep, but she was playing possum. She felt Punky as he throbbed inside Charlie and she was burning up with passion. She wanted this man inside her. Girls had sex when they were young in Japan. She wandered how she could get him to turn over.

Finally she pulled a piece of thread off her dress and tickled Punky's ear. He moved, but didn't turn over. She kept on until he finally turned over. He was still asleep. He was on his side facing her, but his shaft was limp. She lay beside him and stroked him gently. She didn't want him or anyone to else to wake up. When he had a big erection she backed up to him. She spread her legs and reached back to guide his shaft into her hot folds. She backed up until she sheathed all of him. She pushed back and wiggled just a little. She was hot enough to burn his shaft.

She pushed back and forth enough to cause them both to climax. She bit her hand to keep from crying out as she came. Punky was dreaming that he was having a climax in Charlie and it felt so real. Joy Son moved away from Punky and went to sleep. He would never know how she had abused his body if you could call it that.

"Everybody up," said Papa Son.

Punky sat up and looked around. All he could see were naked women. He thought he was in heaven. He then remembered them coming to spend the night. He had never felt so alive in his life, but his body was sore. Charlie sat up and realized she was naked. She put her arms across her chest. "I think every bone in my body is broken."

"Young woman soft not used to hard floor," teased Papa Son.

The young Joy Sons got up and slipped their dresses on. The one that made love with Punky smiled at him and took her time putting her dress on. Punky and Charlie stood up and put their clothes on.

"Sorry, but we have to run. We have to catch a tour bus," explained Punky. He didn't want to tell him they were going to Nagasaki to see where the bomb hit.

They left and found a cab to take them back to the ship. The tour bus was on the dock waiting on everyone. They didn't have time to go onboard and change clothes. They got on the bus and found seats. They didn't know many of the people on the bus.

Charlie leaned on Punky with her head on his shoulder. She was tired and sleepy from sleeping on the floor. Her body protested at what she had done.

Punky pulled her in close, "Are you still hurting?"

"I feel like someone beat my body. Sleeping on the floor is not fun."

"Yes, but you had fun and had an adventure."

"Yes it was fun and I enjoyed staying with the family."

"You know that they asked us to come again."

"We visit in the daytime and go back to a bed at night."

"Papa Son was right you are soft," he laughed.

"Yes I guess I am, I don't want to sleep on a hard floor again."

They were out of Sasebo and driving through green countryside. Women were working in the fields while men were on banks of creeks fishing. The women were more of a workhorse than a sex symbol. They wore simple clothes and worked hard in the fields. If they had one small bowl of rice each day they thought they were lucky. Times were hard for most of the people.

"Charlie what are you thinking you have a frown on your face?"

"I think the women should be in the house doing woman's work and those lazy men should be in the field doing the work."

"Those lazy men are trying to put some meat on the table to go with the rice."

"I never thought of that."

Suddenly the bus pulled over to the side of the road. The driver had stopped so people could relieve themselves. The men went first. They lined up facing away from the highway and relived themselves. When Punky returned he smiled at Charlie, "Your turn sweetheart."

"I am not going to squat and pull down my panties out on the side of the road."

"It is still a long ways to Nagasaki."

"I'll hold it if it kills me, but I won't squat beside the road."

Some of the girls on the bus decided they couldn't hold it any longer. Charlie glanced outside the bus. The girls squatted facing the bus and their rear ends toward the field.

"You got to go, you got to go," laughed Punky.

"It's not funny," She jabbed him in the ribs.

The pit stop over the driver drove on toward Nagasaki. They arrived in Nagasaki and went straight to the museum. The bus stopped and let everybody off the bus. Ground zero was beside the museum. The Japanese had built a park where the bomb hit.

Charlie made a run for the museum looking for a bathroom. She couldn't believe her eyes when she found it. There weren't any doors on the entrance and men, women, and children all used the same bathroom. She couldn't hold it any longer. She went into the bathroom and dropped her panties modest be dammed.

When she came out Punky was leaning against the wall with a smile on his face. She would like to wipe that smile off his face. "Why didn't you warn me that everybody uses the same bathroom?"

"And spoil the fun no way. Better get used to it. I don't know any places in Japan that have private bathrooms."

They toured the museum and walked out to the middle of the park which had been ground zero. "Did you know thousands of people died here?"

"Yes and thousands more died at Hiroshima."

"It only took two bombs to end the war."

"I guess it saved a lot of American lives."

"Yes it did, but I hope we never use it again."

They walked hand in hand back to the bus. Some old Japanese protested them being there. They walked up and down beside the bus. After the bus was loaded the driver found them a place to eat.

When they were seated Charlie looked around at the other tables. "I see something that looks good at that table."

Punky looked over at the table, "Looks good to me."

A young girl asked for their orders. Punky pointed to the food on the other table. The girl got the drift. Charlie did the same.

"What are we going to drink," asked Charlie.

"Do you want a beer to drink?"

"It sounds good to me."

Punky pointed to a picture on the wall of a of draft beer. He pointed to Charlie and himself. The girl hurried away to fill their order.

"Now that wasn't so hard and we know what we are getting."

The girl brought two big glasses of draft beer. Punky held his glass up. "Here's to you kid."

Charlie picked up her glass and touched his glass. The beer was ice cold and went down easy. They had to have a refill by the time their food arrived. They sat by a window with a beautiful garden of flowers. They sat on pillows at a short table. Charlie tucked her legs under her while Punky didn't know what to do with his legs.

"Having trouble," giggled Charlie.

"Yes I don't know how to sit on a pillow. What do I do with my legs?"

"Tuck them under you."

He finally straightened his legs out on the floor and propped his arm on the table. The food was good and they put it away. After they finished eating they walked up and down the streets. They held hands everywhere they went. They had an hour of free time to do what they wanted to do. They saw a huge statue with his arms bent and his hands pointing up. They moved closer to the stature. Their guide from the bus was standing by the stature. "What does the stature mean?" asked Punky.

"It stands for peace."

"Thank you."

Punky and Charlie stared at the huge statue for a long time. It seemed strange to them after the war they had fought.

"We better get back to the bus," said Charlie.

"Do you want to buy something in the stores?" asked Punky.

"I'll wait and shop in Sasebo or Yokosuka."

"Ok let's get back to the bus."

They sat in the bus waiting for the rest of the group. Punky was staring at Charlie. He liked to just look at her. He watched her breasts rise and fall.

"What are you staring at?"

"You I never get tired of watching you."

Charlie blushed, "I feel the same about you."

"What are we going to do about us when the cruise is over?"

"I don't have a clue."

The rest of the group loaded aboard the bus. The tour guide announced they were going on top of a mountain by a trolley car. They traveled a distance before the bus pulled into a parking lot. They unloaded and walked over to a wheelhouse.

"Before we load onto the trolley car I would like to say a few words. If you are afraid of heights sat in the middle of the car and don't look down. If you have motion sickness we will give you a pill now. The car will swing back and forth when we take off and when we stop. Don't throw trash out of the car because we pass over people' yards and homes. When we reach the top you can see for miles. You can see the bay and your ship. They will look like toys from up there. Ok everybody can load now."

Punky and Charlie sat in the front of the car. When the car left the wheelhouse and started to climb to the top Charlie looked down.

"We are a heck of ways up the homes below look like dollhouses. They are small from up here."

When they reached the wheelhouse at the top everyone unloaded and walked around taking in the sights. It was like being on top of the world.

"Our ship looks like a model from up here," remarked Punky.

"It looks like that when we come in for a landing. I think it looks like a postage stamp when we are coming in for a landing."

"What's the name of the mountain?" asked Charlie.

"I read the name on the sign over there, but it is in Japanese and I can't pronounce it."

Charlie looked at the sign, "I can't read it either. We'll just call it a mountain."

When everyone was ready they loaded onto the car for the ride back. It had been an exciting ride up and down. When they reached the bottom the tour guide and driver went into a shrine to worship their God Buddha.

They came out shortly and told everyone to load back on the bus. The driver drove them down to the docks. "This is like what you call a grocery store in American. Over here most of the food is bought here at the docks. Since a big portion of our diet is fish and other seafood this is where peddlers bring wares for the public to buy. The difference being it is outside in the open and lain out on the ground or on tables. The fish are fresh, caught daily and sold before the day is over. Toward the end of the day, prices drop. The real poor people buy the last of the catch."

The driver drove the bus through the city while the tour guide pointed out places of interest. After a while the driver headed the bus back toward Sasebo. Charlie was tired and put her head on Punky's shoulder and dosed off to sleep. Halfway through the trip the driver pulled over for a pit stop. Punky left the bus and took a leak. He came back on the bus and smiled at Charlie. "Now it's your turn sweetheart."

"Yeah right I guess I will." She surprised him by leaving the bus to relieve her bladder.

"I didn't think you would pull your panties down on the side of the road."

"Well things change and I needed to go real bad. I would have probably wet my pants before we got back."

"I thought girls could hold it longer than guys."

"That's probably an old wives tale."

"Did you enjoy your trip?"

"Yes very much."

"How much longer will we be in port?"

"A couple more days, but I have Shore Patrol tomorrow and I thought we would hit the night life the last day in port."

"Sounds like fun to me."

"There is a large section of the city where every business is a bar or club. A lot of them are named after places in America. They like to name their bars after states. I want to visit the Texas Bar."

"Why do they name them after places in America?"

"I think they do it to attract Sailors and tourists."

"That's a good idea."

The bus pulled in on the dock next to the carrier. The bus unloaded a tired bunch of people. Punky and Charlie went straight to their cabins. They decide they would make love by dreams since they were so tired. Charlie wanted Punky to hold her while she slept. She opened the hatch to his cabin and peaked in. "Would you like a bed partner? I sleep better with you beside me."

"Sure, but you know how you turn me on. You may not get much sleep."

"I'll take that chance."

Punky slept naked. "You can sleep with me if you sleep naked."

Charlie only had a robe on. She slipped out of the robe and stood before him naked. Punky had a hard on in a second.

"Now can I come to bed?" she teased.

Punky moved over and held the covers up for her to slide into bed. She slid in beside him. They cuddled, he kissed her softly and she turned her back to him. He moved close to her back and put his arm around here resting his hand on her breast. She felt his hard erection close to her folds. They fit together like two spoons. They were both tired and dozed off to sleep. They would make love when they were both fresh and rested. It would be so much better.

Punky had to get up early and go on Shore Patrol. He had it all day. He got up and took a shower, shaved and dressed. He came over to the bed and kissed Charlie on the neck. She turned over and stared into his eyes. Punky could see love and passion in her eyes. "I got to go, sleep as long as you like."

"I will have fun."

"Yeah right I'm sure I will."

Punky wanted to crawl back in bed and make love to Charlie, but duty calls. He went to the hanger deck where the rest of the Shore Patrol was getting ready to leave the ship. It was going to be a long day.

Punky picked the biggest Sailor in the group for his partner. He hoped they wouldn't have trouble, but he wanted the power if they did. They didn't look for any trouble during the day, but the night might get rough. There were so many bars and clubs to patrol. He hoped there wouldn't be any fights, but when Sailors got drunk anything could happen.

"I hope we have a quiet night," said Punky.

"Not likely sir, we have too many Sailors on the beach."

The ship was on three section duty. Two thirds of the ship could be on liberty at one time. That was a lot of Sailors on the beach to stir up trouble. Punky and his partner checked out one bar after another. During the daytime it was quiet, but as the sun went down trouble started. Their first problem was a Sailor and a Japanese girl. The girl had promised to have sex with him. She had accepted four thousand yen from him which was the going price, but decided she didn't want to go with him. She had been offered eight thousand by another Sailor. He had bought drinks all evening in the bar where she worked.

"Joy Son, give back his money."

"He no care about money I try to give back."

"I want her to do what she said should would."

"I'm sorry, but the lady changed her mind. Give the Sailor his money back."

She gave back his money. Punky told the Sailor to take off. He learned a hard lesson. Never trust a prostitute. He had bought her drinks all evening and then lost out. Punky felt sorry for the young Sailor, but there anything he could do. I would suggest you go back to the ship and call it a night. You are so mad that if you stay on liberty you will probably end up in trouble," advised Punky.

"Do I have to go back to the ship?"

"No, but you need to leave the area. Find another bar and don't be too quick to give your money away."

"Thank you sir I won't."

They went to another bar. A Sailor was on the floor on his back staring up a girl's dress that was standing over him. Punky and his partner stood against the wall and watched.

"Should we break it up?" asked his partner.

"No he isn't causing any trouble yet. Let's watch the show and if it looks like trouble we'll take care of it."

The girl stepped back and reached under her short dress. She pulled off her panties and dropped them on the floor. She stepped back over the Sailor. He was staring straight up at her cat. She did bumps and grinds as she lowered her cat toward him until she covered his head with her dress. Everybody watched and knew what the Sailor was doing. Everybody watched as the Sailor brought her to a climax. She moved over and sat on the floor beside him.

He grinned at her. "Did you enjoy what I did to you?"

"Yes you go home with me tonight."

The Sailor jumped to his feet. "Hot dang you mean it."

"Yes we make much love tonight."

"I'll be right back."

He went over to a table and laughed, "Ok guys pay up." They had bet him he couldn't make out with a girl. She was beautiful and he had made out. They handed him their money. The sailor went back over to her. He smiled at her, "We got money to blow let's go buy you something nice. We can buy food and drinks on the way to your place." She hooked her arm in his and they left the bar.

"That Sailor is going to have a fun night," said Punky.

"Yeah I wish I wasn't stuck on Shore Patrol maybe I could make out."

"We are in port one more night maybe you will make out."

"If I don't it won't be for me not trying."

They left the bar and continued to patrol. They found two Sailors falling down drunk sitting on the ground. Punky called for a jeep to take them back to the ship. After the jeep arrived they went into another bar. It was called the Texas Bar.

"This is my home state. I want to see what it like," said Punky.

They entered the bar and stood close to the front door. The bar had decorations from Texas. Two girls in short skirts and low cut blouses approached them. "Want to have good time?"

"Sorry girls, but we are on Shore Patrol."

"I show what missing." She popped a breast out of her blouse.

"Come on we got to patrol before I do something an Officer shouldn't do."

When they were outside the bar, "Sir you must have nerves of steel. I would have taken the nipple in my mouth."

"Don't think I didn't want to."

"Tomorrow night I'm coming back to this bat and see if she wants to try that on me."

It was twenty three hundred hours and one more hour to go before their shift would be over. "Looks like, our night is almost over and not much trouble so far."

"Sir the last hour is the worst."

"Maybe we will get lucky."

They heard screaming and saw people pouring out of a bar two doors down. They knew it was big trouble. Punky ran down to the door and peaked in. There were six Sailors locked in battle. Drunk, Sailors were fighting.

"What is happening sir?"

"We got as fight in progress."

"What are we going to do?"

"Nothing, when the fight is over we'll take them back to the ship. Call for a backup and a van to take them back to the ship."

"The backup is on the way. Shouldn't we try to break up the fight?"

"If we had got here before they started swinging yes, but after the fight starts we will sit it out until it's over."

The van arrived and two other Shore Patrol. They got out of the van, "Sir what do you want us to do?"

"Stand by the door."

One of the Sailors was knocked close to the door. Punky reached in the door, grabbed him and dragged him out the door. The two, Shore Patrol shoved him into the van.

"That's one down and five to go."

Punky waited at the door for another one. One had been knocked silly and staggered around close to the door. Punky pointed to him and the two Shore Patrol pulled him out of the bar putting him in the van.

"That's two down and four to go."

They pulled two more out of the bar. The other two stood looking at each other and wandered what was happening.

"Ok you can go in and get the last two."

The Three Shore Patrol went in with clubs drawn. The two Sailors gave up without a fight. They marched the two Sailors outside. "Sir we were just having a little fun."

"Get in the van now. You will pay for the damages."

Punky went in, surveyed the damage and walked over to the bartender. He discussed the damage and they came to a figure that they agreed on. He had divided the damage bill by six.

The sailors dug out the money and gave it to Punky. He slammed the door on the van. He told, the two Shore Patrol take the Sailors back to the ship. He went in the bar and settled the bill with the bartender. It wasn't a big deal because they had fights in the bars all the time.

Punky and his partner worked their way back to where all the Shore Patrol was picked up for a ride back to the ship. There was a curfew after midnight and no Sailors could be on the street. They had to have a place to stay in town or go back to the ship.

Jerry was in the Oklahoma Bar just before midnight. He left the bar looking for a cab to take him back to the ship. A pretty young Joy Son approached him. "You stay in town with me."

"I don't think so you look very young."

"I eighteen old enough I give you good time."

Jerry didn't really want to go back to the ship and sleep alone. He knew she would want him to pay. "How much do you want to spend the night with you?"

She smiled, "Only four thousand yen."

Jerry calculated the price and it was just a little over ten dollars. She was wearing a short skirt and a low cut blouse. That was what most girls wore to entice customers. The slant eyes just made her more appealing to Jerry. Her body was tiny and she probably weighed less than a hundred pounds. A cab stopped to pick Jerry up. He held out his hand and she put her small hand in his. They got in the cab and she gave the cab driver directions. She reached over and put her hand on his erection. She smiled at him and felt him grow to full size.

"We make much love tonight."

Jerry shuttered as she ran her hand down the full length of him. The cab pulled in behind a large building and stopped. Jerry paid the cabdriver and he drove off. The Joy Son took his hand and led him inside. "Are you hungry?"

"Yes I am all I have done is drink."

"Come we eat."

She led him into a large room with short tables and pillows around them. They sat down and a Joy Son came over with a big platter of food for them. There were other couples in the room eating.

"You eat."

Jerry had trouble with the chopsticks, but she helped him until he could use them fairly well. He could at least get some of the food in his mouth. There was a small stage in front of the room.

Geisha girls filed out onto the stage. They danced to the sound of Japanese music. Well dressed, Japanese and American men came in and sat down at the couple of tables.

"You like to watch dance?"

"Yes it's the first time I ever seen a Geisha girl."

"Train since small child to be Geisha girl."

"They are beautiful."

"There are only few chosen for Geisha."

"Do they only dance or do they sell their bodies?"

"Sell also, but very high, see men?" She pointed to the men at the two tables.

"I get the picture."

"Girls dance pleasure, men bid on them highest get girl."

"Have you ever danced as a Geisha?"

"No, I was not chosen for Geisha."

They watched the girls until they quit dancing. They were told which man had bought them for the night and they joined the man at the table.

"We go to my room now."

She took Jerry's hand and led him down a hall to her room. It was small and had a mat on the floor. She had a small dressing table and a rack for her clothes. That was all she owned to her name. "I sorry I have no bed."

Jerry opened his arms and she went into them. He held her close and he had this urge to protect her. They stayed that way for a long time. Finally she stepped back and stared at him. She pulled off her skirt, blouse, panties and sandals.

"I undress you."

Jerry stood passive while she took off his shirt, pants, shoes, socks and shorts. She walked back into his arms and they stood naked together. She was short her head rested under Jerry's chin. Her nipples dug into his belly. His erection hit her above her belly. They didn't fit too well together because of their difference in size. It was hard for Jerry to think of her as a woman. She looked up at Jerry and smiled, "We make love."

"Yes we make love."

"You lay on back I make love."

Straddled Jerry guiding his shaft into her folds until, she slowly sheathed all of him. She sat still for a while adjusting to his size. Jerry reached up and cupped her breast with one hand and teased her nipple with the other hand. She moaned and started to ride him. She rode him hard and he thought he would die of pleasure before they both climaxed. She rolled off and lay breathing hard. "We do again when rested."

"That may be a while you wore me out."

She smiled and curled up next to him. They went off to sleep. About four hours later Jerry woke up with a big hard on. He looked up as she straddled again and took all of him in her hot passion. After she had made love to him again they went back to sleep again. Just before daylight Jerry looked up again to find her on top.

They ate breakfast together and she called a cab for Jerry to take him back to the ship. He gave her a very large bonus for her night with him. She went out to the cab with him and watched as he left. She realized she would follow Jerry anywhere. He was the first man to get to her heart.

Jerry looked back and felt like he was leaving part of himself behind. She stood there until the cab was out of sight before going inside. He was just a customer, but somehow he became more than a customer. She couldn't be in love with him.

Mammy Son stared at her when she came inside. She could see the Joy Son was very sad. "What's wrong with you?"

"I don't know feel like part of me is missing."

"Oh no, fall for Sailorman."

"I didn't mean to but, he so nice."

Punky was tired when he finally got back to the ship. He went straight to his cabin. Charlie lay on his pillow her hair fanned out around her head. It was like coming home when he slid in naked beside her. She was naked also. She turned over with her back to him. He eased up against her spoon fashion and put his arm around her. He was so tired he was asleep in seconds. He awoke to someone knocking on his hatch. Charlie slid under the covers and covered her head.

"Come in," said Punky.

"Sorry to bother you this morning, but I need someone to talk to. I got a big problem and need some advice," said Jerry.

"What is your problem?"

Charlie was so close to Punky's back that Jerry didn't know she was in bed with Punky. She lay very still and hoped Jerry wouldn't know she was there.

"I went out last night and met a girl. I spent the night with her in a Geisha house. We watched the Geisha girls dance and made love several times during the night. We couldn't get enough of each other."

"Sounds like you had a good time. So what's the problem?"

"She is a hooker."

""So what is wrong with that?"

"I think I fell in love with her."

Charlie pushed the cover from over her head, "You can't be serious."

"What are you doing in Punky's bed?"

"Would you believe sleeping? I don't like to sleep by myself," she grinned at Jerry.

"Yeah right, you know you two could get in a lot of trouble."

"What are they going to do? They going to kick me out of the Navy for things I did unbecoming an Officer."

"Punky you are a maverick and you never follow rules."

"Heck rules are made to be broken."

"Are you going to tell on us?" asked Charlie.

"Of course not, now about my problem."

"The only advice I can give you is follow your heart. Now who is crazy? After only one night with a girl and you are in love with her."

"I can't explain it, it just happened."

"Well good luck on what you decide."

"Thanks."

"By the way where does she work?"

"She works at the Oklahoma Bar."

"Funny that's where Charlie and I are going tonight. We are going to the Texas Bar just across the street from the Oklahoma Bar."

"Will we see you there tonight?" asked Charlie.

"I don't know. I haven't decided yet."

"What's her name?"

"Would you believe I forgot to ask?"

"Jerry you are crazy like Punky. I can't believe you are in love with a girl and don't even know her name."

"That's funny, I can't believe it myself."

"I don't know about you two, but I'm going back to sleep." Charlie turned over with her back to them.

"I'll see you two later."

Jerry left and went back to his cabin to think about last night. It was not an easy decision to make. Was he in love with her? She was a hooker and could he live with that, knowing she had been with other men? In modern day time ninety nine percent lost their cherry before they were out of high school. So what was the problem? Could he take a Japanese girl home as his wife? What would his Mother say? She would say he had lost his mind. He would say he had lost his heart. He lay on the bed and stared at the ceiling, but no answers came to his questions.

Punky shook Charlie, "Wake up sleepy head."

"I want to sleep in and I'm hungry."

"Get up and we'll go get breakfast."

"How about if you serve me, breakfast in bed."

"Charlie, where am I going to get food?"

"Steal it from the Officer's Mess."

"Honey I'm an Officer and a gentleman and you want me to steal?"

"Lover you never go by rules unless it is for your benefit."

"You are going to owe me."

"Hurry up, I'm starving to death."

Punky came back with two trays of food and coffee. "I had a hard time pulling this one off. I didn't steal the food I bribed the cook and he helped me sneak the food out of the mess."

"Poor baby I'll make it up to you."

They had bacon, eggs, grits and toast. After they finished eating they were full and took a nap. When they woke up Charlie made love to Punky to pay him for their breakfast.

"Do you want me to steal lunch?"

"No silly it's time for us to get up and get going. We can take some food and things with us. We can visit the Japanese couple. They didn't have much and they shared with us."

Charlie went back to her room. After taking a shower she dressed for the day. She applied a small amount of makeup. She added a drop of perfume behind her ear and between her breasts. She wanted to keep Punky's attention. She knew the two young Joy Sons mooned over Punky. They could look, but don't touch.

Punky went to the Officer's Mess and bribed the cook again for a large sack of food. He tapped on Charlie's door. She opened the door and he stared at her. He never got tired of looking at her.

Charlie smiled, "Do you see something you like?"

"Yes I do I never get tired of looking at you because you are so beautiful."

She blushed at the comment. She liked it when Punky called her beautiful. She never got tired of looking at him either. "You don't look so bad yourself."

Punky took her arm and they left the ship. He asked permission to leave the ship and saluted the flag.

"Why do you salute the every time you leave the ship and come back on board?"

"It is a military custom the same as colors."

They caught a cab into downtown and went shopping for some clothes for the family. They bought Japanese style clothes for the adults and western style for the girls. They bought some candles and a blanket for the Mother.

They walked the short distance to the Japanese couple's home. They were met at the door by one of the Joy Sons. She screamed with joy at seeing them. The rest of the family came from the bedroom. They were so happy to see them. Charlie passed out the gifts to the family. The girls couldn't believe their eyes when Charlie handed them their new outfits. The girls started taking off their clothes to try on their new outfits. Charlie pushed Punky into the living area. He took the food with him.

Father Son followed letting the girls have some time together. When the girls finished dressing they went into the other room to show Punky and their Father.

They were beautiful and Punky told them so. They were wearing American style dresses and with their trim bodies they were beautiful.

Mommy Son took the sack of food and started supper. They had brought a huge ham, sweet potatoes, corn, rolls and an assortment of fruit. They had also brought a large tin of coffee, sugar and can milk. The family had never seen so much food.

Punky and Charlie enjoyed their visit with the family and promised to visit again if they came back to Japan. It was dark by the time they left and headed for the bars. As they approached the bars Charlie was staring at the girls out front of the bars.

"Are they what I think they are?"

"Yes do you want to make us some spending money?"

Charlie poked him in the side, "Don't you wish? If I did I wouldn't spend it on you."

"Now I'm really hurt. You don't love me anymore."

They stopped in front of the Texas Bar. The girls greeted them and one opened the door for them. A girl approached them from the bar, "Buy a girl a drink?"

"Sure why not."

If looks could kill Punky would be dead. Charlie glared at him. How could he pick up a girl with her with him? The young woman led them to a booth. "I fix drinks what want?"

They both took draft beer. She left them and headed for the bar. She was a drink hustler and got part of the take.

"Why did you pick up that girl?"

"Three reasons, first we have our own private waitress, second she gets a little of the drink money and third she can give us a rundown about things. "

"Now I'm not mad at you." "All we do is to buy her a drink and it is probably watered down."

The young woman returned with their drinks. She sat beside Punky while Charlie sat across from them.

"How do you like working here?" asked Charlie.

"It ok part time I school teacher. I make extra money and practice American talk."

"Do the other girls outside have other jobs."

"Most have jobs some school teacher like me."

Charlie stared at Punky, "I can't believe it. They would get fired in a minute back home if they were caught working like this."

"Hookers are legal in Japan and it's looked on as just another job to make ends meet."

"Are you married?"

"Yes."

"Where is your husband?"

"Papa Son home taking care of little Joy Son while I work."

"He doesn't mind you working in a bar?"

"Have little money have to work to make ends meet as you say."

Jerry walked in the door and saw them. He came over and sat down beside Charlie. He looked at Charlie and back at Punky. "Am I missing something here? Why do you have two girls?"

Charlie giggled and explained it to Jerry. He asked for a beer and told the young woman to get, herself a drink. He looked very nervous.

"Have you been across the street yet?" asked Punky.

"No not yet I can't make up my mind."

"Talk to the young woman with us. She is a school teacher."

The young woman returned with their drinks. She thanked Jerry for buying her a drink. The more drinks they bought the more money she made.

Jerry stared at her for a moment, "Could I ask you a personal question?"

"Yes."

"Do you think a hooker could make me a good wife?"

"Very good wife, love and respect you forever for picking her."

"Do you think she would leave Japan and come to America with me?"

"Yes many girls go to America. Make good wife take good care of you."

"What do you think guys?"

"Follow your heart," advised Punky.

"I'll see you guys in a few minutes. I got to see a girl about a lovesick guy."

Jerry left the bar and headed across the street to the Oklahoma Bar. He stood outside and looked around. She was standing at the corner of the building. She walked slowly toward him. Jerry opened his arms and she ran to him.

"You come back."

"Yes I come back. We have to talk. I want you to come with me over to the Texas Bar. I have friends that I want you to meet." Jerry took her hand and they went across the street. They entered the bar and Jerry led her over to the booth. He told the other girl to bring drinks all around. Charlie watched the young woman and could see love in her eyes every time she looked at Jerry. Maybe it wasn't a bad thing for Jerry.

Jerry started at the girl. Do you know I don't know your name?"

"Kim Lou my name."

"This may come as a shock to you, but I love you."

She stared at him, "Kim Lou love you too. I hurt other morning when left. I felt part of me missing."

"I felt the same way." He opened his arms and she went into them.

"Isn't love grand? I'll have to try it sometime," said Punky.

"Yeah right," Charlie punched him in the ribs.

"You know my ribs are going to be sore tomorrow."

"Good enough for you."

The girl came back with drinks for everyone and they toasted Jerry and Kim Lou. They all sat and talked while Jerry and Kim Lou made plans. Jerry gave her money and told her she was his girl and didn't work anymore. He told her to meet the ship in Yokosuka and they would get married by the ship's Chaplain. As soon as the paperwork went through she would fly to America.

Kim Lou wanted Jerry to stay with her, but the ship was leaving early the next morning and Jerry didn't want to miss it.

"We have the rest of our lives to spend together."

At eleven thirty, Punky, Charlie and Jerry caught a cab back to the ship. Kim Lou watched the cab until it was out of sight. She couldn't believe the young American Officer was in love with her. She would do anything to make him as good wife. They were trained from little girls to honor the man and please him. Kim Lou smiled she would please him very much. She would make love to him every night and have beautiful children together. She had read about America and their customs. They were so different from Japan, but she loved Jerry and would do anything to fit in. She walked across the street and shouted to the girls in front of the Oklahoma Bar.

"I don't have to be a hooker anymore, I'm going to America."

The girls gathered around her and wanted to know all about her good fortune. They couldn't believe she had an Officer for her Own. Some girls had married enlisted men and went to America, but this was the first Officer to fall in love with a hooker.

"See you later girls." She would work where she lived, but not as a hooker. She would cook and clean for her rent and food until she went to Yokosuka to marry Jerry. She would save Jerry's money and use only what she had to.

McDaniel and Morgan were at the dock with their girls when Punky, Charlie, and Jerry got out of the cab. They told about their leave and where the girls took them. They had seen a lot of Japan while on leave. Finally the girls took a cab and left.

"Well guys here we go again until the next port," said Punky.

"What is our next port?" asked McDaniel.

"Kobe and I heard we are the first carrier to ever pull in there."

"That should be fun."

"I'm not so sure they say not many of the people speak English." They loaded back aboard ship.

CHAPTER SEVEN

At zero six hundred preparations were made to get underway. The gangways were removed, lines taken in and the order given to get underway. Punky and crew had flight deck parade as usual. Air Group stood flight deck parade while the ship's crew got the ship underway. As soon as flight deck parade was dismissed Punky and crew went to the ready room to check the flight schedule. They had a flight at sixteen hundred to screen for the carrier.

McDonald and Morgan went to their shops to work. Punky, Charlie and Jerry went to the Officer Mess for coffee. The seas were rough as the ship headed north. The UH-2A had been replaced while in port and they didn't have to do plane guard until it broke down again.

When they launched and started screen duty it was hard to get back in the swing of things. After an hour, sonar picked up a target and they gave directions for a bomb run by another helicopter. They bombed it, but they knew what it was. Their target left the area at a fast speed. The rest of the flight was normal routine.

Punky told Daniel and Morgan what happen while they were on leave and how glad he was to have them back. The next few days were normal routine until disaster struck.

"Battle stations, man your battle stations, fire on the hanger deck by number one elevator this is not a drill."

Punky and Charlie just made it to the ready room before the hatches were closed. A damage control team fought the fire with foam. It was spilled fuel that had caught fire. They laid a blanket of foam over the whole area and finally put the fire out. A couple of planes were damaged, but not too bad. They could be repaired, but it would take time. The foam was a mess to clean up. Fire is the ship's worst enemy. You have to stand and fight it. You don't have anywhere to go. After everything was back to ship shape general quarters were called off. There would be an inquiry into the cause of the fire and try to keep it from happening again.

Punky looked at Charlie, "Coffee time."

"I'm ready, let's go to the mess."

They got their coffee sat and stared at each other. They would do this for long periods of time and never say anything. They loved each other and let it show in their eyes.

"I don't know about you, but I'm ready to pull into port again for some fun and relaxation," said Punky.

"Do you realize we haven't made love in a long time?"

"Yes I know and I may break another rule."

"And what is that?"

"Come to your cabin tonight even if we are out at sea and make love to you."

Charlie became hot just thinking about making love to Punky and rubbed his leg under the table with her ankle. She smiled at him as she inched her ankle higher up his leg. He got an instant hard on.

"You better cool it or I might take you here on the table with God and everybody watching."

"Promises, promises," She was having fun teasing him.

"Fun's over, we have a flight in about an hour. We better go to the ready room and get ready."

That was the trouble being at sea all you did was eat, sleep and fly. It got to be boring after a while. McDaniel and Morgan were shop supervisors and had to work in their shops along with their flying. They didn't get much rest or sleep.

The brief was about a submarine in the area and they didn't know whom it belonged to. He would stay clear of the fleet unless he wants to play the game.

They lifted off at eighteen hundred and took the screen forward and starboard of the carrier. Punky flew the helicopter into a fifty foot hover.

"Sonar pilot commence standard sonar search. Watch out for that submarine in the area. We don't want him near the carrier."

"Pilot sonar standard search."

Every fifteen minutes they would move on to the next search area. The S-2E aircraft used mad to try and find the sub. They flew low over the water searching for the sub. The destroyers used sonar to try and find the sub. It was the submarine against the fleet with all the equipment used against him, but he was still hard to detect. He was a silent killer who stalked his prey.

Punky and crew had searched for two hours and nothing so far. They were in the air when an S-2E reported a possible mad contact and gave bearing and range. Jerry called the S-2E pilot and told him we were on it. Punky flew into a hover and sonar went to work. Sonar had the transducer down to one hundred feet and on active search. He picked up the contact moving away fast.

"Pilot sonar I have a target one hundred fifty yards, one eight degrees and moving away at twenty knots."

Jerry called the S-2E aircraft and they lined up for a bombing run on the submarine. They dropped a smoke, P.D.C. and smoke. The submarine didn't make contact, but high tailed it from the area.

"We got his attention let's give him a little more reason to leave the area," said Punky.

"Sonar pilot raise the ball and let's go after him again."

Punky flew the helicopter into another hover, "Sonar pilot down dome."

"Pilot, sonar roger down dome."

When the transducer reached one hundred feet, "pilot sonar I have a target at one hundred yards, one eight five degrees, speed twenty five knots. He's trying to get away."

"Sonar pilot stay on him."

Jerry called the S-2E with speed and bearing. He could read it off the meters in the front, but the sonar operator had to keep the cursor on the target. The S-2E made another run on the submarine dropping another smoke, P.D.C. smoke.

"Pilot sonar they landed right on target."

Jerry called the S-2E crew and gave them the good news. The bad news was they didn't know which country the submarine belonged to. They had chased him away from the fleet. If the submarine had persisted trying to get in range of the carrier they would have dropped real bombs on him. They would protect the carrier at all cost. Any aircraft that wasn't part of the fleet was met and turned away from the fleet. The A-4B aircraft fully armed would turn them away from the fleet.

"Well our flight is over and here comes our relief time to go home," said Jerry.

Charlie had sat through the whole flight and hadn't said a word. "Why haven't you said anything?" asked Punky.

"You guys were too busy doing your job for me to butt in. I enjoyed watching you work. Would you have dropped real bombs on the submarine if he had gone after the carrier?"

"Yes we would. Nobody goes near the carrier unless we know who they are."

Punky was bringing the helicopter in for a landing when it started to go ballistic. He fought the controls to get it over the flight deck. "Hang on guys it's going to be rough."

The helicopter hit hard and did a lot of structural damage to the helicopter. Jerry shut off the engines with the rotors still spread. The crew was shook up, but no one was hurt. They exited the helicopter and surveyed the damage. It had jammed the struts up into the body of the aircraft. Punky looked at Charlie, "Well you wanted a crashed aircraft to find out the problem on the aircraft."

"Yes, but I didn't want to be in a crash to find it."

"Do you have any idea what caused the crash?"

"It acted like a stuck control valve. Now I got to find out for sure."

The Air Boss came out to the aircraft, "Well Mr. Wilson I see you are at it again. This one being your, third crash."

Charlie's anger rose and she jumped in front of Punky. "Sir whoever you are this was not Mr. Wilson's fault. The controls locked up we were lucky he landed the aircraft on the carrier and not in the water. Now maybe I can find out why the controls go crazy on the aircraft."

"I'm sorry I didn't know you were on the aircraft. From where I was standing it looked like pilot error."

"Well it wasn't. The controls were locked. I was sitting next to him while he fought the controls to land the aircraft."

"Maybe crash the aircraft would be more like it," said Punky.

"You always told me landing aboard an aircraft carrier was a controlled crash."

"Yes, but I didn't control this one."

The Air Boss shook his head and walked off. The helicopter was moved below to the hanger deck. Charlie would try to find the cause of the locked controls. The helicopter looked like someone had stomped on it. They went to the ready room for a de brief and fill out an accident report. Charlie wanted to get started on the helicopter and find out what caused the crash. This was her job. This was why she came on the cruise to find out what caused the controls to go crazy.

"Do you want me to help you with your investigation?" asked Punky.

"No, but could you get me a man from airframes, electric, and the mechanic shop. They can take things apart when I need it."

"You got it. When do you want to start on the investigation?"

"Right now, while the controls are locked."

"I'll get the men and their tools."

"Thank you."

Charlie put on her work clothes and started on her investigation. A little later three men showed up with tool boxes. She started a list of possible causes and assigned them to the men. The electric checked ok. The hydraulics checked ok. They checked the complete system, but the controls were still locked. They moved the rotor wing and the controls unlocked and worked normal. Charlie still didn't have a clue as to what caused the lockup of the controls. She crawled upon the engine platform and started to inspect the rotor wing. After inspecting the rotor wing and controls she still didn't have a clue.

"Change the pitch on the rotor wing."

Charlie watched as they changed the pitch over and over. She still didn't find the problem. "Ok guys let's knock off for now. We'll work on it more tomorrow."

The Sailors went back to their shops. Charlie stood staring at the rotor head. Whatever was causing the problem was acting like a closed valve, but all the valves were working normal. What would cause the same effect?

Charlie went to her cabin and pulled off her dirty clothes. She went down the hall and took a shower. She dressed in a skirt and blouse. It made her almost human again. She went next door and knocked on Punky's hatch, but he didn't answer. She went looking for him and found him in the Officer Mess drinking coffee.

"You know that stuff is bad for your health." The coffee was so black and thick you could cut it with a knife.

"OH well we have to die of something."

"I can think of better ways to die," she giggled.

"Charlie you got your mind in the gutter."

"Do you want to come down in the gutter with me?"

"Yes, but I don't want to get all hot and not be able to take care of the problem. Just you wait until we get back in port we are going to catch up on our love making."

"Promises, promises, that's all I get."

"How is your investigation coming?"

"It's not we have checked the complete system and can't find the problem. It acts like a stuck valve, but they all check normal."

"How about a pinched line, wouldn't that act like a closed valve?"

I didn't see any pinched lines."

"Well I would look harder I bet that is the problem."

"Well smart ass you can help me look."

"When do you want my help?"

"Tomorrow morning."

"I'll be there, but right now I need my beauty sleep."

"Punky did anyone ever tell you were crazy?"

"Sometimes they call me crazy."

"I'm going to get some sleep. Would you like to walk me to my cabin?"

"Only, if you kiss me goodnight."

"I think I can handle that."

Punky walked Charlie to her hatch and opened his arms. She walked into them and put her arms around his neck. It always seemed so natural. It seemed she had known him all her life not just a few weeks. He put his arms around her waist and pulled her tight against his body. She could feel his hard on pressing into her belly and it made her hot with desire. She looked into his eyes and saw passion and love. He lowered his head and covered her mouth with his. He thrust his tongue deep into her mouth and teased her tongue. It built her passion even more. Finally they came up for air. They were breathing hard. If they didn't stop Punky would take her in the passageway.

They kissed one more time and went to their own cabins. Charlie undressed and stood in front of a mirror. She touched her nipples and found them hard as marbles. She liked what Punky did to her, but now she would have a hard time sleeping.

Punky lay naked on his bunk thinking about Charlie. They had to work out a solution to their problem. He didn't know how he could live without Charlie. He was sure that she was his, sole mate.

Bright and early the next day Punky and Charlie plus the three Sailors were hard at it again trying to solve the problem. They had overlooked it the day before. Punky and Charlie climbed upon the engine platform. Charlie was on one side and Punky was on the other side. They were looking the rotor head over with a fine tooth comb. Punky told the Sailors to move the rotor blades. It was hard to do manually. They worked at it for a while. Just when they were about ready to give up Charlie told them to hold it. "Guess what guys? I think I found the problem."

Punky came around to the other side of the engine.

He stood beside Charlie as she pointed to a hydraulic line which was in a bind. "Punky I hate to admit it, but I think you were right. That line goes into a bind when the rotor wing changes pitch."

"How will you fix it?"

"Very simple reroute the line and that will solve the problem. We have to inspect all the other helicopters for the same problem."

Charlie showed the airframe Sailor how to reroute the line. After he had completed the job Charlie inspected his work. There were two more helicopters on the hanger deck. Charlie inspected them and found one with the same problem. The other helicopter was ok.

"What do we do now?" asked Punky.

"Write a directive to inspect all Sh-3A helicopters for the problem. Then we send it out to all the squadrons."

"Does that mean your job is finished?"

"Yes, but I am going to ask to finish the cruise just to be sure."

"Do you think your company will let you?"

"They normally let me be the judge and there isn't too much of the cruise left."

"We got three more port calls before we head home."

"What are the ports?"

"Kobe, Hong Kong and back to Yokosuka, then we head home."

"Home sounds so good, but what about us?"

"I don't know what to say. I can't see my life without you in it, but I don't have an answer to our, problem."

The next two days were routine eat, sleep and fly. The next morning the carrier pulled in off shore and dropped anchor. To go on liberty they would have to go by boat. The enlisted went by an open boat called a whaleboat while the Officers boat was covered. It looked like a cabin cruiser, but not as fancy. The boats were referred to as liberty launches. Punky and Charlie stood on the flight deck looking at the city of Kobe.

"Do you want to sight see today?" asked Punky.

"Only if we come back early, I'm going to make wild passionate love to you tonight."

"We could go to my cabin now and make love."

"If we went to your cabin we would never make it off the ship. The longer we wait the better it will be when we do make love."

"Ok I'll meet you in the passageway in thirty minutes. Will that be enough time for you to get ready?"

"Yes thank you."

They walked down the steps on the side of the ship and got into the Officer's liberty launch. The water was choppy and made the ride in a little rough. Charlie thought she would be seasick by the time they tied up to the dock. She was fine as soon as she had her feet on dry land.

"I never get airsick, but for some reason riding in a bouncing boat makes me seasick."

"Are you ok now?"

"Yes let's get on with our sightseeing."

They took a cab into the middle of the city. They had a hard time making the cab driver understand them. The city was modern compared to a lot of Japan. They went into several stores and tried to shop, but gave it up as a bad idea.

"Doesn't anyone in this city speak English?" asked Charlie.

"I don't think we will find many that do. Ships don't pull in here and tourists go to other parts of Japan."

"Now I know how someone feels that is in America and we don't speak their language."

"Let's find a place to eat and get a cold beer."

They found a nice restaurant to eat at, but had trouble ordering. When they were in Sasebo and Yokosuka a lot of people spoke English, but not in Kobe. They finally manage to get some food and beer, but not what they wanted.

People stared at them from other tables. They hadn't seen many Americans in their city. They finished eating and went back to strolling down streets. They were approached by children wanting their autograph. At first they didn't know what the kids wanted, finally when the kids handed them paper they figured it out. Charlie dug into her purse for a pen.

"Has anyone ever asked you for your autograph?" asked Charlie.

"Only to sign a speeding ticket when, I was in high school."

"Did you get many tickets?"

"Yes I did."

"You must have been a bad boy with hot wheels. The one mother's didn't want their daughters to date."

"Guilty as charged."

They wandered around all over town until it started to get dark. They were close to the water when they decided to go back to the ship. They had wandered off the beaten path and couldn't find a cab. They walked out on an old pier and was confronted by two men with knifes. They didn't know if they wanted to rob them or just didn't like Americans. One man took a swipe at Punky with his knife, but he sidestepped him and shoved him, off the pier. The other one lunged at him. He managed to grab the hand with the knife in it and twisted it out of his hand, but he was getting the best of Punky.

Charlie came up from behind and hit the man with her purse. He let go of Punky and turned on her. He hit her in the face sending her sprawling on her buttocks. Punky recovered and the fight was on again. This guy was tough and wouldn't go down.

"Charlie, get out of here."

"Not without you."

The fight raged on, they were evenly matched. Punky could feel blood running down his face. Charlie came up behind the man again and hit him with her purse. He turned to hit Charlie, but Punky bulldozed him off the pier into the water. Charlie looked down the pier and saw two men running toward them.

"We had better get out of here."

"Good idea."

They took off down the pier trying to outrun the two men. They entered a dark area and suddenly Charlie screamed. She fell through space and hit the water. She had fallen through a hole in the pier. Punky heard her hit the water. He dropped into the hole after her and hit the water beside her. When he came up she threw her arms around his neck. It was dark under the pier. Punky grabbed a pole holding up the pier. The other two men had got out of the water and they could hear all four of them running around on the pier looking for them.

"We got to get out of here," whispered Punky.

"How are we going to do that?"

"We swim in the direction of the ship. It should be to the right."

"Yes, but how far?"

"I have no idea, but we can't stay here."

Punky led the way and Charlie followed. They swam until they were exhausted before Punky grabbed another pole.

"Why don't we get back on the pier?" asked Charlie.

"The mugs may still be looking for us and where would you like to get out? I don't see a ladder to crawl up."

They took off swimming again. It seemed like hours and they were still under the pier. They would stop and rest then swim some more. Finally they found an old rowboat under the pier. Punky pulled himself into the boat and helped Charlie get in the boat. It had only one old paddle, but it would have to do. Punky started paddling in the direction of the ship.

Punky I'm cold."

"We'll take turns paddling and that will warm you up."

"Punky I see a liberty launch coming from the ship. The dock can't be too far now. Let me row awhile so I can get warm."

"Ok you can row out from under the pier now. I think we are safe from the mugs."

Charlie rowed as fast as she could. It helped her stay warm. Punky took the last turn and rowed them in beside the loading dock. They got out of the boat and let it drift away. The Officer's liberty launch pulled in and docked.

"What happened to you guys?" asked the boat Officer.

"We decided to take a swim," replied Punky.

"I don't buy it. What really happened?"

"We were mugged."

"Come on in the cabin. I think there are some blankets to wrap you in."

"Thank you."

They took the blankets and sat in the back of the boat. They huddled together and slowly warmed up. There were only a few Officers returning to the ship. The Air Boss recognized Punky and came to the back of the boat.

"Mr. Wilson what happened, did you crash another aircraft?"

It wasn't funny to Punky, "No sir we were mugged."

He then noticed the blood running down Punky's face. Charlie had a split lip and bruises on her face.

"My God you two look awful. Tell me what happen."

After they told their story the Air Boss told them how sorry he was. "We need to post that area off limits to the Sailors. Do you remember where you were?" "Not really we were under the pier most of the time and everything happened so fast."

"You two report to sick bay when we get to the ship."

"Yes sir we will," replied Punky.

Punky and Charlie had a hard time climbing the ladder up to the ship. They were sore all over. Punky thought he had a broken rib or two. They headed for sickbay. It was below the hanger deck. They were put in separate rooms for an exam.

Charlie had a split lip and bruises to her face. She also had splinters in her buttocks where she slid across the pier. They told her to take a shower and come back to get patched up. Punky was worse off. His ribs weren't broken, but badly bruised. He had small cuts on his face, a fat lip and one eye almost closed. He also had a few small cuts on his body. They told him to take a shower and come back. Punky and Charlie helped each other back to their cabins. They took showers and went back to sickbay.

The Doctor took two stiches in Charlie's lip, put cream on her bruises and pulled some splinters out of her buttocks. He put something that set her on fire on her rear end. She stood in the waiting room and waited on Punky.

Punky had to have several stiches on his face and body. The Doctor wrapped his ribs in a wrap-a-round bandage. He was given a shot for pain before he left and some pain pills. He felt like he had been run over by a truck. Charlie was waiting for him when he came into the waiting room.

"Punky you look like hell."

"I feel like every bone in my body is broken, but they say I don't have anything broken."

They climbed the stairs again and went to their cabins. They tried to kiss in the passageway, but couldn't manage it. Charlie went to her cabin and undressed. She looked at herself in the mirror. She didn't like what she saw. She lay on her bed naked thinking about what a close call they had. They could be dead now.

Punky lay naked on his bed hurting all over. He decided he didn't want to sleep by himself. He started to get up when he heard a faint knock on his cabin door. Charlie peeked in the door. "I don't want to sleep by myself tonight."

Punky opened his arms to her. She slipped out of her robe and joined him on the bed. She didn't want to hurt him. "This was the night I was going to make love to you."

"Yes I know, but I don't think I can be much help."

Charlie lay beside him and reached for his penis. She stroked it softly while Punky lay still on his back. When he was hard she straddled him and guided his shaft into her folds. She slowly sheathed all of him. She sat not moving to see if it hurt him. She was content to sit there with his shaft in her. "I'm going to try and move on you. Call out if it hurts."

She pulled out until only the tip of his shaft was inside her. She started to bounce up and down on him. It hurt, but Punky bit his lip and let Charlie have her way with him. It hurt and felt good at the same time. She came first, but he was right behind her. She sat on him until she felt him go limp.

Charlie lay beside Punky and was content to go to sleep. She needed the release from tension after the scare she had today. She was so tired now she didn't think she would have any bad dreams.

Punky laid his arm across her naked body and went to sleep. They slept almost until noon the next day before Charlie opened one eye and stared at Punky. He had more bruises on his body than he did last night. One eye was almost closed shut and his lip was huge. It would take a while for her and Punky to be back to normal.

"Wake up sleepy head."

Punky opened one eye the good one, "Do I have to?"

"Punky you look like hell."

"Sweetheart you don't look too good yourself. Have you looked in the mirror?"

"I'm afraid to."

"Well we won't look any batter later so let's get up, I'm hungry."

Charlie got up and put on her robe. She peaked out in the passageway to see if it was clear. "I'll meet you in the hall in fifteen minutes." She ran across the hall to her cabin.

Punky wasn't sure he could get out of bed. He hurt all over his body. He was finally able to get dressed and meet Charlie in the passageway. His ribs hurt like hell. They entered the Officer Mess and all eyes turned their way. Jerry motioned for them to join him at his table. He took one look at them and shook his head.

"Do I dare ask what happened to you two, did you have a fight?"

"Funny, no we were mugged last night."

Punky explained how stupid they were wandering into a bad part of the city and how they ended up under the pier. He told them how they had to swim and finally found a boat.

"What does the other guy look like?"

"Probably a lot better than I do."

"Are you going out tonight for some more fun and games?"

"Not likely I'm staying on board until we leave port unless I have to stand Shore Patrol."

"How about you Charlie, are you going on liberty?"

"I'm staying on board. I've had enough of this port."

"Well I'm going on liberty, see you later and don't do anything I wouldn't do."

They finished eating and went back to Punky's cabin. They pulled their clothes off and went back to bed. Charlie cuddled up next to Punky and rubbed his back. He was asleep in minutes. Charlie lay staring at the celling. She wanted to make love, but she didn't want to hurt him.

They were in port four more days. Punky had Shore Patrol on the last day, but was relieved when he reported for duty. His eye was open, but was a little dark his lips were almost back to normal. His ribs still hurt sometimes.

The last night in port and Punky was going to enjoy it. He came back and tapped on Charlie's cabin door. He opened the door and peaked inside. "I'm scared to sleep by myself."

"I'll be right over," giggled Charlie.

A few minutes later Charlie entered Punky's cabin in her robe which she pulled off and let drop to the floor. She stood naked before him. She liked to tease him before she got in bed with him. He was naked under the sheet. She could see the sheet rise where his manhood was. She loved the effect she had on him. She also liked the effect he was having on her. She moaned as her nipples harden. Her body became hot and she knew she was slick and moist. Punky raised the sheet and she slid in beside him. She turned her back to him so he could enter her from the back and not hurt his ribs.

Punky eased up to her and entered her wetness. He grabbed her hips and gave her all he had to give. She moaned his name. "It feels so good Punky."

"Yes it does sweetheart," He picked up the pace.

They made love several times that night before they finally went to sleep. The ship was underway early the next day. They checked the flight schedule. They had a flight that evening.

"Charlie you don't have to fly with me now if you don't want to. You found your trouble on the helicopter."

"You're not getting rid of me that easy. I want to be with you."

Punky liked the sound of her wanting to be with her man. He hoped they would be together forever and grow old together. He wanted to be on the porch rock in his rocking chair and her in a rocking chair when they were old. Where did thought come from? They were still young and weren't married yet. He knew she was his, sole mate.

"Punky what are you thinking? You seemed a million miles away."

"I was thinking how much I love you and what we would do when we are old."

"What will we do when we are old?"

"Sit on the front porch rock in our rocking chairs and watch the cars go by."

"Punky, are you turning into a romantic?"

"Where you are concerned I guess I am."

When they reported to the ready room the word was watch for Russian aircraft, ships and subs. They were not to penetrate the task force. The cold war could get heated up at times. Saying to watch out for Russian threats was the understatement. Punky and crew launched for screening duty. They were on station a few minutes when the A-4B aircraft was launched to intercept two Russian Bear coming in from the south. They were fully armed and ready for action. The three A-4B aircraft spread out to meet the Russian Bear head on. Just before they got with range of the fleet they turned off and flew on past the fleet.

Everything was normal for a while. Punky and crew did several dips with their sonar and didn't have any contacts. Then all hell broke loose. An unknown helicopter flew over the top of Punky's helicopter headed for the carrier.

"Sonar pilot raise the dome."

"Pilot sonar roger dome raised."

Punky pulled the helicopter up fast and gave chase. Another helicopter was ahead of Punky hot on the tail of the unknown helicopter. When they were closer to the unknown helicopter Jerry recognized it.

"It's a Russian helicopter the one that can land or takeoff out of the wind. A crewman is opening the hatch and has a camera in his hand. The Admiral isn't going to like this."

The Russian helicopter stopped suddenly and the American helicopter just missed slamming into him. The Russian stopped out of the wind and the American helicopter went over the top of him missing him by inches. Punky came real close to the Russian and he retreated, but he had got his pictures. He had broken through their defenses. If it had been an attack he would have had a shot at the carrier. He was close enough to have launched a torpedo. That was not good.

When they returned to the carrier and went to the ready room they were showing movies of the Russian helicopter and how close he was to the carrier. The Admiral was pissed off to say the least. He wanted answers as how the Russian was able to fly right up to the carrier.

Combat center thought he was one of our helicopters. They didn't know where he came from or what his range was. The helicopter didn't have I.F.F. gear so why wasn't he asked for identification? They thought it had quit working. There was a lot of butt chewing in Combat Control. Punky was glad for once he wasn't on the hot seat. He had more than his share already. "

"Well that was fun let's get something to eat."

"Don't you think the Admiral was a little hard on everybody?"

"He has to be being responsible for all the ships in the task force."

They ate and went back to their cabins. Charlie came over for a while, but they only talked about their future together, but couldn't make any decisions as how they would work it out. They talked about Jerry and how he made a split decision about taking a Japanese girl back to the states to marry her.

"His parents will come unglued," said Charlie.

"Yeah like if I brought a black girl home to meet my Mother."

"Well I wish him luck."

They talked a while longer before Charlie went back to her cabin. She would like to stay the night with Punky, but they were operating at sea and anything could happen. They needed to stay sharp at all times. Duty came first and loving second. They were having so much contact with the Russians that the ship started to have battle station drills regularly. Just as Charlie closed her cabin door one was sounded.

"Battle stations, battle stations all hands man your battle station."

Punky met Charlie in the passageway on the way to the ready room. They had to go up to the hanger deck and up to the level just below the flight deck. They checked in and sat down to wait until it was over. They would man aircraft if they were ordered to.

All stations called in to Combat Control Center as they were manned and ready. The drill lasted about thirty minutes before it was called off. "All hands secure from drill."

"Do you want to get some coffee before we go back to our cabins?" asked Punky.

"Sure I'm wide awake now."

They went to the Officer's mess and had coffee. Then they decided to return to their cabins. They stood in the passageway and held hands for a while before going into their cabins. "You can go to bed and dream about a beautiful girl," teased Charlie.

"Do you have someone in mind?"

"Me you silly ass, it had better be"

"Now be nice and I might do just that."

Punky took the chance and pulled Charlie into his arms for a goodnight kiss. She felt something pressing against her belly, but she knew what it was. She liked the fact that she had so much effect on him, but he had the same effect on her. Her nipples were as hard as marbles her folds were hot and wet. He broke the kiss. "We better stop while we can," warned Punky.

"Yeah I might take you down in the passageway and have my way with you," giggled Charlie.

One last kiss and they went their separate ways. It was a good thing they went to bed alone. Three o'clock in the morning Punky was shook awake by a Sailor. "Sir a pilot is sick and they want you to take his place. The launch time is in an hour." He wasn't too happy about the news, but he rolled out of his bunk and started dressing. "I'll be in the ready room shortly."

"Yes sir."

The Sailor left and Punky finished dressing. He didn't like flying with another crew, but sometimes it happen. He went to the ready room and met his new crew. They seemed fine as far as he could tell, but you never knew how a person would act under pressure. He didn't like manning an aircraft in the dark and trying to check the aircraft with a flashlight, but it had to be done.

Punky started the engines while the crewman checked the hoist. You never knew when you might need the hoist. The Copilot called for permission to lift off. "Bennington tower 05, permission to lift off."

"05 Bennington tower you are cleared for lift off." He gave them weather, ship's position and the position they would be at when they returned to the ship. The Copilot dialed in on the plotting board their position and put an X where the ship would be when their flight was over.

If the gear worked as expected and the ship was on course it would be a piece of cake, but if the gear quit working or the ship didn't stay on course it could be fun. Everything worked as advertised and they came back to the ship after a very boring flight.

When they landed the crew thanked him for being their pilot. Their crew flew together all the time also. They didn't know what to expect from Punky, but everything worked out fine.

Punky found Charlie in the ready room waiting on him. She had held off on breakfast until he got back off his flight. "Well how was your flight?"

"It was very boring."

"That's because I wasn't there to cheer you up." she grinned at him.

"You're right I missed you."

"I waited breakfast on you."

"Good let's go eat I'm starved."

After they ate Punky went back to his cabin to try and catch forty winks. Charlie decided to hang around the ready room and read. Jerry found her there and they talked awhile.

"I hope Mom and Dad don't flip out when I bring Kim Lou home to be my wife. I can't believe it myself."

"Maybe they won't take it so bad. After all she is a beautiful young woman. I think she loves you very much."

"I still don't know how it happened. I just know I love being with her and I think she feels the same way about me."

"Will it bother you knowing she was a hooker?"

"I don't think so Japanese people don't look on her as bad. They think it is just another way to make a living. She hasn't been a hooker very long."

"Their way of living is certainly different from our life style. Can you see only one bathroom at home and everyone using it?"

"Not really," laughed Jerry. "I'll let you get back to your book."

Charlie read until she got sleepy. She lowered her chair and took a nap. She slept right through lunch. Punky came into the ready room and sat down beside Charlie. He liked to just sit and watch her. She had a smile on her face. He wandered what she was dreaming. He hoped she was dreaming about him.

"Wake up sleepy head you going to sleep all day?"

Charlie groaned and opened one eye. "What time is it?"

"Suppertime you must have slept through lunch."

"I can't believe I did that."

"Well let's make up for it. I slept through lunch also."

"By the way we have another night hop. We take off at eight."

The weather turned bad before their flight. They had to do a preflight in the rain and high winds. It was times like these when you would like to curl up in bed and sleep.

"Ok crew tonight is going to be a bummer. I'll try and keep the helicopter from pitching and rolling as much as possible."

Jerry called for permission to lift off. As the ship dropped from going over a large wave Punky lifted off before it hit bottom. It made for a smooth takeoff. They had the starboard aft section for screening. Punky managed to fly the helicopter into a hover while the sonar operator went to work. The automatic pilot had a hard time holding a hover. He had to keep his hand on the stick all the time.

"I don't think we have to worry about our Russian friends tonight. We are the stupid ones to be out in this weather."

The wind came harder and the helicopter shuttered. Charlie reached forward and put a hand on Punky's shoulder. He glanced back at her. "Are we going to be alright," she asked.

"They say these birds are all weather birds I hope they are right. We are sure taking a beating."

Suddenly the automatic hover fell apart and the helicopter dropped almost touching the waves. Punky recovered in time to keep them out of the water. "Sonar pilot bring up dome."

"Pilot sonar dome coming up."

"I'm going to fly along and not dip until the wind dies down."

Just before the flight was over the winds died down and Punky made a smooth landing. They were glad to be back safe and sound. Punky and Charlie went for coffee after they had debriefed from their flight. They then went back to their cabins. They were tired and exhausted from the flight. Punky lay in bed and thought about

Charlie. They would be in the port of Hong Kong in a couple more days. He wanted to take Charlie all over the city. He heard the city was something else to see. There were so many different people that lived in Hong Kong.

There were many people living in cardboard boxes on the side of a hill. There were people starving on the streets of Hong Kong. There were rich people and very poor people that were starving. Punky wanted to see the San Pan Village that he had heard about.

The next two days was all bad weather. The carrier pitched and rolled all the time. There were a lot of seasick Sailors. Finally the carrier headed toward Hong Kong. When they were close to Hong Kong the ocean finally settled down. The ship knocked off flight operations.

Charlie and Punky went out on the flight deck and watched as the ship approached Hong Kong. There were all types of fishing vessels in the water. There were a few large ships going and coming from the port. The carrier was too big to go into Hong Kong. It would anchor out in the bay. They would have to ride a liberty launch if they wanted to go on liberty.

"Did you get in the anchor pool?" asked Punky.

"No what is an anchor pool?"

"Everyone puts money in the pool and draws a number which is the time the anchor is dropped. The one with the closet time to the anchor drop wins the money. There are usually several anchor pools throughout the ship."

"Did you get a time for the anchor drop?"

"I got ten o'clock, but I'm never lucky."

"What happens if two of you get the same number?"

"Then you split it. But the numbers are divided in minutes so there is never a tie."

"What time is it?"

"Nine thirty five and they will be dropping the anchor any minute now."

"Poor baby, how much are you going to lose?"

"I will lose twenty dollars."

The ship dropped anchor at nine forty seven. Punky wasn't even close. Well easy come easy go was his motto.

Boats came from every direction to meet the carrier. Hong Kong sent word to the carrier that they would run a ferry to and from the carrier to make it easy to go ashore. Word was sent back thanking them and the carrier would donate water from the ship to put in their water supply. The carrier made its own water and wouldn't need as much since a lot of the Sailors would be ashore on liberty.

A small tanker would come along side and the water would be pumped aboard and took back to the city water supply. Hong Kong was on water hours a lot. The city was always short on water.

"Are you ready to see Hong Kong?" asked Punky.

"I'm ready I have always wanted to come to Hong Kong."

"Then let's get dressed and hit the beach. I don't have duty for two days. I got Shore Patrol the third day in port. That should be interesting. I hope I get a better part of the city. They say some of it is real mean."

They went to their cabins and got dressed to hit the beach. They could ride the Officer launch, but they went down the enlisted ladder and got on the ferry. They could see the city real good from the ferry. It was an enjoyable ride to the shore. When they got off the ferry they didn't know where they wanted to start. They could see the Hong Kong Hilton in the distance.

"How would you like to spend the night in Hong Kong?"

"Oh Punky I think it would be fun."

"Then let's go and get a room before they are all taken."

They walked into the Hilton hand in hand. Punky went to the desk and asked for a room. They were lucky to get a room because the hotel was almost full. They got a room on the third floor facing the front of the hotel. Punky took the key in one hand and Charlie's in the other. They took the elevator to the third floor. "What's our room number?" asked Charlie.

"We are in room 305."

Punky took the key and opened the door. Charlie stepped inside and glanced around. It had a large king size bed, a couch, another large chair, dresser, television, and thick brown carpet on the floor. Charlie kicked off her shoes and walked across the carpet. It was expensively decorated. "I like to feel the carpet on my feet."

Punky jumped in the middle of the bed. "I love a big bed. I'm going to sleep good tonight."

"Yeah right and it's going to snow tonight."

"Well part of it anyway." He was grinning like a possum.

Charlie sat down on the bed. "I guess you know we didn't bring anything to stay the night."

"We can buy anything we need downstairs. All we need is a toothbrush and toothpaste. I like to travel light."

"We better get going if we are going to see Hong Kong."

"Just one kiss before we go."

"No kissing Punky, you know what would happen if we had one kiss. We would never leave the room."

"You are a spoiled sport."

Charlie pulled Punky up out of the bed and turned toward the door. He knew she was right. He had a hard on just looking at her and the king size bed. They went down to the lobby and looked around. They decided to eat before leaving the hotel. Punky knew it would be expensive, but it was nice to know what you were eating. He looked around at the people. This was where the rich people came. Punky had been saving his money and he wanted them to have a good time.

The hostess seated them and a waitress came to take their order. She handed them the wine menu first. Charlie selected the wine. Punky didn't drink much wine since he got sick on it in high school. He had been drunk for two days. Every time he drank water he was drunk all over again. He ordered a large t-bone steak, baked potato and a salad. That was his favorite meal. Charlie ordered a full rack of baby back ribs, baked potato and a salad.

A couple came in flanked by two mean looking men in black suits. Punky could see the bulge in their suits and knew they were packing guns. The woman looked to be in her late twenties. She was about five feet six, long legs showing from the split in her dress. She had natural blond hair and her complexion was flawless. She had on a small amount of makeup. She looked to be British. She was the most beautiful woman he had ever seen. She had a string of diamonds around her neck that cost a fortune. The man was dressed in a black tuck. The couple looked like they could buy Fort Knox. Punky couldn't take his eyes off of her.

Charlie punched him in the ribs, "Don't you know it is impolite to stare?"

"Sorry I have never seen anything like that couple."

"She has a beauty mark on her left cheek."

"So what if she has a beauty mark?"

"She wasn't perfect. She had one flaw."

Punky turned his attention back to Charlie. "Where do you want to start when we leave here?"

"Let's wander down the middle of the city and see where it takes us."

When they left the hotel there were a bunch of dirty ragged kids hanging around in front. They wanted money and tried to tear Punky's pockets off his pants. He reached in his pocket and pulled out some Hong Kong dollars. He threw them into the street. The kids broke and went after them. He glanced at Charlie. "Let's get the hell out of here."

"I'm with you."

They took off running and didn't stop until they were out of sight of the kids. The kids were starving and attacked anyone they thought they could get money from.

"Now that was different being attacked by kids."

"I guess you will do anything if you are starving," replied Charlie.

They wandered further into the city. They saw all kinds of people. Hong Kong had a mixture of all the different countries. A little girl of about twelve came up to Punky and took his hand. "You come with me and I show you good time, I cherry you be first."

"Honey I have a girl to show me a good time and you are too young to be doing this."

"I not too young show you better time than her."

"No, I'm sorry."

"You can have mamma she cherry."

Punky pulled out some more Hong Kong dollars and gave them to her. "Take the money and go home."

"Have no home live in box on side of hill. You come see on other side town."

Punky glanced at Charlie and she nodded. They had wanted to see the people living in boxes. This way they had a guide. He took her hand and motioned for her to lead on. She smiled at Punky and led the way. She was full of information. "See family on sidewalk wait turn to use room to eat and sleep. They live in one room."

"Sometimes several families live in one room, take turns eat and sleep. They wander around until it is their turn."

They were close to the edge of town. They saw people on the sidewalks waiting to die. They had no hope. Punky and Charlie would like to help, but they couldn't help very little. They didn't have much money.

They were high up on a hillside and could see the ship in the bay. It was almost like being on top of the world. "See down there that San Pan Village people live on small boats, very poor people."

"How could anyone live on something that small?" asked Charlie.

"I guess you do what you got to do," replied Punky.

There was a large cluster of small boats in a tight group. They tried to count how many, but gave up. "A whole family will live on one boat."

Charlie looked amazed, "Those boats can't be over eight feet. How can they eat, sleep or use the bathroom?"

"Use water when go."

"In bad weather, don't some of the people fall overboard in the water?" asked Punky.

"Yes they drown."

"That's terrible."

"Life cheap here more room in boat for others."

They could see the shacks on the side of the hill. They were made of anything they could find to keep the weather off them. Most of them were made of cardboard. A few of them had some wood. They stopped in front of a small shack. "Live here," she motioned for them to enter the small door.

On the floor were a woman and a small boy. They were both dirty and ragged. They looked up as they entered. "Hun-Ying," the woman said.

"Mamma Son, say welcome."

The mother or little boy didn't speak any English. The mother was young, but hard times were telling on her and she liked much older. She motioned for them to sit down. They sat in a circle facing each other. The little girl said most of the people crossed the border from China to be free, but now that they were free what could they do now? Some found jobs in the city and women became whores to survive. Punky looked around and saw a small bag of rice. If they cooked they had to be careful not to set the whole place on fire. He didn't see any more food. He reached in his pocket and pulled out some more Hong Kong dollars and gave them to the woman. She started crying from happiness. They could survive a long time on the money he gave them.

The young girl hugged Punky and thanked him for giving her Mother money. She said they would use it wisely and make it last a long time. They got up to leave and the little girl walked them to the edge of the shacks. Punky and Charlie walked down the hill toward the city. It was hard to believe people had to live like that.

"I feel so helpless not being able to help these poor people."

"The government should help them, but they won't."

They walked back toward the city and watched the people in San Pan Village as they moved around. It was another horrible place. "I'm glad we live in the land of the plenty," said Charlie.

"These countries are nice to visit, but give me the good old U.S.A."

"It makes me sad to see all the food that is wasted back home and could be used to feed these poor people."

They walked back into the city and went into shops to shop around. Charlie was so sad at the things they had seen she didn't even like to shop. When she started to buy something all she could think about were the poor people of Hong Kong. They worked their way back toward the hotel. When they got back to the hotel they went straight to their room.

"Let's take a nap before supper," suggested Charlie. "I'm tired from all that walking. I feel like we walked fifty miles."

"It sounds good to me."

Charlie undressed down to her bra and panties and looked at Punky. He had everything off except his shorts.

"What the heck," she pulled off her bra and panties and jumped in bed.

"What the heck," he took his shorts off.

He jumped in bed beside her. He pulled her into his arms and held her. They were asleep in about five minutes. They were exhausted.

Charlie woke up first and looked at the time on the clock radio. They had slept for four hours and it was dark outside. Punky was sleeping on his back. She reached over and stroked his manhood. It stood up and he smiled, but he was still sleeping. Charlie eased over and straddled him. She eased up and lowered herself until she sheathed all of Punky's erection. She started to move slowly and he opened his eyes.

"What are you doing?"

"I'm abusing your body."

"Well don't stop."

"I won't," she picked up the pace.

After she finished with Punky she fell off and lay beside him. They were both breathing hard. They had gone to the edge of the world and fallen off. Slowly their breathing returned to normal.

"After all the exercise I'm hungry," said Charlie.

"Me too let's get dressed and try to find something to eat."

They were walking down a hall toward the restaurant when they passed a party in a banquet room. It was a bunch of British. A young woman saw them pass and came out into the hall. "Where are you going? The party is in here."

"We aren't part of your party," replied Charlie.

"You are now I'm inviting you to party with us."

She led them into the room and called for everyone's attention. She told them they had two Americans at their party and to make them feel at home. British people liked Americans and liked to party with them. Before they knew what was going on they were seated at a table with several other couples, a plate of food in front of them and a beer in their hand. The night turned out to be a fun night. The British were off a cruise ship docked at the pier.

They stayed at the party until two in the morning. They danced, eat and drank until they were starting to get drunk. Punky helped Charlie up from the table and she leaned on him as they said goodnight to their party friends. They took the elevator up to their floor. They had a hard time walking to their room. They sang as they walked.

When they finally entered their room they fell, face down on the thick carpet. Punky rolled over and stared at Charlie. "Sweetheart I think you are drunk."

"I am not it's you with the big feet that tripped me."

"I did not."

"You did too."

"I did not."

Charlie eased over and laid half on top of Punky. They were both sleepy and they passed out on the carpet. It had been a long day. Punky woke up at four in the morning. Charlie was still on top of him. He eased her over to his side then picked her up and laid her on the bed. He lay beside her and went back to sleep.

Sunshine shined on them through the window facing east. Charlie opened one eye and thought her head would fall off. She glanced at Punky and he was still sleeping. She got up and used the bathroom, took a long hot shower. They had to be out of the room by noon. She let Punky sleep on and she sat by the window looking out over the city. Looking out over the city you never knew all the hardships and heartache that went on in Hong Kong. She thought about the brave little girl and her Mother. She hoped they would be all right, but you never knew.

Charlie called room service and ordered some breakfast. She went and tickled Punky's feet to wake him up. He sat up in bed and looked around.

"Get up sleepy head breakfast will be here shortly."

"I can't move my head will fall off."

"Get up."

"Ok, ok, I'm getting up"

Punky got up and went to the bathroom then took a shower. He came back into the room and dropped the towel. He had a big hard on. "Do you want to work off our headaches?"

"I think it would make it worse."

"Last chance," he put on his pants and shirt, but left the shirt unbuttoned. Charlie stared at his hairy chest. She liked to lay on him and run her nipples through the hair. It made her hot thinking about it.

"Button your shirt our breakfast should be coming."

A knock sounded at the door and Charlie went to the door. The waiter wheeled the cart into the room. She tipped him and he left. Charlie had ordered coffee, eggs, bacon, hash browns and toast. They were both hungry and started eating right away. "How do you want your coffee?" asked Charlie.

"Black and did you get some aspirins?"

"Yes they are on the tray."

"That was a fun party with the British, but I hate hangovers."

"How did I get off the floor? I don't remember getting in bed."

"I woke up about four and I picked you up then put you to bed."

"Did we make love last night?"

"No we both passed out on the carpet."

"We were going to make love all night."

"Sorry about that there will be other times."

"What are we going to do today?"

"Go back to the ship I got Shore Patrol tonight."

They checked out of the hotel and went to catch the ferry back to the ship. The rocking motion of the ferry made Charlie sick. As soon as they made it onboard she made it for her cabin. Punky would do the same, but he had to go on Shore Patrol.

He went to his cabin and put on his uniform to go on Shore Patrol. An hour later he was back in Hong Kong walking the streets on patrol. He didn't like the area he would be on patrol. It was close to San Pan Village in a bad section of the city. He had a First Class ordnance man for a partner. Nightsticks were all they had for protection. He didn't like patrolling that area at night, but they didn't have a choice. In the daytime they didn't have any problems.

It turned out to be a dark night. Two, backup Shore Patrol met up with them on patrol. It seemed safe enough with four of them. They were called into a bar where a fight had broken out. Chairs and bottles were flying everywhere. "We better get this one under control before they destroy the place. I would like to wait until it is over, but we don't have a choice," explained Punky.

Two of the Shore Patrol went in and pulled one of the Sailors outside. Punky and the First Class put handcuffs on him and waited. A few minutes later they came out with a second Sailor. With the two hard cases out of the fight it stopped the fight. They took the two Sailors back to the ship and left Punky and the First Class to patrol.

Things were quiet for a while. They were walking down a dark street when they noticed two men following them. They walked faster and the two men walked faster. "I think we are in trouble," said Punky.

"I think you are right. What are we going to do?"

"I don't have a clue. I hope we can get off this street before they catch us."

They were almost to the end of the street when two more men stepped out in front of them blocking their exit. They were boxed in. Punky noticed that they had knifes or a club. The men were slowly closing in on him and his partner. "Cover my back," said Punky.

"It doesn't look good sir."

"If you get a chance to break go for it. If you make it bring help."

All four rushed them at the same time. The First Class decked the first man, but the other one took him down with a club. Punky had managed to keep his feet and backed over toward a wall. The other man got to his feet and now he was facing four of them. They were slowing moving in for the kill like a pack of wolves. All, Punky had was a nightstick for protection. He used it like a knife and jabbed them keeping them at bay, but for how long. He didn't want to end up dead on a street in Hong Kong. He kept jabbing, but he was getting tired. He knew he couldn't last much longer.

Suddenly a young woman called to the men and they turned to face her. She walked by them and stood in front of Punky. They argued with her and he thought she would back down. She stood her ground and took a karate pose. The men looked at her and laughed. Punky didn't know what was being said, but he almost laughed at the girl ready to take on four bad guys.

They were tired of talking. One man came at the girl and she hit him so many times Punky couldn't count them. With a final kick she brought him down. She struck a karate pose again. Another man rushed her and she sidestepped him smashing his nose and giving him neck chop as he went down. He hit the ground hard and didn't get up. She struck her karate pose again. She motioned for the next man to do battle. He rushed her and she did a flip over him. When he turned around she smashed him in the face with the palm of her hand. She twisted in the air and struck him on the side of the head with her foot. He stood there dazed while she finished him off with a couple more kicks to the side of the head. He fell to the ground and didn't get up. She struck her karate pose again and motioned for the last man to do battle. He wasn't a fool. He turned and ran as fast as he could. Punky looked around and none of the three men were moving.

"Are you alright?" she asked.

"I think so just a little sore here and there."

"Your arm is cut. You are bleeding. Tear a piece off your tee shirt."

Punky ripped his tee shirt and handed her a piece of it. She bound it around his arm to stop the bleeding.

"We got to get away from here fast he come back with more men."

"Help me with my partner."

They picked him up between them and moved down the street. Two blocks down she motioned for Punky to go into a building. She lived in one room, but now they were safe. The men didn't know where she lived. They laid the First Class on her bed on the floor. She got a wet rag and washed his face. He started to come around. "How did we get out of that fight?"

"You are looking at the one who saved our ass. She is an army of one. She whipped three of them and sent the forth one packing."

"Wow."

"You stay the night and leave in the morning."

"We can't put you out and we have to report back in at midnight."

"Better late going back or not going back at all, men see you on the street tonight and they will kill you."

"Good point we will stay the night."

She looked at Punky and stared at his jacket. She reached and touched the wings on his chest.

"You pilot?"

"Yes I am a pilot."

"You owe me your life."

"Yes I guess I do."

"I collect debt."

Punky stared at her, "What?"

"You go close to Viet Nam?"

"I don't know if the ship will go close to Viet Nam."

"If you go, close to Vietnam save my family, Mother, Father, and Brother."

"What are you talking about?"

"My village is just inside South Vietnam close to the border. When Viet Cong cross border they go by village. They say our men join Viet Cong or they destroy village and kill everyone. My Father head of village and he will not give in to Viet Cong. They will kill family and destroy village. Need you to fly them out you fly helicopter yes."

"Yes I fly helicopter, but I could never convince my superiors to let me fly into Vietnam for that kind of mission. I don't know if the ship will even go close enough anyway."

"You owe me your life yes?"

"Yes I owe you my life."

"Promise if you get close enough you will try to save my family."

"Ok I promise."

"You honest man I see in eyes you will do it."

Punky had made a promise and he would keep it somehow. He couldn't believe what he had just done.

"Is he with you?"

"No he isn't part of my crew. We are just standing Shore Patrol together."

She was wearing a top and bottom that looked like pajamas and it didn't look like she had anything on under them. Her nipples strained at the pajama top. She was small only around five feet two inches.

Her face was round with slant eyes. She had long black hair and weighed less than a hundred pounds. She looked very young.

"How old are you?" asked Punky.

"I am twenty three."

"You look about sixteen."

"Thank you."

"You are also very pretty."

She slipped off her top and threw it over to the side. She started to slip out of her bottom.

"What are you doing?"

"Get ready for bed and make love if you want to."

Punky stared at the beautiful young body and got a hard on. He couldn't help himself, but it ended there. "I'm sorry I have a girlfriend back at the ship."

"I no tell if you no tell."

"I'm sorry I can't cheat on her. I love her too much."

She looked at the First Class, "You have girlfriend?"

"No I'm single."

"Pull off clothes I sleep with you."

Punky slept on one side of the room on a pallet and they slept on the other side. He turned his body toward the wall, but he could hear them making love. It was going to be a long night. He couldn't believe he had turned down such a beautiful woman to make love, after all he wasn't married yet, but he would feel guilty. He must really have the love bug. He was finally able to drift off to sleep.

The next morning they reported back to the ship and told them what happened to them last night. Punky went to sickbay and got three stiches in his arm. The First Class was checked for a concession, but he had a hard head and was fine. They didn't say anything about the sex or what the girl asked Punky to do.

Punky found Charlie in the ready room reading a love story. When he entered she saw the bandage on his arm.

"What happened to you?"

"I ran into some trouble last night. I guess the men didn't like Americans. They wanted kill us and rob us, but a young woman saved our ass."

"This I got to hear."

"She used karate and was very good at it."

Punky told the story again leaving out the sex part and the promise he made. He didn't want to involve her in it if it happened.

"Are you hungry?"

"Yes I haven't eaten since I left the ship yesterday."

"Then I'll take you to breakfast," said Charlie.

"I thought we were pulling out today, but we will be in port two more days."

"What do you want to do today?"

"Get some sleep after last night."

They finished breakfast and went back to their cabins. He took a shower and shaved. Punky lay in bed staring at the overhead. Charlie waited until she knew Punky was cleaned up. She tapped on the door and entered.

"Can I sleep with you?" I don't like to sleep by myself," giggled Charlie.

Punky was on his bed and all he was wearing was his shorts. Charlie had her robe on and slipped it off. She had nothing on under the robe. Punky had an instant hard on. Charlie walked over to the bed and reached for his shorts. She slipped them off over his hips.

"Now we are dressed the same both naked."

Charlie stared at Punky and his erection. It made her hot looking at his very male body. She liked what she saw. "Where do you hurt?"

"I hurt all over."

She put her hand on his shoulder, "Ouch." She touched the other shoulder, back, chest and each time he moaned. "You are in pretty bad shape. I'll kiss your hurt spots and make it better." She kissed him on the lips and moved to his shoulder. She kissed the other shoulder, back, and down the front. She teased a nipple with her tongue, kissed his belly and moved lower. She kissed down one leg and up the other. She stared at his shaft. She reached over and took it in her hand. "Well you got one part that isn't hurt."

"I guarded that part carefully."

Charlie stroked his erection and finally kissed the head. She took as much as she could in her mouth and wrapped her tongue around it. That got Punky's attention. She straddled him and lowered herself until his erection was fully sheaved. She started to move slowly and stopped. "Am I hurting you?"

"Who cares move your butt."

Charlie rode him hard. Punky thought this was what his sore body needed to make him well. They made love two more times that night. Finally after they were exhausted Charlie curled up beside him and they went to sleep.

They stayed aboard the ship the next day. They wandered around the ship and spent a lot of time on the flight deck watching the ships go by. They watched a movie and worked out. Punky was feeling much better. That night they curled up together and talked way into the night. They were still trying to figure a way to be together after the cruise was over.

CHAPTER EIGHT

The ship upped anchor early the next morning and headed out to sea. The task force joined up and everything was back to normal. Punky and his crew had a flight that night and did screen duty for the carrier. The task force started round the clock operations and war games.

The first five days passed without any problems, but on the sixth day the weather turned bad. The ship pitched and rolled through the waves. Flights were few or called off. Punky, Charlie and crew were in the ready room on standby. It started to rain hard and Punky was glad they weren't flying in the mess.

The Operations Officer walked to the front of the ready room. He had a sheet of paper in his hand and was reading it.

"Gentlemen we have a serious problem. Two medium size ships have run together. One has a big hole in the side and is sinking. The other ship has a lot of damage on the bow and isn't sure they can make it back to port. They are located about ten miles north of our position. The carrier is turning toward them as we speak. At this time the weather is terrible and we should hold off on launching our helicopters, but if we wait a lot of Sailors will die. Anybody who wants to launch his helicopter may launch at this time."

Punky glanced at his crew and they gave him thumbs up. They gathered their gear and headed for the flight deck. Their helicopter was ready to go since they were on standby. They lifted off in a few minutes and the ship directed them toward the ships in trouble.

McDaniel, Morgan and Charlie went to the back to put on gunner belts. The helicopter was pitching and rolling all over the sky.

"I see the ships," said jerry. He called the carrier and told them they were going in. The ship was sinking slowly. They had to get the crew off as fast as possible. Punky started an approach to the sinking ship. "This is going to be a rough one, hang on."

McDaniel slid the back hath open. Charlie gave Punky directions. It was too rough to use the joy stick. She would talk him in.

"You are coming up on the ship. Easy forward, easy forward, hold, hold, the hoist is going down, steady, steady, the hoist is down, one man in the sling, hoist coming up, hoist is up and survivor is in the aircraft."

"Hoist is going down."

They did the same thing over and over. They now had seven survivors in the helicopter. Jerry pointed south of them. They could see four more helicopters approaching the ship. Jerry called the other helicopters. "We are pulling out. We have a full load and will be back shortly. Help yourself."

Punky pulled up and headed for the carrier. Jerry called the ship and asked for landing instructions. Two helicopters went in over the ship. One went in on the starboard side and one on the port side. They had a lot of Sailors to get off the ship before it sunk. They looked like bees gathering honey. As soon as the two were loaded the other two took their place. Punky landed and let the survivors out. He lifted off and headed back. He met two helicopters coming in. Punky made it back to the ship just as the other two helicopters were leaving.

Punky flew in over the ship. The ship was almost under water. They pulled the last two Sailors aboard as the ship went down. The Captain and the First Mate were the last to be picked up. Both ships were from Japan. The other ship limped toward Japan. The weather started to clear as Punky came in for a landing. The Helicopters had rescued thirty two Sailors off the sinking ship.

A ship was headed toward the carrier from Japan to pick up the survivors. The survivors were given dry clothes and food. They would look funny when they left the ship in American Sailor outfits. They didn't care they were glad to be alive. They were gathered on the hanger deck and the helicopter crews went down to see them. They visited with them while they waited on the ship to pick them up and take them back home.

Several of the Sailors invited the helicopter crews to come to their homes when our carrier pulled back into Japan. When the ship arrived a hoist was rigged between the ships and the survivors were transferred from the carrier.

"Well that was fun," said Charlie.

"Yeah right we could have gotten killed in that storm."

"Yes, but we didn't and don't it make you feel good knowing you saved a lot of lives?"

"That it does. How about I buy you a cup of coffee?"

"I'm hungry let's eat something."

They went to the Officer Mess for a full meal. Charlie could put away the food and Punky wandered how she could eat like that and keep a beautiful figure.

"What?"

"How can you eat like that and keep your figure?"

"I don't know I eat whatever I want and don't gain weight."

"If I ate like that I would look like the Good Year blimp."

After a good meal they went to their cabins for some needed rest. They were so tired they didn't think of sex. After a couple more days of round the clock operations they went into a day stand down. A ring was set up on the hanger deck for boxing. Movies were played on the hanger deck. The Marines always like to challenge the Sailors in sports and usually won. The Marines couldn't get any takers and bragged about it. Punky talked to his flight crew and they decided to take on the Marines. Jerry was a good boxer and Morgan was fair. Punky was thinking, you dumb ass, you're going to get your ass kicked. It wouldn't be the first time.

That evening after supper they paired off for the match. Punky went first. The first round he managed to hang in there, but by the fourth round he was dead on his feet and taking a beating. Before the round was over the Marine put his lights out.

Jerry went next and surprised everybody. He was trading punch for punch and staying in there. The Sailors went wild urging him on. Nobody went down, but Jerry won the match. He won on most punches and best punches. The Marines were mad and would take it out the next two matches.

The next match McDaniel took a beating, but hung in there for the whole match. He lost the match, but at least he made a showing. Charlie was their cheerleader and urged them on even when they were getting beat.

The final match Morgan and the Marine were the same size. Charlie was screaming her head off for Morgan to kick the Marine's ass. All the Sailors including the Captain and Admiral were stating at her.

Punky sat, down beside, her laughing. "I guess the Marines know who you are for."

Morgan and the Marine went together. Morgan knocked the Marine out with his second punch.

The navy went wild. The Marine officer approached the Captain and suggested another fight to break the tie.

"How about a no rules fight?"

The Marines picked their best fighter and he stepped into the ring. The Captain asked for a Sailor to take the challenge. Nobody wanted to fight that kind of fight. If someone didn't take the challenge the Marines would lose by default. The Captain looked around for someone to go against the Marine. A young Sailor from VA-93 stepped up to the ring.

"Sir I'm not a boxer, but I am a bar brawler. I'll take on the Marine."

Everybody laughed at the young Sailor. He was only about five feet six inches. When he stepped into the ring and pulled off his shirt nobody laughed anymore. He had muscles on top of muscles. His legs were large as tree trunks. The Marine looked down at the short Sailor.

The boxing gloves were put on each man. They met in the center of the ring. The referee looked from one man to the other, "Now I want a good clean fight. Hell what am I doing? There are no rules, at the sound of the bell come out fighting."

At the sound of the bell they came to the center of the ring and sized each other up. The Marine punched at the Sailor and he blocked the punches. The Marine landed a good punch that staggered the Sailor. He came in for the kill, but the Sailor stomped him on the foot and kicked him on a leg followed by solid blow to the ribs. The Marine backed off hurting to regroup. He thought it was going to be an easy win, but it didn't look so easy now. The Marine tried to use karate on the Sailor, but he didn't fall for any of the moves.

The Sailor short to the ground and short arms close to his body was hard to penetrate his defense. The Sailor advanced on the Marine with short jabs and kicked him in the balls. The Marine went down. The referee started to say something, but remembered that there weren't any rules. He counted to eight before the Marine was on his feet.

The Marine tried to use his long reach to batter the Sailor. It was working. He was getting in some good punches. The Sailor charged the Marine catching him off guard. He drove up under his arms and held on slamming the Marine in the stomach. He grabbed the Marine's arms and fell backwards with him putting his short legs up heaving the Marine high in the air. He landed flat on his back. He flipped around and slammed a leg across the Marine's stomach knocking the wind out of him.

The sailor jumped up and kicked the Marine in the side a couple of times before he could get up. The Marine got to his feet and both men started swinging. They were now trading punches to the head. It was a big mistake for the Marine. The Sailor being a brawler and could take the punches.

The Marine realized his mistake too late. The Sailor pressed his advantage until the Marine went down for the count. The Sailors won the fights. The captain and Admiral were happy as larks. When the ship pulled back into port the Sailors wouldn't have any duty the whole time. This was the first time the Sailors had won the boxing games. The Marines didn't like losing, but they were good sports about it.

Punky and Charlie went back upon the flight deck to stare at the stars. It had turned out to be a beautiful night. They were thrilled that the Sailors had won. They walked to the outside of an S-2E so the plane was between them and the island. Punky pulled Charlie into his arms for a long kiss.

"I been, wanting to kiss you all day."

"I have you to."

"Let's find a helicopter and play like it the back seat of a car."

"Punky you are crazy."

"Yes crazy about you. Do you want to find a place to neck?"

"Yes."

They crawled into a helicopter in the middle of the pack. It would be hard to make out the way the seats were arranged. Charlie sat in Punky's lap and they necked. They were getting worked up when they saw the flight deck watch coming toward the aircraft. "Well it was fun while it lasted." Charlie crawled out of his lap.

The Sailor came by and Punky knew him from the Electronic shop. He waved at him and the Sailor went on down the flight deck. The mood was broken. They got out of the aircraft and went into the island. "I'll buy you a cup of coffee before we go to bed."

"Sounds good, I could use a cup."

They went to the Officer mess and had coffee. They sat and starred at each other. They didn't have to talk. They could read each other's mind. They loved each other and it showed in their eyes. "We better check the flight schedule for tomorrow."

They left the mess and went to the ready room. Punky was sure they would be on the schedule and he was right. "We got an eight o'clock flight."

They didn't catch screen duty. They had mail delivery to all the ships including a submarine in the area. The submarine would only surface long enough for the mail drop. At least it was different from the regular screen duty. The mail was loaded by the time they manned the helicopter. They also had plane guard for the launch since they weren't on screen duty.

Jerry called the tower and asked permission to lift off. Permission was granted and they lifted off and assumed plane guard. After all the aircraft were launched they headed for the cruiser off the port side.

Charlie, Morgan and McDaniel went to the back and put on gunner belts. Morgan slid the back hatch open and McDaniel looked for the cruiser's sack of mail. When they were close to the cruiser Charlie took control of the helicopter using the joystick to bring the helicopter over the cruiser.

McDaniel and Morgan operated the hoist lowering the sack of mail and picking up a sack of mail to go out. Next they delivered to several destroyers and picked up mail to go out. The last delivery was to the submarine. When it surfaced Charlie eased in over the submarine. McDaniel and Morgan dropped the mail and picked up mail going out. A sailor came out on deck with his duffer bag. Charlie called Punky to let him know they were picking up a passenger. Morgan put the sling on the hoist and McDaniel lowered the hoist. The Sailor slipped into the sling and McDaniel raised the hoist. Charlie called Punky when the Sailor was in the helicopter. Punky took control of the aircraft. The Sailor was strapped in the drop seat in back and the crew returned to their seats.

It was a long hop and the crew was tired. Jerry called the tower for permission to land. Permission was granted and Punky made a smooth landing. They left the helicopter, went to the ready room while the blue shirts unloaded the mail and secured the helicopter. Punky checked the flight schedule and they had a night hop. They usually only had one flight a day, but sometimes they got stuck.

"Come on Charlie I'll buy you lunch." They had missed lunch, but they would still eat.

"I'm starved," replied Charlie.

"We better eat and get some sleep before the night hop."

They went to their cabins and tried to sleep, but their minds were on each other. Punky would like to make love to Charlie, but when they were at sea they stayed in their own cabins. They had a couple more days at sea before they pulled back into port. Yokosuka was their last port before going home. Punky remembered the promise he had made and pulled out a scrap of paper with the girl's address on it. He didn't think he would be able to keep his promise. The night hop was screen duty and they didn't get any unknown targets. A couple of days concluded their war games. The fleet headed for Yokosuka, their last port before going home.

The carrier pulled in and docked. The crew would buy all the things they wanted to take back home with them. There hadn't been any word about going to Vietnam. The next port was home. Motorcycles were the big thing. They were cheap compared to the same price in the states. Motorcycle after motorcycle was pushed up the ramp made for that purpose. You would think the ship would sink with all the junk the Sailors brought onboard.

Charlie knocked on Punky's door and stuck her head in. "What are you doing?"

"Getting ready to go on liberty and spend a lot of money. I got to shop for everyone at home. Are you going with me?"

"I thought you would never ask. I'm ready when you are."

They left the ship and headed downtown. They hit store after store until they could hardly carry all the junk they had bought. They were ready to head back to the ship.

"Would you like to eat one more time in Japan?" asked Punky.

"Yes, but will they let us in their place with all the packages with us?"

"We can try anyway."

When they entered a small eating place the waiter didn't say a word about their packages. They looked around the large room and almost everybody had packages with them.

"I guess everyone is shopping today," said Charlie.

"It sure looks that way."

They used their old method of ordering. They looked around the room until they seen a dish that someone was eating that they liked. When the waiter took their order they pointed to the dish they liked. They pointed to a picture of the drink they wanted. This was the easy way to order since they couldn't read the menu.

The waiter brought their drinks and they sipped on them waiting for their food. When the food arrived they dug in. "Have you seen Jerry today?" asked Charlie.

"No, he is going to meet Kim Lou today. She was coming from Sasebo. They want to get married before the ship leaves Japan for home."

"Do you think it will work out for them?"

"Yes I believe it will. I don't know how his parents will take the news. They may freak out and they may take to her."

"I hope they like her for Jerry's sake."

They finished eating and Punky paid for their meal. Back on the street they looked up and down the street. "Do you want to shop some more?" asked Punky.

"My feet are killing me. Let's go back to the ship."

Jerry met Kim Lou downtown when she arrived from Sasebo. They stared at each other for a moment before Kim Lou ran into Jerry's arms. She loved this man with all her heart. She would follow him anywhere. They got a room for the night. They would have two nights together before the ship pulled out. They made love until they were exhausted and then went to sleep. In the middle of the night they made love again. "I love you Kim Lou."

"I love you Jerry."

"Whatever happens I will be with you always."

"Yes Jerry I will be with you always."

The next morning Jerry and Kim Lou finished getting everything she needed to marry Jerry. She had her passport to go to America. Jerry knocked on Punky's door. Charlie and Punky were still in bed. Charlie grabbed her robe while Punky put on his pants.

"Who the heck could that be?" asked Punky.

"Do you want me to hide?"

"No I don't care if the Captain or anyone else knows we are together. What will they do, kick us off the ship?" Punky opened the hatch.

"May we come in?"

"Well I'll be a monkey's uncle."

"Is that a yes?" asked Jerry.

Punky opened the hatch for Jerry and Kim Lou. He looked at Kim Lou and knew why Jerry fell in love with her. She was a beautiful young woman.

"I need to ask a favor," said Jerry.

"Anything you want you got it."

"We are getting married in an hour and I need you to be my best man. Charlie can stand in for Kim Lou."

Charlie grabbed Kim Lou by the hand and led her toward the door. "Come with me to my cabin and help me get dressed."

Punky dressed in slacks and a shirt. "Jerry, are you sure about this?"

"I'm sure it's meant to be. Here take the rings."

"Where did you get the rings?"

"Mom sent her wedding rings and Dad sent his."

"Does that mean they approve of the wedding?"

"Mom said that any girl that could make me happy had to be alright. They sent their blessings. They are looking forward to meeting Kim Lou when she arrives in America."

"Hey we better get going or you will be late for your own wedding."

Punky knocked on Charlie's hatch and she opened it for them. They were both dressed in a skirt and blouse. They were both beautiful.

The wedding took place in a small chapel with the Chaplin doing the honors. Charlie looked at Jerry and Kim Lou. She dreamed it was Punky and her getting married. Maybe someday it would be a girl could dream couldn't she?

Jerry kissed the bride. He took a long time.

"Ok that's enough of that. It's time to find a place to party," laughed Punky.

They left the ship and found a bar with live Japanese music. They partied into the night until Jerry reminded them this was his wedding night. They left and went back to their room. Punky and Jerry had a round for the road, before going back to the ship.

Charlie came to Punky's room and they made love like there was no tomorrow. They still didn't know if they had a future.

CHAPTER NINE

Preparations were being made to get underway. Jerry ran up the gangway just before it was removed. Kim Lou stood on the dock watching until the ship was out of sight. She couldn't wait to be in Jerry's arms again. She couldn't believe it was happening. It was like a dream. She had to be at the airport in two hours for her fight to America.

"I'm going to America, oh God, I'm going to America." She had forgot about her God and called on Jerry's God.

The fleet assembled for the voyage home. They had been on their way home for an hour when the word came down. "Now hear this, now hear this, this is the Captain speaking. We have a change in our orders. We are to change our course and go by Vietnam. We are to pick up a group of advisors and take them home. It looks like we will be at war soon. Things have heated up in South Vietnam. The V. C. has started coming across the border in large numbers. That is all for now. I will advise the crew as I get news."

Punky thought about what the Captain just said. He had to find out just how close they would come to South Vietnam. He remembered his promise to the girl about helping her family. Punky and Charlie were in the ready. She was watching the expression on Punky's face.

"Punky what's wrong?"

'Nothing," he lied.

"You looked like you just got bad news."

"I did, I thought we were going home."

"I got to go see a man about a dog," he joked, "see you at lunch."

Punky left and Charlie wandered why he didn't ask her to tag along. Punky went to operations to try and find out how close they would come to the coast of Vietnam. He found out they would be out of range of the helicopter. He thought that was great and then he remembered the sad eyes of the girl begging him to save her family.

Punky found Morgan in his shop relaxing since the war games were over. He asked Morgan to take a walk.

"What's up sir?"

"What we talk about is not to be repeated."

"Yes sir."

"Is there any way to increase the range of the helicopter?"

"Sure you add a bladder for more fuel. It's like adding another fuel tank."

"How much range are we talking about?"

"Almost double the range why?"

"With the added fuel it will put us in range of Vietnam."

"So are you planning a trip to Vietnam?"

Punky stared at Morgan, "Yes I am."

"Sir, have you gone crazy?"

"You remember when I got beat up on Shore Patrol? Well the girl saved my life and I made a promise to her. If we came close enough to Vietnam I would try to rescue her family from the V.C. Now you know what I'm planning to do."

"Sir the ship won't authorize a flight like that."

"I know and I don't plan on asking them."

"I need a crew, but I won't ask you to go. I need a crew of rebels who don't care about rank."

"Sir you don't get rid of me that easy and you know the whole crew will back you."

"It will be dangerous and I don't want Charlie to go, so I won't tell her about it."

"She will be mad."

"Better mad than dead."

"Will it be that bad sir?"

"Yes I think we will be flying into a hornet's nest. If you want out I will understand."

"Count me in."

Punky left and went to the ordnance shop. He pulled the First Cass in charge aside for private talks. He wanted the helicopter armed to the hilt. He told him what he was planning.

"I need rocket launchers on the helicopter and machine guns in the hatches. I need small arms for the crew. Will you do it?"

He stared at Punky like he was crazy, "Only if you take me with you as part of the crew."

"You got it. You will have to arm the bird just before we get in range. It should be night when we get there."

"I'll tell my men it is a drill."

"I'll let you know when it's time."

Punky left and went to the Marine quarters. He wanted to have someone with him that had been to Vietnam and was good with weapons. One Sargent had been there as an advisor. Punky asked him to take a walk. He told him what he told him wasn't to be repeated. He told him he needed him on the crew and what he was planning. To his surprise the Marine told him he would go on the mission of mercy with him.

Punky got the crew together that night to plan the mission. The crew of six would launch in the dark just as soon as they were in range. The ship was taking its time on the way to Vietnam. Punky still hoped they would arrive at night. If they didn't he would have to come up with a plan B.

"Where were you last night," asked Charlie.

"We had a poker game going," he lied.

"Are you playing again tonight?"

"No I don't have any money left." He didn't lie about that.

"Good we can take a stroll on the flight deck tonight and look at the stars."

"I had rather look at you, you are so beautiful."

Charlie blushed and her body became hot. She didn't like sleeping by herself. She wanted Punky in her tonight even if it broke their rules. They didn't have that many more days on the cruise and she wanted enough dreams to last a lifetime if things didn't work out.

Charlie came to Punky's room that night and he didn't send her away. They made love like there was no tomorrow. There may not be a tomorrow for him. He knew the mission would be dangerous.

Charlie loved the fact that Punky made love to her like he couldn't get enough of her, but she sensed something was wrong. She knew he had something very heavy on his mind. She wished he would tell her, but she wouldn't push him. The next night was more of the same. "Punky what's wrong?"

"What do you mean?"

"I don't know, but there is something troubling you."

"I'm afraid of losing you when we get home."

"You won't lose me, I love you. We will work something out."

"Yeah like what?"

"I don't know, but we will find a way."

Charlie curled up with her backside to Punky, "Good night lover."

The next morning Punky checked to see how close they were to Vietnam. He calculated that around four the next night they could launch on their mission. The next day he checked with his crew to be sure everything would be ready.

Punky spent the day with Charlie hoping it wasn't his last. He told her he had thought about getting out of the Navy. She told him she didn't want him to give up his career for her.

Nighttime came and they went to bed early. Punky said he was sleepy. They made mad passionate love again. He stared at the ceiling having a hard time going to sleep. Charlie sensed something was wrong, but Punky said there wasn't anything wrong. Charlie finally drifted off to sleep.

Three in the morning Punky slipped out of bed and went to the ready room and got his flight gear. There wasn't anyone manning the ready room. When they reached the flight deck the plane handling crew was getting the helicopter ready for flight. The bladder inside the helicopter was filled with fuel. The electronics that was for submarine hunting was stripped clean to take weight off the helicopter. The helicopter was fully armed with rockets, machine guns in the hatches and plenty small arms for the crew.

Plane handlers pulled the helicopter out of the pack. Power was plugged in and they were ready to go. The crew of six manned the helicopter. Punky told Jerry to call the tower and request permission to launch. He told Jerry to tell the tower it was a test hop and may not be on the schedule.

"Bennington tower, 07 request permission to launch on a test hop. It may not be on the schedule yet."

"07 Bennington tower you are clear to launch."

"Let's get out of here before they get wise."

Punky lifted off and headed straight toward Vietnam. Bennington tower called them to let them know they were almost out of radar range and headed for Vietnam. Jerry answered and told them they were breaking up.

Punky to crew "Keep a sharp eye out for enemy aircraft or gun boats."

The Ordnance man and Marine manned the machineguns in the front and back hatch. McDaniel watched out the window by the sonar and Morgan the left side window.

"We should be coming up on the coast soon," said Jerry.

Everybody was watching for land. Punky wanted to come as close to the village as possible. The village was just across the border on the South Vietnam side. It was located on a little river. He wanted to get in fast and get out. He was keeping the helicopter close to the water. He didn't want to attract attention.

"There it is," said Jerry.

It was the first time any of them except the Marine had seen Vietnam. Punky brought the helicopter up a little higher. He didn't want to crash in a tree. Suddenly they heard small arms fire and knew they were being fired on. Punky made a sharp turn and headed back out to sea.

"Well we got more than a normal flight. If any of you want to turn back I will understand."

"We are with you all the way," replied the crew.

Then it's time I call the ship and let them know what is going on. Punky circled out of range of the small fire. "Bennington tower 07, I would like to speak to the Operations Officer."

"07 what the hell do you think you are doing? Where are you?"

"Sir we are off the coast of Vietnam and we are on a mercy mission."

"You are not authorized for this mission. Get your tail back to the ship this minute."

Punky explained why he took the helicopter and the mission to save a family. The Operations Officer still didn't buy it. He told Punky he was in big trouble, but if he came on back to the ship it would be signed off as a test hop.

"I can't do that sir, we are going in."

"You get back to the ship. That is an order."

"Sorry sir, we have to do this."

"What is that noise in the background? It sounds like small arms fire."

"Yes sir, we are being fired on."

"Who is firing on you?"

"I think it is V. C. from North Vietnam. I think they have crossed into South Vietnam."

"Have you fired back?"

"No sir not yet, we are out of range."

"What are you going to do?"

"Fly down the coast and come in at a different direction."

"If you have to do this stay in contact with the ship and keep us posted at all times. I want to know if that is V. C. in South Vietnam."

"Yes sir we will stay in contact at all times."

"The ship should be within radar range by this evening, good luck."

"Thank you, sir."

Punky turned the helicopter and flew down the coast. He turned toward the coast and flew in over land. They didn't receive any hostile fire. He turned the helicopter and headed back toward the village. He saw the small river and followed it. They saw the village in the distance and smoke. Punky saw a small area beside the river.

"I'm going to set the helicopter down in that small area beside the river. We will walk up the river to the village."

Punky set the helicopter down. They scanned the area watching for V.C., but it was quiet. He shut down the rotors, but kept the engines running at low power.

"Jerry you stay with the helicopter and if you see us coming fast start the rotors. Morgan you man a machinegun and give us cover fire if we need it. The rest of you, arm yourselves and follow me."

They dropped down the embankment close to the water. They headed up river to the village. When they were even with the village Punky crawled up the bank and looked around the village. Several of the huts had been on fire.

Punky gave the signal to enter the village to check it out. He didn't see anyone out of the huts until he saw bodies on the ground. He found the Chief hanging in front of his hut.

His wife and boy were dead inside the hut. They had been shot, but not before the woman had been raped. She was naked from the waist down in as pool of blood. Punky realized he was too late to save the family.

The rest of the crew was checking bodies trying to find someone alive when Punky came outside. The V. C. had destroyed the village and killed everyone. Suddenly they heard screams from some of the huts. They split up and slowly approached the huts. Punky gave the signal and they charged inside the huts. Some of the V.C. was still having their fun with the women. They looked up in surprise, but too late. Punky shot two V.C. while they were still pumping the women. They fell on top of them. He pulled them off the women.

"It's alright we are American. You are safe now."

Punky went outside with the two naked women behind him. The rest of the crew killed five more V.C. the Marine confirmed the kill was all V.C. One lone V.C. came charging out of another hut, but the Marine cut him down.

The Marine spoke their language and asked what happened. There had been a large force of men come through the village heading into South Vietnam. They had killed the men, raped the women, killed the children and destroyed the village, taking all the food with them. The Marine told the women to leave the village and go inland, then turn south.

"Let's get back to the helicopter and make a report," said Punky.

Punky called the ship and made a full report. They were told to return to the ship. The men were fighting mad at what the V.C. had done. The marine was the first to give his two cents worth. "The V.C. is only a little ways from here. We have a lot of firepower with us. I suggest we use it up."

"I'm with you. What about the rest of you?" They were ready to do battle. They wanted revenge for what the V.C. had done to the village.

"Ok lock and load. Man the machine guns."

Punky lifted the helicopter off and the crew dropped the extra fuel tank out the back hatch. He followed the trail the V.C. had made. Jerry armed the rocket launcher.

"There they are," said Jerry.

Punky fired three rockets into the formation of men. The machineguns opened up on them also killing a large number of V.C. and kept firing. The V.C. returned fire striking the helicopter knocking out one engine. The helicopter was taking a beating. Punky fired the rest of the rockets into the V.C. and turned to make a run for it.

"We got a problem, we are going to crash. I'll get us as far away from the V.C. as the bird will take us. Jerry, call the carrier."

"Bennington tower 07 mayday, mayday, we are going down."

"07 Bennington tower can you make it back to the ocean?"

"Bennington tower that is a negative, I say that is a negative. We are passing through one hundred feet and going down. We are headed inland to get away from the V.C., but we killed a lot of V.C. before they got us. I guess we started a war."

That was the last message they got off before they crashed. Punky found an area where the trees weren't too big, but the helicopter still flew apart. The tail broke off and next the rotor wing went to pieces. The wheels broke off and by the time they came to a stop there wasn't anything left but the cabin.

"Is everybody alright? We had better get away from the helicopter in case it blows up."

Everyone piled out of the helicopter taking as much gear as possible. They took their weapons, signal flares and survival gear. They had water, but no food.

"Where is Jerry?" asked Punky.

"I'm over here under the helicopter."

He was pinned in by part of the cabin. Fuel was leaking from the fuel tank. Jerry had blood running down his left arm. "You guys leave me before the helicopter blows."

"No way do we leave a man behind," said the Marine.

They tried to lift the piece of the helicopter, but it was too heavy. Punky looked around for something to use as a lever, but there wasn't anything. McDaniel grabbed a machine gun and went over to a small tree. He cut it down with the machinegun. Morgan helped him drag the tree over while Punky and the Ordnance man pulled a tire over to the helicopter. They put the tree under the aircraft and the tire under the tree.

"Give me a big enough lever and I can move the world," quoted McDaniel.

They all got on the tree and slowly raised the aircraft enough for Jerry to crawl out from under it.

"Let's get the hell out of here," yelled Morgan.

They had just got away from the helicopter when it caught fire and blew up. They hit the deck as parts flew everywhere. Punky checked Jerry over.

"You been shot."

"You think?"

"Yes Jerry you have a hole through your shoulder. Did anyone save the first aid kit?"

"I got it," said Morgan.

Morgan treated Jerry's shoulder and put it in a sling. He gave him a shot of morphine to ease the pain.

"We got to move," said Punky, "The V.C. will see the smoke and come after us. "

"Which way?" asked Jerry.

Punky thought about it for a moment. "The V. C. will be looking for us to head south and try to cut us off. I think we should go further inland and head north into North Vietnam. They won't think of looking for us in their own back yard."

"Sounds like a good idea," said the Marine.

"Grab your gear and let's get out of here," said Punky.

"I'll take point," said the Marine.

The Marine took point followed by Punky, Jerry, McDaniel, Morgan and the Ordnance man bringing up the rear. They moved at a fast pace. They wanted to put as much distance between them and the V.C. as possible. They tried not to leave a trail. They were lucky the V.C. headed south to cut them off. It was getting dark and the Marine turned north. They crossed a small river and decided they were in North Vietnam. They decided to go deep into North Vietnam before turning toward the coast.

Finally they stopped for the night. They didn't have any food and were very hungry. Jerry's shoulder had started to bleed through the dressing. Morgan broke out the first aid kit and fixed Jerry with a clean bandage.

"Sorry guys, but we have to have a cold camp. Maybe we can kill some animal for food."

"We should have brought food with us," said the Marine.

"Actually we do have some food," said Morgan.

"What is it?"

Morgan produced several bars of chocolate and passed them around. Jerry thought he had never tasted anything so good. Chocolate gives the body energy. They didn't feel so bad after they had something in their stomach. They didn't have much water and they only took a small drink.

"Tomorrow we look for food and drink. We have to stay in shape. We may be here a long time," said the Marine.

"We got to find a way to get back to the ship or it will leave without us. They probably think we are dead anyway," replied Punky.

"Anyway we had better get some sleep."

Back aboard the carrier they did think the helicopter was gone and the crew was probably killed. Charlie had heard the word when she came to the ready room. She couldn't believe what was happening. She went back to her cabin to cry. She found a note from Punky telling her what they were doing. His last words were I love you. He promised he would be back.

The carrier would be on station for a while waiting to see what was going to happen in South Vietnam. It didn't look good. It was beginning to look like the United States would be in another war.

The men didn't get much sleep that night. The next day they planned to get food and drink first. The next was to plan a way to get back to the ship. They were in North Vietnam and if they got caught they would be executed.

Joe the Marine became the leader because he had the experience. Punky was highest ranking, but at a time like this who cared about rank. They were worried about survival.

"What do you think we should do first?" asked Punky.

"We need to find some clothes and get out of this flight gear. We need their weapons and get rid of our weapons. We need to blend into the countryside."

"Well lead out Joe and we will follow you."

They were in a jungle type area and the going was tough. Joe was point and they followed. It was almost noon when they came into some woods. They could hear loud voices in the distance. They crawled up close and scanned the area. They had run upon an army camp. It was a large force and they were well armed.

"What do we do now," asked Jerry.

"We go back into the woods and hide until dark."

They retreated back into the woods and looked for a place to hold up until dark. They found a high place on a hill above the camp and hid in the bushes. They could see the whole camp from their position. They could see men going into the buildings and coming out with weapons.

"I think that is their store house. Tonight we can steal what we need."

"Jerry and I will find out what is in the building," said Punky.

Bob the Ordnance man said, "Joe and I will try to steal some food and something to drink."

"We want to get in and get out without them seeing us. We don't want them to know we are in the area. Whatever you do, don't fire on them unless it is to save your life."

"What do you want us to do?" asked Morgan.

"You and McDaniel cover us from the edge of the woods. Right now we need to try and get some sleep before dark. Morgan, take the first watch and I will relieve you in four hours."

They wanted to wait until after midnight before entering the camp. They wanted to be sure everyone was asleep. They were getting hungry.

"I hope they don't hear my stomach making noise from the camp," laughed Jerry.

"I hope we find something to eat." said Bob.

"We will be lucky to find rice," said Joe.

They settled down and tried to sleep, but it was hard knowing what they had to do when it got dark. Time went at a snail's pace. Finally it was after midnight and the camp was quiet. They could see only three guards and they sat at a campfire drinking and laughing. They moved down to the edge of the woods. Punky and Jerry crawled toward the back of the building. Joe and Bob crawled toward the guards. Joe wanted to hear what they were saying. He knew the language.

Punky and jerry reached the back of the building. Punky slid open, a window and crawled inside. He told Jerry to wait at the window. It was a store house. Punky picked out six Ak-47 rifles and a case of ammunition. He handed the rest of the loot out to Jerry. He found powder kegs in one corner. Joe said not to kill anyone he didn't say anything about blowing up the place. He took a case of power and ran a trail around the room to the clothes. He put the rest of the powder on the clothes. That should start a good fire and maybe they wouldn't think anyone blew up the place. Jerry had crawled back to the woods with part of the loot and crawled back for more.

Punky told Jerry to go back to the woods and take what he could. He hung around behind the building waiting until Joe and bob were back in the woods. He didn't want to light the powder until he was sure Joe and Bob were safe back in the woods.

Joe and Bob crawled close to the guards and listened to them talk. Then they crawled over to another building and found it was the mess hall. They eased inside and found the food. It wasn't great, but it would be filling.

"We got enough," said Joe, "Let's get the hell out of here."

They crawled past the guards and into the woods. Joe looked around doing a head count. He didn't see Punky. "Where is Punky?"

"He is over by the store room."

"What is he doing?"

"I don't have a clue. He told me to come on ahead."

Punky lit an old rag and tossed it in the window on the gunpowder trail. He quickly crawled back to the woods.

"Let's get the hell out of here."

Nobody asked what was going to happen. They had figured it out already. Joe took point and they slipped back into the woods.

They headed for the jungle. A few minutes later they heard them call fire.

"Punky what did you do?"

"I made a small fire and hoped they couldn't put it out. I wanted them to think it was just an accident."

A few minutes later, they heard a loud explosion. They didn't hear anyone coming into the woods after them. Punky had made it look like an accident.

"Now wasn't that fun?"

"What if they thought it was a raid?" asked Joe. "They would be on our trail by now."

"Well they didn't," argued Punky.

"How did you ever become an Officer?" asked Joe, "You are a maverick."

"So I've been told."

"Well let's get the hell out of here."

They faded back into the jungle. They found a place to stop and divide the loot. Punky passed out the clothes and weapons. They pulled off their flight suits and gear. They changed into clothes that the V.C. wore. They made fun of each other.

"Joe what did you get us to eat?" asked Punky.

"We had to take leftovers. We got fish heads and rice. We found a bottle of wine and something that looks like bread."

"They don't, eat too good."

"Sorry we didn't find the Officer's mess," laughed Joe.

"Well it's better than nothing." They ate their fill and had wine to drink. They didn't find any water.

"What were the guards talking about?" questioned Punky.

"They were bragging about raping the women and taking anything they wanted when they got to South Vietnam. They were talking about a big invasion."

"Then we need to get back to the ship as soon as possible."

"And how do you plan to do that?"

"Steal a plane or a boat, I don't know."

"Then we better get rid of our gear and weapons. We'll keep our pistols and anything else we can hide in these new clothes. With AK-47 weapons we should look like the rest of the V.C. at a distance."

Morgan found a hollow tree and they hid their weapons and flight gear. They didn't want to destroy them in case they needed them again. Joe suggested they move at night and hold up in the daytime. They put their sloppy hats on and Joe took point. He looked at his compass and headed toward the coast. They walked until just before daylight. They came upon a sleepy little village. There didn't seem to be anyone up yet.

"Should we go around the village?" asked Jerry.

"No we will walk through like we are V.C. and going someplace. That will test our new clothes."

Halfway through the village they found a well and drank water until they were full. They found a couple of jugs near the well and filled them. They needed food. They found a young girl at the edge of the village baking bread and cooking rice. She gave them food without being asked. They took the food and walked on without saying a word. She went back to her cooking.

They found an old building just outside the village and hid out in it. They ate their fill and then lay down to get some sleep. Punky took the first watch. It was too open country to try and move in the daytime.

While on watch Punky was thinking of a way to get back to the ship. He would like to steal a helicopter, but they hadn't seen a plane or helicopter yet. If they could make it to the coast maybe they could steal a boat. If they could get past the patrol boats maybe they could make it back to the ship. Then if they got to the carrier maybe they wouldn't sink them for the enemy. There were a lot of maybes.

Joe relieved Punky and he was trying to get some sleep. About two in the afternoon there was the sound of approaching trucks. The crew watched as a convoy passed right by the old building.

The trucks were filled with soldiers and the trucks were heading south. They were getting ready for something big, like an invasion.

"Since we can't get to the ship maybe we could steal a radio and let the ship know we are alive. We need to let them know about the troop movement and what it means." said Punky.

"Ok we steal a radio," replied Joe.

"You know when we use the radio they will be coming after us."

"Yes I know. We will have to move fast and stay ahead of them."

"We could split up to confuse them."

"No we stay together."

"It will be dark soon and we can move out."

They slept until it was dark before moving out. Joe took point as usual and headed toward the coast. They ran into camps all along the way. The whole area was flooded with troops getting ready to move south. Finally Joe saw a truck with a radio attached to it. He scanned the area looking for troops. The only one close to the truck was the radio operator on duty. This proved to be as problem.

"We better move on," said Punky.

"No we may not get another chance."

"How are we going to get the radio?"

"I'll get the radio this is what I was trained for."

"Good luck," whispered Punky, as Joe crawled toward the truck

Joe crawled slowly toward his target not making a sound. Punky and the rest of the crew watched and brought their weapons in place in case Joe needed backup. He moved up behind the radio operator and took him out with his knife. He removed the radio from the truck and made his way to where the crew waited for him.

"Let's get out of here before they find the radio operator."

Punky took point and headed toward the coast. "Your wish is my command." He led the way into a jungle area. It wasn't too dense so they could move fast. Punky called a halt to the march.

"McDaniel do you think you can raise the ship with this radio?" asked Punky.

"I don't know sir, but I will give it a try."

He played with dials trying to find a frequency that the ship would pick up. It was a low frequency transmitter-receiver. After some time he finally found a frequency he thought the ship would be monitoring. "I think I got it sir."

"Well give the tower a call and ask for the Operations Officer."

"Bennington tower this is McDaniel of the downed helicopter, can you hear me? I am using a piece of V.C. equipment trying to reach you. Do you read me?"

"McDaniel Bennington tower I can hardly hear you, rotate your antenna."

After adjusting the antenna, "Do you hear me now?"

"I read you loud and clear."

"May I talk to the Operations Officer?"

"Operations here give me your report."

Punky took the mike. "Sir we were shot down and all the crew is still alive. We are seeing a huge buildup of troops getting ready to invade South Vietnam. We are somewhere in North Vietnam. We will be on the run after this transmission. We are trying to find a way to get back to the ship. If you see an odd aircraft or boat coming toward the ship please don't shoot us."

"We will keep a close watch for you."

"We better be on the move, over and out."

"Good luck."

"We better change directions," said Joe.

"Let's go north deeper into North Vietnam. They won't be expecting us to go that way," replied Punky.

"Good idea, let's move out."

Joe took point and the rest of the crew followed. They tried not to leave a trail for the V.C. to follow. They headed north all night. They looked for a place to hide before daylight.

"Look there is an old barn," said Bob.

The barn was old, but it had animals in it. They took stock of what was in the barn. There were chickens, a pig, a nanny goat and water for the animals. They found some eggs also.

"I vote for fried chicken," said Jerry.

"I vote for roasted pig," said Morgan.

"I'm sorry guys, but we can't have a fire. We have raw eggs, milk from the goat and some water," said Joe.

"I think I'm hungry enough to eat a chicken raw," replied Bob.

"Well, have at it."

"I know what we will do. Bob kill your chicken. I'll build a small fire in the center of the dirt floor. We keep the doors closed and keep the light and smoke confined. It will be worth it for a good meal."

Bob killed a chicken and plucked the feathers off the chicken while Joe built a small fire. Bob cut up the chicken and found wire to put the chicken on. They used water pans to milk the nanny goat. Morgan broke some eggs in a pan and scrambled them. They ended up with a pretty good meal. The barn was smoky, but it was worth it for some cooked food. Joe cracked a door and let the smoke out slowly. They bedded down for the night with Morgan taking the first watch. The next morning Joe scanned the area and didn't like what he saw. They were in open country.

"We got a problem. We are in open country. We can stay the day here and move out tonight or take a chance looking like V.C. and moving out now."

"The farmer will be checking his animals pretty soon. We better move out now," replied Punky.

"Then let's move out now and hope they take us for V.C. or we will be in deep trouble."

Joe led them down a dirt road hoping not to attract any attention. They spotted an old helicopter off to their left in a field. "Do you think that piece of junk will fly?" asked Joe.

"I don't know, but I don't see anyone around so let's go find out."

"I wonder who it belongs to?" asked Jerry.

They made for the helicopter. Joe and bob stood guard while the crew looked over the helicopter. Punky looked over the cockpit. "It full of fuel and looks like it will fly."

"Sir I know who this copper belongs to. I would say a drug lord because it is full of drugs."

"Maybe he won't mind us borrowing it for a while," laughed Punky.

Shots were fired from the outside. Punky looked outside and saw a truck headed toward them. It was loaded with men and they were firing at Joe and Bob. Joe stuck his head inside, "Get us out of her sir."

Punky jumped into the pilot seat while Jerry slid into the copilot seat. He was having some trouble figuring out the instrument panel. He finally got the engine running and rotors turning. The truck was getting close and still firing at them. Joe and bob crawled inside the helicopter.

"Jerry get the throttle, I'm talking her up."

"You better make it quick or we will be junk in a few minutes."

Punky lifted the helicopter off and headed away from the truck. They were out of range with only a few holes in the cabin.

"We made it," yelled Jerry.

"We're not out of the woods yet."

Punky turned the helicopter toward the coast. Maybe they would make it back to the carrier. Things were looking good.

"Sir there is a missile fired at us from seven o'clock."

"I see it."

Punky rolled the helicopter over on its right side trying to avoid the heat seeking missile. He almost made it, but the missile exploded close to the helicopter damaging the engine and cargo area.

"Here we go again, hang on we're going down."

The helicopter came all to pieces as it hit trees and bushes. It finally came to a halt. Punky scrambled out of the chopper and looked around for rest of the crew. Joe and Morgan were thrown out of the helicopter and lay on the ground. Bob came out what was left of the tail section. Jerry crawled out through the cockpit window.

"Is everybody alright," asked Punky.

"Bob where is McDaniel?"

"I'll check on him sir."

Bob came out of the helicopter and looked grim. "McDaniel didn't make it sir. One of the stray pieces of metal hit him in the chest. He is dead. I got his dog tags."

"We got to get out of here sir," yelled Joe.

"We can't just leave him?"

Punky started back to the chopper. He is my crew I don't want to leave him.

"Sir we have to. I'm sorry I know how you cared about your crew, but we got to move or we will be dead meat ourselves.

"Ok Joe, take point."

Joe took off with the crew hot on his tail. They were out in the open and a long ways from the woods in the distance. He looked around and saw a rice patty off to their left. He headed for the rice patty. He stopped a good distance into the rice patty.

"Dig yourself a long trench and cover yourself with rice seedlings. In other words plant yourself. We will stay out here until dark. I don't think they will look for us out here. From the distance it will look like just a flat rice patty without a place to hide."

Punky dug into the wet soil and water, and found it easy. He was planted in just a few minutes. He thought about Charlie and wondered if she missed him. He had to be in mud, but at least he could dream.

Jerry lay there and wondered about his new bride. He wondered if she had made it to the United States. He hoped his Mother and Father would accept her and love her as much as he did. He wandered if he would ever hold her in his arms again. Bob thought of his wife waiting for him at home and his young son. Why had he taken on this mission? Would he ever see them again? They had lost one man so far, but at least he was single. Morgan thought of his wife back home. Why did he go on a mission he didn't have to, go on. What was the rule to never volunteer for anything? He had to be stupid. He grieved for the friend he had lost. Joe didn't have anyone waiting on him. He had gotten a Dear John letter while they were in Japan. His wife said she couldn't take being alone anymore and found a man that wasn't in the military. She had sent divorce papers. He signed them and sent them back wishing her a happy future.

It was getting dark. Joe raised up and scanned the area. "It's time to get up and get out of here."

Joe took point and led them toward the woods. It was a long ways to the woods and they were tired by the time they entered the woods. The further north they got the more open the country was. They were getting too far into North Vietnam. They needed to head for the coast. They rested and planned what to do next.

"Punky do you have any ideas?" asked Joe.

"If we had money we could move on and buy what we need. We need to change clothes. We have been in these too long. This far into North Vietnam we could wear civilian clothes."

"How about we rob a bank?"

"I don't think we better go that far. I don't know if they even have banks. We could find us a rich civilian or a store to rob. Joe you speak the language so you can go into the village and scout out a place to rob."

"Sounds like a plan, let's move out."

Joe took point and they stayed in the edge of the woods as they worked their way toward the coast. They walked and rested taking a break at midnight.

"The first thing we need to buy is a truck. I'm tired of walking." complained Jerry.

"How is your shoulder?" asked Punky

"It's healing and I don't need a sling."

"I would like something to eat besides rice," said Bob.

"I would like a bath and clean clothes," said Morgan.

After their break they continued their march toward the coast. They didn't have a clue how far they were from the coast. They had changed directions many times. After a long march again they spotted a small town.

"What do you think?" asked Joe.

"What time is it?" asked Punky.

"It's about three in the morning."

"Joe, go scout it out."

Joe walked toward the town while the rest of them waited in the woods. He walked down Main Street checking out each type of store. He turned and walked slowly back to the woods.

"Well what did you find out?" asked Punky.

"I saw a store that sells anything you want. That should be the one we rob."

"Then let's do it."

Bob and Jerry found a place to cover them. They watched Joe, Punky and Morgan move slowly down the street. Joe found an old sack and wound it around his hand. He knocked out a pane of glass on the door and reached inside to open the front door. They slipped inside and looked around. Joe found the moneybox in a desk. It was locked up, but with a knife Joe had it out in just a couple of minutes. Joe held up the bills for them to see.

"Look what I found, money and quite a lot of it. The storeowner was doing a good business. I wonder what he, was selling to make this kind of money?"

"For one thing he was selling dope. I found a box full back here," said Morgan.

"Guess what I found in a small room back here? It was looked so I broke in. It is full of weapons of all kinds," said Punky.

Joe stuck his head in the room, "Wow, you could start a war with all this. He even has land mines."

"Ok guys find some sacks for out goodies and let's get out of here."

Morgan took the moneybox. He sacked up can foods and some beer he found in a cooler. He found water in jugs and took a couple. Jerry shopped for new clothes for them to wear. He didn't know what they would want so he filled a large toe sack. Punky and

Joe loaded up on weapons. They got a couple of machine guns, ammunition, land mines and hand grenades. They lugged their booty to the front door. Morgan left with his booty.

Punky looked at Joe. He knew what Punky had in mind. He smiled at him. "Do it, it will cover our robbery."

"Your wish is my command."

Joe left with his sack of weapons. Punky hunted for something to start a fire with. He found a candle and put it among the clothes. He put paper around the candle. It would take a while for the candle to burn down. It was like a slow fuse. They would be long gone before the fire started. Punky lit the candle and made it for the door. He joined the other men and they left in a hurry. They were a long ways from town when they saw the sky light up followed by explosions. The fire and explosions wiped out most of the town.

"Let's make tracks in case someone gets the idea that fire wasn't an accident." explained Joe.

They started off at a fast pace. They were putting some distance between them and the town. Suddenly they heard trucks coming down the road. Joe pointed to the trees and they got off the road as fast as they could. Two trucks loaded with soldiers passed as they watched from the trees.

"There must be a base near, by," said Joe.

"It can't be too far away. It didn't take long for those trucks to get here," replied Punky.

"We better stay in the woods and work our way on down the road. That is the direction of the coast."

"The guy that owned the store is in big trouble," said Punky.

"Yes I would say so. I'm sure he was doing black market. If he isn't dead already he will be shortly when the solders figure out what he was doing."

Joe took point and they moved down the road staying in the woods. At four in the morning Joe called a halt to their march. They were in a dense wooded area. They were tired and needed a rest and some sleep. Punky took the money and divided it among the crew. He wanted everyone to have some in case they got separated.

Joe and Punky took a machine gun each with several clips of ammunition. Joe passed out the hand grenades to everyone. He kept the land mines in a sack to carry himself. He didn't think anyone else knew how to set the land mines.

Morgan passed out can meat and peaches. The guys, eyes lit up when they saw the beer. They feasted on their booty. It had been a good raid. After everyone was full Jerry took the first watch and they settled in for a good sleep. They slept the rest of the night. The next morning Jerry dumped the clothes on the ground and told them to help themselves. Some were fancy and some were work clothes. They decided to wear the work clothes. Morgan gave them a jug of water and a bar of soap.

"I thought we might wash up some before putting on our new clothes," explained Morgan.

They all were all starting to grow beards. They took turns stripping down and washing their bodies before putting on their clean clothes.

"I'm going to scout the area," said Joe.

"I'll go with you," replied Punky.

"We need some faster transportation."

"You can say that again. I got blisters on top of blisters. I don't make a very good Soldier."

"We need a truck and a map to know where we are."

"How do we get a map?"

"We may have to sneak on a military base and find their operations office."

"You are kidding."

"No I'm serious."

They walked back to their camp. The men had put on work clothes. Joe and Punky washed up and put on work clothes. They put their weapons in sacks along with the leftover food. Joe checked his compass and they headed toward the coast again. Since it was daylight they stayed in the woods.

"How far do you think we are from the coast?" asked Jerry.

"I have no idea since we have changed directions so many times," replied Joe.

They walked until noon and noticed another army camp. They surveyed the camp from the woods. There was only one guard on the gate. It had a wire fence around the camp. They eased further back into the woods.

"Joe what do you think?" asked Punky.

"I think we wait until dark and then I will sneak in and try to find a map. I'll steal a truck if I can."

"Are you sure you want to try it?"

"I don't think we have a choice. We don't know where we are and could wander around until we get caught."

They settled down to rest and get some sleep. They would wait until dark before doing anything. Morgan took the first watch. They waited until midnight and the camp was settled down for the night. Joe said he would slip past the guard and try to find a map. Punky was to distract the guard while Joe sneaked in the base. Joe sneaked up close to the gate. Punky threw a can in the road and the guard looked that way. It was just enough time for Joe to sneak past him. Punky eased over to the side Joe had gone in. There were some bushes for him to hide in. Joe went from building to building until he found the one he was looking for. He used his knife to open the door and went in. He was lucky it was the planning room with maps everywhere. He found a map of the area and several of South Vietnam. It showed troop movement and gun placement. He took that also.

Joe found a small truck by the mess hall with the key in it. It was a civilian truck. He decided to steal it. He started the engine and headed for the gate. When he got to the gate the guard signaled for him to stop. Joe hoped Punky knew what to do. Punky eased up behind the guard and put a knife between his ribs. He jumped in the truck with Joe and headed for the woods. The rest of the men jumped into the truck bed with their supplies. Jerry handed Punky his machinegun and ammunition. Jerry drove down the road like the devil was after him. They knew as soon as the guard's relief found the dead guard all hell would break loose.

"Joe did you get a map," asked Punky.

"Yes and we are a long way from the coast. There is an airfield off to the left not far from the coast. There is a boat dock with patrol boats at the end of this road. Maybe if we are lucky we can steal a boat."

"That sounds like a plan. What kind of aircraft are at the airfield?"

"The map only showed aircraft. It didn't show what kind."

"When we get close to the airfield I want to have a peak and see what they got."

"Well right now we better get the hell out of here."

"Is there any more army camps ahead of us?"

"No we are lucky there."

"Then we need some way to slow them down from following us."

Joe kept his foot to the floor on the gas. They were making good time. They hoped they wouldn't find the guard for a long time. They didn't know the guards rotation. The old dirt road was full of holes and jarred their teeth when they hit a hole. It was late in the afternoon when they came to a bridge over a small river. Joe slowed down on the bridge and looked it over, he looked at Punky.

"Are you thinking what I'm thinking?"

"Yeah do you think we could rig the land mines to blow the bridge?"

"I don't know, but it is worth a try."

Joe stopped the truck and went around to the back of the truck. He took two land mines and went to the middle of the bridge. Now all he had to do was find a way to set them off. There had to be a way to set them off. "I want to take out the bridge when they blow."

Joe took two bags and eased one land mine in each bag. He placed them so that a truck was bound to run over them crossing the bridge. They could stop if they saw them, but they may still set them off.

"What do you think Punky?"

"Joe I think it will work."

"I think I'll rig a couple of surprises just in case the whole bridge doesn't blow."

Past the center of the bridge Joe ran a string across the bridge. He attached the string to the pins on two hand grenades. He stood back and looked at his handy work. "That should give them a good surprise if the land mines don't work."

"I would hate to trip one of those hand grenades," replied Punky.

Suddenly a hail of bullets rained down around them some hitting the truck. One hit Morgan in the leg, but went on through. Joe jumped in the driver seat and took off across the bridge. Punky jumped in back and was returning fire with his machinegun. Jerry and bob returned fire with him.

"Aim for their tires," yelled Punky.

They all consecrated their fire on hitting the front tires of the lead truck. Someone was lucky and blew out a front tire. The driver lost control and left the road. That only brought up another truck. Joe had the pedal to the floor, but the old truck wasn't very fast. They still weren't out of range. The truck full of soldiers came onto the bridge moving fast.

The driver didn't see the sacks in the road until it was too late. He ran across both sacks and the mines exploded under the truck. It took out part of the bridge and the truck. The two hand grenades exploded and took out all the soldiers that weren't killed in the truck. That stopped the firing on the fleeing truck.

"That got their attention," said Joe.

Bob split Morgan's pants up the leg and worked on his wound. It was hard with the truck hitting every bump in the road. Joe, peddle on the floor, driving as fast as he could make the old truck go.

"We were lucky to get away. Look at all the bullet holes in the truck and we only had one man hit," said Punky.

"Yeah we might not be so lucky next time," replied Jerry.

"Won't this old truck go any faster?" asked Bob.

"That's all I can get out of this old truck. We don't have much gas left and a long ways to go. Keep an eye out for anyplace to get some gas," instructed Joe.

"How far are from the air field?" asked Punky.

Jerry took the map and found the airfield. "We are still a long ways away. It's hard to tell. I haven't seen any signs to tell us where we are and how far we are away."

All they could do was move as fast as they could. They were low on fuel and didn't know when the old truck would run out of gas.

CHAPTER TEN

"Joe look up ahead, there's a truck beside the road. Could we be lucky and get another truck."

Joe pulled the truck in behind the other truck. There wasn't anyone with the truck. Then they noticed the right front jacked up and the tire missing. They didn't have a spare," said Jerry.

"Check the gas tank and see if there is any fuel," said Joe.

"I'm on it."

Jerry checked the fuel tank and returned, "We're in luck. It has half a tank of fuel."

Morgan started to get out of the truck, "I'll get the fuel."

"You stay in the truck you are hurt I'll get the fuel," said Bob.

Bob grabbed a water jug and poured out the last of the water. He cut the fuel line with his knife and filled the jug with fuel. He crimped the line and handed Jerry the jug. Jerry dumped the fuel into the tank. "It's going to take a long time to fill the tank like this," said Jerry.

"Can't be helped we got to have fuel."

Jerry handed the empty jug to Bob. It would take a long time. They got twenty five gallons of fuel out of the truck. Bob and Jerry jumped back into the truck. "That's all there is so how much do we show?"

"It shows half a tank. It must have been the same size tank. We should have enough fuel to make it to the coast."

"I just hope we aren't being followed," said Punky. "You can bet they are and they may be close since we lost so much time fueling."

Joe stopped the truck. "Maybe we should use the rest of the lined mines."

"It will take time to plant them," replied Punky.

"But it will be worth it if they run over them."

Joe and Punky jumped out of the truck. Punky dug holes in the dirt road while Joe covered the mines. This would also serve as a warning. They would hear the mines blow and know how far the soldiers we behind them.

"That should do it," said Joe.

"Let's get the hell out of here."

Joe took the driver seat and Punky took shotgun. Joe took off as fast as the old truck would go. Joe pulled off the road around midnight for a pit stop. Everyone relieved himself. They only had a little food left which they finished off. Joe and Punky studied the map. He pointed to the map. "We passed that place about an hour ago so we should be almost there."

"That makes the airfield only a few miles up the road. It will still be dark so we can take a look at the field."

"Let's get trucking before it gets daylight."

They loaded up and hit the road again. They had gone a few miles when Jerry spotted a flagpole and a tower. "That has to be the airfield." It was just a short distance off the road. There was a small hill close to the airfield. Punky, Jerry and Joe went up the hill to take a look. It wasn't a big airstrip, but they could see four jets parked off the runway. They were fully loaded with weapons.

"What kind of planes are they?" asked Jerry.

"They look like a Mig-17. I think they are Mig-17's, but I'm not sure," replied Punky.

"Well now you have seen the aircraft let's get out of here and find a boat to steal because I want to go home," said Joe.

"I want a Mig-17," said Punky.

"You are crazy," replied Jerry.

"Well I can wish can't I?"

"Yes and I can wish we are back on the ship."

"Let's get out of here. It will be daylight soon and we need to find us a boat."

They got back in the truck and headed down the road. It wasn't but a couple of miles to the end of the road. They saw a boat dock in the distance and small patrol boats tied up to the dock. Daylight would soon be upon them so they had to act fast. They couldn't afford to wait another day. The soldiers behind them might catch up. Joe pulled the truck over to the side of the road into some bushes.

They hid the truck as best as possible. Joe, Punky, and Jerry went to scope out the area. They crawled up within fifty yards of the boat dock. There were several boats and a lot of Sailors milling around. There were three docks with several boats tied up to each dock. It wasn't going to be easy to steal a boat. "We need a plan," whispered Joe.

They walked down the hill back to truck. They were trying to come up with a way to steal a boat. "We could buy a boat we have money," suggested Jerry.

"If we could find one to buy it would be some old fishing boat which couldn't outrun those Patrol boats," explained Punky.

"Well we better come up with something soon."

"We need a distraction of some kind," said Joe.

"What kind of a distraction," asked Punky.

"We need something big to get them away from the boats."

"You mean like a big explosion."

"Yes a big explosion. What have you got in mind?"

"How about I blow up that fuel tank in the edge of the woods? That should get their attention long enough for you to steal a boat."

"And how do you get on the boat?"

"I don't. I run back to the truck and go back to the airfield."

"I guess you are going to steal a plane?"

"Yeah I thought maybe I would."

"You are crazy."

"Maybe, but do you have a better idea?"

Jerry looked at Punky, "We can't leave you here."

"Sure you can, don't worry I'll catch up to you and protect you with the Mig-17."

"Now I know you are crazy. You have never flown a jet."

"If it has wings I can fly it."

"Are you sure?"

"Yes Daddy I want my Mig-17. I want my toy."

They went back to the truck. The plan was for Joe, Bob, Jerry and Morgan to get as close to the end boat as possible. Punky would blow the fuel tank which would be their signal to rush the end boat. If they were lucky all the sailors would rush toward the fuel tank.

"Good luck guys, I'll see you on the carrier."

Punky made his way down to the fuel tank. Jerry and crew crawled as close as they could to the dock and waited for the fuel tank to blow. Punky crawled upon the tank and opened the filler hatch. He was thinking about dropping a hand grenade in the opening, but he didn't think he could get away before the tank blew. He opened a valve on the side and cut the hose attached to it. He cut the hose going down to the dock. He set the fuel on fire and stepped back from the tank. He looked at the hole in the top of the tank.

"I can do it, I can do it."

He pulled the pin on a hand grenade and lobbed it at the tank. It hit the lip of the opening and fell into the tank. Punky turned and ran for his truck. The explosion rocked the whole area.

"Let's get our boat," yelled Joe.

All the Sailors but two had left the boat when the explosion went off. Joe shot the two Sailors that were on the boat. Bob cast off the bowline and Jerry cast off the stern line. Morgan dragged the gangway away from the boat. By the time they were all on the boat Joe had the engine running and pulled away from the dock. He headed the boat out to sea. Bob and Jerry tossed the two dead sailors over the side.

"They are going to be real mad at us and will come after us," said Joe.

"Well I hope we picked the fastest boat," replied Jerry.

"We have a small lead on them. I hope we are out of range of their machineguns."

"If these boats run the same speed we should be safe. God help us if the engine quits."

"They are pulling away from the dock and coming after us," said Morgan.

"How many do you make out?" asked Joe.

"It looks like four boats."

Punky made it to the truck and left the area as fast as he could. He was almost to the airfield when he heard a rumble in the distance. That would be the soldiers and trucks. He left the road and ran the truck into the woods. He jumped out and ran for the airfield.

He crawled upon the hill and could see the jets getting ready for takeoff. He had to move fast. He ran down the hill to a building that looked like the locker room and ready room. He looked in the window and saw four pilots suiting up. The pilot leaving the building first looked about his size. The pilot walked out of the building. Punky grabbed the pilot, slit his throat and dragged him around the back of the building. He undressed him and took his flight gear. He made it out to the flight line first. Punky walked up to the first aircraft. A plane Captain was checking over the plane to make sure it was ready for flight. He motioned for the Plane captain to pull the chocks. He did as he was told even if it was not the normal thing to do. Punky crawled up into the cockpit and looked it over. He had better learn the controls and instruments fast or he was in trouble. The Plane Captain came to the cockpit and helped him strap in. He kept his head down and didn't speak. The Plane Captain crawled off the plane and stood by for instructions. Punky gave the signal to plug in power to start the plane. He hoped it was the right signal. The Plan Captain plugged in the power unit and he gave the signal to start. After the engine caught, Punky gave the signal to pull power. He taxied out to the runway and applied full power. He shot down the runway and lifted off. He made a run toward the coast. He looked down at the airfield and saw the other pilots manning their aircraft. He knew they would be airborne in a few minutes and after him like a nest of hornets.

Joe was pushing the boat as fast as it would go. Things were looking good. They were keeping their distance from the other boats. They fired at them, but they were out of range. Suddenly a shell exploited just behind the boat. One of the boats had a cannon mounted on the bow. Joe started moving back and forth so their boat wouldn't be an easy target.

"Joe what can we do?"

"We could slow down until they are in range of our machineguns and try to knock out the cannon, but we would also be in range of their machineguns. It's a catch 22."

"We better do something fast, here comes another shell."

Suddenly a jet passed right over them. He turned to make a run on the boat firing the cannon.

"Punky the crazy maverick did it."

They watched as Punky made his run on the boat. He fired on the boat with his 30MM cannon and the boat went dead in the water. He turned back toward the carrier. The radar operator on the carrier had dots all over his screen. He reported to the Operations Officer who reported to the Captain. A few minutes later the Captain and Operations Officer were watching the scope.

"What's happening asked the Captain?"

"I'm not sure, but it looked like one of the boats was firing on the lead boat. They look like patrol boats. Then a plane fired on the boat that was firing on the first boat and that boat is dead in the water."

"Launch the A-4 aircraft," ordered the Captain.

"Sir I now have three more aircraft coming fast."

"Get the A-4s in the air now."

The Pilots manned the aircraft while the carrier turned into the wind and picked up speed. They had two aircraft on the cats and two waiting to launch.

"Well I guess this is what I always wanted to do, fly a jet fighter and fight enemy aircraft in a dogfight."

Punky turned the jet in a sharp turn and headed head on with the three Migs following him. It caught the Migs by surprise. He got a lock on the middle aircraft and fired a missile. He was lucky and took out the middle aircraft.

"Sir the lead aircraft just turned and headed toward the three aircraft. He fired a missile and took out one of the aircraft."

"That can only be one person flying that aircraft. It's that maverick Punky," stated the Operation Officer.

The A-4 aircraft launched and headed toward the beach. They were a ways off and would take time to get to where the dogfight raged.

Punky had a Mig on his tail and was having a hard time shaking him. The Mig fired a missile at him. He faked right, turned left and dove for the deck. The missile just missed him. He made a sharp turn and got a side angle on the Mig. The Mig pilot saw what Punky was trying to do and turned away. The other Mig was now on his tail firing at him. He pulled back on the power and hit the speed brake. The Mig went right by him. He got a missile lock and fired. His missile took out the Mig.

"Sir the aircraft took out another one of the aircraft."

"That Maverick is good."

"Sir they are in a dogfight again."

"How close are the A-4 aircraft?"

"Five minutes to target."

"Sir I see two more aircraft coming from the beach."

Jerry and the crew watched the dogfight from their boat as they ran full speed toward the carrier. The two Migs circled each other like two boxers looking for an opening.

"Punky was wrong about the Migs. He is flying a Mig-21," said Jerry.

"How do you know?" asked Joe.

"The Mig-17 doesn't have missiles. It has one 37 mm cannon and two 23 mm cannon for armament."

"Well he is flying it like he has been flying them all his life."

"That crazy maverick is going to get himself killed."

"I hear planes," said Joe.

"Look toward the carrier they are ours," shouted Jerry.

"It looks like we are home free."

"Now if Punky can take care of that Mig."

The radar operator watched as all the aircraft were on a collision course. He was going to have a hard time telling who was who in a few minutes. He could tell the boat was still headed for the carrier. The Operations Officer gave the order for the Angel helicopter to stand by in case he was needed for a pickup.

"Blue Blazer leader this is the Captain, fly between the Migs and the two more coming from the coast."

Blue Blazer roger we are circling the two in the dogfight."

The Mig launched a missile at Punky, but he turned sharp and the missile missed. He went after the Mig. He took his time and waited for a good shot. He followed him in several turns. The Mig couldn't get Punky off his tail. The Mig made a dive for the deck and turned right. Punky led him and fired in front of him with his 30 mm cannon. He timed it just right and took out the Mig. He pulled out and came up beside the A-4 leader. He came up on emergency frequency. "Blue Blazer leader Maverick Mig, do you think the other two Migs want to play?"

"Maverick Mig Blue Blazer, give our friends a call and find out."

Before Punky could figure what frequency to call the two Migs turned and headed back toward the coast. "I guess they don't want to play."

The five planes turned in formation and headed back to the carrier. The Mig shuddered and Punky was losing control of the plane. "Bennington tower Maverick Mig I'm having a little trouble. I just lost part of my wing. Mayday, mayday, mayday, I'm going down."

Punky finally figured out how to eject from the Mig and punched out. His shoot opened and he floated down. The Angel heard the mayday and headed toward the downed pilot. Almost as soon as He hit the water the Angel helicopter was there to pick him up.

They lowered the hoist and Punky crawled into the hoist. They brought him up and pulled him into the helicopter.

"Sir you have had a busy day. You shot down three Migs and destroyed a patrol boat."

"I just want to get back to the carrier."

The Angel helicopter set down on the carrier and let Punky out. It lifted back off and flew to the boat. It hovered over the patrol boat and picked up the four other men. It flew back to the carrier and dropped off the men. It lifted off and stood plane guard for the A-4 aircraft while they landed.

Punky and his men went to the ready room. They were welcomed back to the carrier. The pilots who had never flown against a Mig bombarded Punky with questions about the Mig. The Captain and Operations Officer headed straight toward him.

"Attention on deck," said Jerry.

The Captain walked up in front of Punky. "You have had quite a day Lieutenant Wilson."

"Yes sir."

"You got a lot of explaining to do, but first you and your crew get cleaned up and in uniform. Get something to eat and report back here in two hours."

"Yes sir."

Punky headed to his cabin to get cleaned up. He opened the hatch and Charlie was waiting on him. "You stink." "Well good evening to you too."

Stink or not she flew into his arms and kissed him hard. She was afraid she had lost him and was shaking all over. "I thought I had lost you."

"I told you I would be back."

"They thought you were dead."

"We almost were."

"Was it worth the mission?"

"No it was all for nothing. The family was dead when we got there and the village was destroyed. I lost one of my men, my aircraft, and my career for nothing."

"Punky I'm so sorry."

"There will be investigation. I was not on an authorized mission. They may Court Marshal all of us. They may just kick me out of the Navy. Who knows what they will do. I got to meet with the Captain in two hours so I need a shower, clean clothes and some good food, I'm starving."

"I'll be here when you get back." She left and went to her cabin.

Everywhere he went everyone treated him like a hero. While he was trying to eat he was covered up with pilots wanting to know about the Migs. He knew he was in deep trouble. Punky entered the ready room and Commander Owens was waiting on him. He wanted to know what happened and why? He told him his story before the other Officers arrived. He understood why he did it, but the Navy would still frown on what he did. The Captain and other Officers entered the ready room. It was an informal gathering and everybody seated around Punky. The Captain told him to take his time and tell them the whole story. After he told them the reason why he did what he did and all he saw in Vietnam they discussed what was going on in South Vietnam.

"It looks like all-out war to me," said the Captain.

"How long will we be on station," asked Punky.

"We will be relieved two days and head back to the states. We have to pick up some Advisors before we leave.

A young Officer entered the ready room and came over to the Captain. He whispered something to the Captain.

"Lieutenant Wilson your name and what you did is plastered all over the world. The Navy won't be able to punish you, but you will never get another promotion. Your career is dead."

"Then there won't be any reason for me to stay in the Navy."

"No, I guess not."

"If you keep your nose clean for a few years the Navy might forget all the things you have done."

"I'll have to think about that."

"North Vietnam denies any of this happened. They didn't want to give you credit for shooting down three of their aircraft with one of their own aircraft. It would be very embarrassing to their Air Force."

"I was just lucky."

"Lucky, you are a dam good pilot."

The Captain called an end to the meeting. He told Punky there would be a formal inquest later. He went back to his cabin.

"How did it go?" asked Charlie. She was in his bed naked.

"About like I thought it would except for the world knowing about it already. How do they find out so, quick?"

"Nobody knows, newspapers have a nose for news and that was big news."

Punky started taking off his clothes. Charlie sat up in bed letting the sheet slid to her waist. Her breasts were firm and stood straight out. Her nipples were hard thinking about what was about to happen. Punky stepped out of his shorts and his erection stood at attention. She ran her tongue around her lips and made him go crazy. She threw the sheet back raising her legs and spreading them in invitation.

"You really know how to turn a guy on."

"I sure hope so, I want some loving, think you can handle the job?"

Punky crawled onto the bed and between her legs. He poised above her touching her folds with the head of his erection.

"I don't want foreplay, I'm hot enough to set the bed on fire, I want you inside me now."

"Sock it to me, I can't wait any longer."

Charlie raised her hips taking him deep inside her. Punky slammed into her and she raised her hips to meet each thrust. It had been a long time since they had made love. She wanted him to put out the fire building in her. She knew that she was about to come. She locked her legs around Punky and squeezed his shaft. She wanted them to come together. He felt her shudder as she came and Charlie felt his hot liquid go deep inside her. They hadn't used any protection, but she wanted to feel him inside her and not a rubber. "Oh Punky, that was fantastic."

Punky turned over carrying her with him. She was on top with her nipples digging him in the chest. They were still coupled. "As soon as it rises again you can ride me."

"I would like that."

It didn't take long before Charlie felt Punky filling her again. She began a steady pace and slowly increased the pace. She took her time and slowly brought them to another climax. She rolled off him and turned her back on him. He eased up behind her and slipped his shaft back inside her. They dozed off to sleep both contented and tired.

The next two days the carrier cruised up and down the coast of South Vietnam. They kept the A-4 aircraft in the air in case of any kind of attack from North Vietnam. Migs came out toward the carrier, but A-4 aircraft intercepted them and they would turn back. It was a cat and mouse game they played. They wanted to see how close to the carrier they could get.

This went on for the two days the Bennington had left on station. They used the helicopters to bring the men aboard from South Vietnam that were going home. They got their orders to head home and would be relieved by another carrier with its group of ships.

Punky and crew had been grounded until the formal hearing. He didn't like it. It made him look like a bad guy. He had a bad feeling that his time in the Navy was over. Even if he got out of the mess he was in it would still be in his record. When transferred to a new squadron the Commanding Officer would read his file and think only one thing. He would think he had a maverick on his hands.

Punky, Jerry and crew met on the hanger deck and discussed what would happen to them. The enlisted men would probably be busted in rank, but how far was anyone's guess. Punky was going to take the blame for everything, but the men didn't agree. Nobody made them go on the mission so they would share the blame. He told them the Navy wanted a scapegoat and he would be it. He would tell the inquest that the men went with him out of loyalty to him. He would tell them he was the ringleader and talked everyone into going with him.

The trip back to the states seemed like it would take forever. When the Bennington was close to the coast the aircraft were launched and flew to their home base. They were welcomed home by their families. The carrier finally pulled into Long Beach and the rest of the squadron would take busses home. Trucks would take their gear behind the buses. The helicopters had flown back to Ream Field.

Punky kissed Charlie when they off loaded and she was gone. A car was there from Sikorsky to pick her up. She would go back to her office in L.A. for debrief of her trip. She felt like part of her was left behind. She loved Punky and no matter what happened she still wanted him in her life. They still hadn't settled anything between them. She couldn't see life without Punky in it. She should have told him she would quit her job and go with him.

Punky and Jerry stepped off the bus at Ream Field and Kim Lou threw herself into Jerry's arms. His parents were there with Kim Lou. They were happy when they saw the two together and how happy they were.

Punky didn't have anyone to meet him and he didn't care. The woman he loved had gone back to her life and he had gone back to his. He didn't have a clue, but some way they would be together. They were meant for one another.

Charlie was back in her office at her desk. She should be happy, but all she could think about was Punky. Her supervisor walked in and sat down across from her. Dan knew something was wrong. Charlie was looking at him, but not seeing him.

"Charlie what's wrong. You did a good job on finding the problem with the helicopter so what's wrong?"

She blushed at being caught daydreaming. "Nothing is wrong. I'm just tired from the trip."

"Liar, now tell me what's wrong. You look like you just lost your best friend."

"What makes you think I'm lying?"

"Charlie I have known you for a long time and I can read you like a book, so what gives? You can talk and I will listen."

"I don't want to talk about it."

"Is it that bad?"

"Yes, no, maybe, I don't know."

"Well that is a good start."

"Ok, ok, I met this guy and spent a lot of time with him."

"Do you love him?'

"Yes."

"Does he love you?"

"Yes I think so."

"So what's the problem?"

"Did you read the newspaper?"

"You mean the about the maverick pilot going into North Vietnam?"

"Yes that's the one. He is in big trouble. The public loves him, but the Navy isn't happy with him. He didn't have permission to make the flight."

"Tell me why he made the flight."

Charlie told him the story about the girl saving Punky from a fight where he would have probably died. He owed her his life. She told him about her family in South Vietnam and wanted him to save them from the V.C. from the North. When he got there they had been killed and the village destroyed. A few V.C. were still in the village raping the few women they hadn't killed yet. Punky and his men killed the V.C. and saved the women. They were so mad they took to the air in their helicopter and attacked the V. C. killing a lot of them, but they were shot down.

They fled into North Vietnam to escape the V.C. and find a way to get back to the carrier. They killed several North Vietnam Soldiers and Sailors before they made it back to the carrier.

"How did he get his hands on a Mig?"

"He created a diversion while his crew stole a boat and he went back to the airfield and stole the Mig. The rest is in the newspaper."

"Does the newspaper know the rest of the story?"

"No, only about him shooting down, the Migs."

"Will the Navy give out the information to the newspaper?"

"No they say it is a Navy matter and not a need to know by the public."

"You could leak it to the newspaper."

"No I can't because I promised Punky I wouldn't."

"Have you seen him since you got back?"

"No he went back to his Navy Base and I came back to work."

"Have you called him?"

"Yes, but he isn't in a good mood."

"Are you going to him?"

"No he said to stay away until it's over."

"You can go to him anytime you want to."

"No it may be over between us and he can come here if he wants to see me."

"Charlie I'm here anytime you want to talk."

"Thank you Dan."

Punky sat in his room staring at the walls. He hated waiting for the Navy to make up their mind about what they would do to him. In a couple of days he would have to go to an inquest. He knew they wouldn't be light on him. It wasn't the first he had disobeyed an order. He was known as a maverick. The Navy didn't like a maverick. They wanted Officers that would obey their orders. He hoped the Navy would go light on the men that went with him. One man had been killed and two shot. That was his fault.

He should have turned the helicopter around and headed back to the carrier when they found the family dead and the village destroyed. He was their leader and should have made the decision to go back to the carrier. Such is life he screwed up his career for nothing, got one man killed and two men shot. The men that went with him would have to pay for his screw up. The hardest thing he had ever done in his life was to visit McDaniel's home. He informed his family that their son was with him when he died. They asked questions and he answered as many as he could without telling them they were on a mission that was not suppose, to have happened. He had to tell them their son's body was still in Vietnam. The military would try to get the body back if they could.

"Thank you for coming and telling us about our son."

Punky returned to his base. He thought about getting drunk, but changed his mind at the last minute. He went back to his apartment and stared at four walls. He wanted to call Charlie, but didn't want to cry on her shoulder. He didn't know if they would have a life together. It may be over between them. He couldn't see a life without her in it. The inquest would start tomorrow. There would be big brass on the panel including one Marine Officer since one of the crew was a Marine.

CHAPTER ELEVEN

Punky didn't sleep much that night, his thoughts on the inquest and his dreams about Charlie. What would happen was out of his hands. The next morning he dressed his best. He wanted to look good even if he went down in flames. The inquest was held in a classroom at Ream Field. There were six high ranking Officers seated at a long table. Punky and his crew were seated in front of the table since it was a formal hearing. The Officer in charge asked if anyone wanted a Navy lawyer to speak for him. They all refused.

"Then I call Lieutenant Wilson to give us his story of what happened."

"Sir before I began I would like to say this is all, my fault."

"Lieutenant Wilson the panel will determine who is at fault. Go on with your story."

"It all started when I was on Shore Patrol and a young girl saved my life." Punky took his time and tried not to leave anything out. He got to the part where he decided to make the flight. He told them he asked for men to go with him.

"Lieutenant Wilson, why didn't you ask permission to make the flight?"

"Sir I knew they would refuse me."

"You are right I'm sure your request would have been turned down. Go on with your story."

"I started looking for men to go with me."

"Stop right there," said the Marine Officer. He looked directly at Joe. "I can't believe a Marine would go with you knowing you didn't have permission to go on the flight. Did you know Lieutenant Wilson didn't have clearance to go on the mission?"

"Yes sir I knew," replied Joe.

"And you went anyway?"

"Yes sir I knew he needed someone that knew weapons and had been to Vietnam. It seemed like a good idea at the time."

"Well it wasn't."

The panel asked the rest of the crew the same question. They got about the same answer. The panel was stunned that the men had gone, knowing that they would get in deep trouble. They all referred to the flight as a mercy mission. They wanted to save the lives of the family.

"How did you get the weapons mounted on the helicopter? Did the Sailors know what was going on?"

Bob answered that question, "No sir I told them it was a drill."

"How did you get clearance for a launch?'

"I told the tower we were on a test hop and it just hadn't been posted yet," explained Jerry.

"You guys are a bunch of con artists."

"Thank you, sir."

"It wasn't meant as a compliment."

Punky continued with the story. He told them what they found when they got to the village. "The family was dead, the village destroyed, and V.C. still in the village raping the girls they hadn't killed yet. We killed the V.C. raping the girls. We attacked the large force of V.C."

"Why didn't you turn around and bring the helicopter back to the carrier?" asked the Marine Officer.

"I guess I made a bad call I was so mad at what they had done to the people and the village," explained Punky.

"All of us decided to attack," replied Joe.

"Lieutenant Wilson it was your decision you should have brought your helicopter back to the carrier."

"Yes sir I take full blame for the decision."

"Go on with your story."

"We attacked a large force of V.C. invading South Vietnam. We killed a large number of V.C. before we were shot down."

"Then what happened?"

Punky told them how they decided to go north to throw off the V.C. coming after them. It had worked, but every time they tried to make it for the coast something happened. They got deeper and deeper into North Vietnam.

"We found an old helicopter, but we were shot down again. McDaniel was killed in the crash."

Punky went on with the story about stealing food, clothes and weapons. Then they had stolen a truck. The panel sat on the edge of their seats as they listened to the story.

"Did you kill more people?" asked the Marine Officer.

"Yes sir we killed several soldiers, one pilot at the base, and several Sailors," replied Joe.

"What were you trying to do start a war?"

"Sir the war is already started they are invading South Vietnam as we speak."

"Yes you are right we have been getting reports of fighting from South Vietnam,"

"Sir they plan to conquer South Vietnam. I heard the Soldiers taking about it at one of the Army camps."

Punky continued with his story. He told them about the airfield and how he thought the Migs were Mig-17's. As it turned out they were Mig-21's. He told them how he distracted the Sailors while his crew took over a boat. He then went back to the airfield and stole a Mig-21.

"Is that where you killed the pilot?" ask one of the Navy Officers.

"Yes sir, I needed his flight gear."

"Then what happened?"

"All hell broke loose, sorry sir."

"And then what happened?"

The Migs came after me. I put one of their boats out of order that was firing their cannon at the boat my men were on. Then I turned around and met the Migs head on. It surprised them and I took out one of them. I took out the other two in a dogfight. The rest you know."

"That's an amazing story Lieutenant Wilson. You said you had never flown a jet."

"No sir I had never flown a jet. I wanted a jet squadron out of flight training, but I got into some trouble and ended up in a helicopter squadron."

"Then how were you able to fly a jet and a Mig-21 at that."

"If it has wings and an engine I can fly it sir."

"That's quite a story."

"Yes sir."

"Were your kills confirmed?"

"Yes sir."

The panel asked if any of the men would like to add anything. They declined any further information.

"Sir may I speak to the panel?" asked Punky.

They gave him permission to speak. "Sir we would like for the panel to assess our punishment and not drag it out."

The Officer in charge looked up and down the table. All the Officers nodded yes. They said they would consider all the information given them at the inquest and give them their verdict tomorrow at ten hundred.

"Attention hut."

The panel filed out and left Punky and his crew. They were glad it was over and all they had left was the verdict.

"Guys since I am the cause of all this trouble I would like to take you out on the town tonight. It is probably our last chance to be together. What do you say?"

"Let's do it," they answered at the same time.

"Is it alright if I bring my wife?" asked Jerry.

"Sure and the rest of you can also if you want to bring someone."

Jerry's wife was the only one in the area. That would make her the only woman with five men. Punky would like Charlie to come, but she was back at her job. They decided to meet at the Officer's club, have one drink then paint the town. They met at nineteen hundred at the club and decided to eat before they left. It was good food and would be cheaper. The men ordered steak and Kim Lou ordered fish. They each had a mixed drink or beer. After they finished their meal they met in the parking lot.

Punky, Joe, Bob and Morgan went in one car. Jerry and Kim Lou followed in another car. There was a big Country Western Club in San Diego and they decided to go there.

They entered the club and Punky asked for a table for six close to the dance floor. After they had their drinks they sat and watched the couples on the dance floor. They were dancing a two-step.

"I never see a dance like that," said Kim Lou.

"Sweetheart before the night is over you will know how to dance." replied Jerry.

"You teach me."

"Yes I'll teach you."

Jerry asked Kim Lou to dance a slow dance to get her started. They danced well together. Joe looked around the room looking for a dance partner. A cute blonde looked at Joe. She was smiling with I want to dance look in her eyes.

"See you guys later," said Joe.

He went over to the blonde. He held out his hand and she took it. "Would you like to dance?"

"I thought you would never ask?"

Bob spotted him a fine looking girl and was gone. Punky and Morgan sat and drank their drinks. Punky wasn't in a mood to dance. He was thinking about Charlie. He missed her very much. He had called and left a message on her answering machine to let her know he would be in touch. Morgan didn't want to dance either. The truth was he didn't know how to dance.

"Sir what do you think they will do to us tomorrow?"

"I don't think too much since the newspaper picked up on what happened. It wouldn't look good for the Navy."

The band was good if you liked country western music. Punky figured Morgan would prefer something different, but he didn't say so. It was almost closing time and everyone was back at the table.

Punky ordered one more round for the road. He held up his glass, "To friends when you need them."

They all drank to that. They were finishing their drinks and were about to leave when five guys approached their table.

"Well boys what have we here? A Jap and a Nigger at the same table and I can't stand either one."

Joe stood up to face them, "Watch your mouth and move on."

"Who is going to make us?"

Punky stepped between Joe and the men. "Guys you have had too much to drink so why don't you move on?"

"We'll leave when we are ready. That gal must be good to service all of you. Do you think she could, take on five more?"

That did it. Jerry, Kim Lou, Bob and Morgan came to their feet. Punky turned and slammed a fist into the guy's face breaking his nose. The guy next to the guy hit Punky on the side of his head sending him to the floor.

Battle lines were drawn with each person facing another. All hell broke loose. One guy stood staring at Kim Lou. She was small with a short skirt on and he didn't know what to do with her, his mistake. Kim Lou kicked him in the balls and came around with a flying kick. He went down and didn't get back up. The fight raged on, the owner called the Police and Shore Patrol.

When the Shore Patrol and Police arrived Punky and his group were in a circle with their backs to each other. There were men all over the floor, some out cold, the one with the broken nose bleeding all over the floor and some moaning. The fight was over. The Police asked the owner who started the fight. He pointed to Punky and to the one with the broken nose. The Police told the

Shore Patrol to take care of the military and they would take the men on the floor to Jail.

Punky walked over to the owner and handed the owner some money. "That's to take care of our part of the damage."

"It wasn't your fault that jerk started it."

"Yes but I threw the first punch. Maybe we should have turned around and left."

"They would have followed you outside."

"Anyway for what it's worth I'm sorry it happened in your club."

"You and your friends can come back anytime, but I don't want that bunch in here again. I put them on criminal trespassing."

The Shore Patrol wrote up a report on them and let them leave in their own cars. They stopped at a fast food place for coffee.

"This will be a night to remember when we are old. The Navy and Marine, fighting together," laughed Joe.

"Those punks got what they deserved," replied Punky.

"You should have let me take the guy out."

"It was my pleasure, but I should have ducked after I hit him."

"You got a bump on the side of your head and blood running down your neck. I think the eye on that side of your head is turning black."

"We are going to be a mess tomorrow at the inquest."

"Punky it has been my pleasure being with you and your crew."

"Thank you Joe, that means a lot to us."

"We better go home and get cleaned up. We need some sleep to face tomorrow."

Punky woke up with a headache and a bruised body. He knew the rest of the crew was hurting too. They made it to the inquest early and sat talking. They were wandering if the panel knew about their night out.

"Attention hut."

The panel entered and sat down at the long table. "Stand at ease."

The Officer in charge of the panel looked over at Punky. "I see your group had a fun night out fighting and destroying a night club."

"Sir it's all, my fault I lost my head," explained Punky.

"I can understand a Marine doing something like that, but you are an Officer and a gentleman. How could you start a fight in a club?"

"Sir may I speak?" asked Joe.

"You have the panel's permission, make it good."

"Sir if Lieutenant Wilson hadn't stepped in front of me I would have started the fight. The jerk insulted First Class Morgan and Jerry's wife Kim Lou. He tried to talk the men into leaving us alone, but they kept on."

"The Shore Patrol report confirms your story. It reads when they entered the club your bunch was standing in a circle and with men on the floor all around you. Is that true?"

"Yes sir," replied Joe.

The Marine Officer asked, "It reads that Kim Lou put down one of the men. Is that true?"

"Yes sir she is one tough lady. I would want her on my side anytime in a fight. She knows karate and is good at it."

"Why were you in a circle?"

"We covered each other's back."

"That was good fighting tactics."

"Lieutenant Wilson I would like to show you something interesting. These are two personnel folders, one is yours, one is the Sargent's and notice, the difference in size. The Sargent has been in the Marines several years and you have only been in the Navy a short time. His folder is one third the size of yours. He looks like a Boy Scout compared to you."

"Sorry sir."

"Can you explain why you are always in trouble?"

"I guess being at the wrong place at the wrong time."

"In flight training you were given a direct order to take your flight home."

"Yes sir, but the instructor would have died if I had left him."

"You could have died crashing the plane to save him."

"Yes sir, but it seemed like the thing to do at the time."

"How many planes have you crashed?"

"Sir I kind of, lost count."

"I take it you don't like to follow orders."

"Most of the time I do sir."

"Lieutenant Wilson you are a maverick."

"Yes sir I have been called that a few times."

"I got one thing to say to you, you should have joined the Marines. I like a man who thinks on his feet and does what he thinks is best for his men."

"Thank you, sir."

The Officer in charge of the panel looked at Punky, "Lieutenant Wilson we have reached a decision."

Punky stood up at attention, "Yes sir."

"I have heard talk of a plan to train pilots in a dogfight. I don't know when it will come about. It is in the planning stage. It will be called Top Gun. They will probably want you and your experience. You will have a severe reprimand placed in your record. You will not be eligible for promotion for at least five years if you keep your nose clean."

Jerry was given a reprimand, but not as bad because it was his first offence. Joe, Bob and Morgan were busted down to E-5 pay grade.

"Attention hut."

The panel filed out leaving Punky and his crew. They milled around for a while talking.

"Punky what are you going to do?" asked Jerry.

"I don't know yet, I may get out of the Navy."

"I thought about it myself since I am married and will want a family. The Navy is hard on family life."

"What about you guys?" asked Punky.

"It's no big deal, I've been busted before. I'll just get it back," replied Joe.

Bob and Morgan felt the same way. They would work to get their rank back. It wouldn't be as hard for them as it was for Officers to get their rank back.

"Well guys it's been fun," said Punky.

They all shook hands and went their separate ways. Punky went to the Officer's Club for a beer or two. He sat in a corner by himself nursing his beer. He was down in the dumps. His career in the Navy was in shambles and his girl was gone. He loved Charlie, but what did he have to offer her? She had a good job making more than he did.

Jerry came in and sat down across from Punky. "You look like you lost your best friend. Do you want to talk about it?"

"I don't think it would do any good to talk."

"Well I made up my mind what I'm going to do. I'm getting out of the Navy and going home. I want to be with my wife all the time, not part of the time. I'll work in the family business until Kim Lou and I find jobs we want."

"Well good luck. Now all I have to do is make up my mind what to do."

Jerry had one beer and shook hands. Jerry left and Punky went back to drinking his second beer.

"Lieutenant Wilson there is a phone call for you. You can take it in the bar."

"Thank you."

"Hello this is Lieutenant Wilson."

"Lieutenant Wilson this is Dan Walker at Sikorsky Helicopters. I would like you to come and talk to me this weekend if you can make it."

EPILOGUE

Punky had talked to Dan Walker and told him he would think about the job offer with Sikorsky Helicopters. He had received a call Larry Cooper his friend and classmate to attend his wedding in Dallas. He told Dan he would give him an answer when he got back from Texas.

The wedding was a sight to see. His old classmates were there as grooms, Rex Johnson was in a suit, Mike Love in a country western suit, and Gary Mitchel was in buckskins, Wolf his partner as himself. Punky was in his Navy uniform.

Punky watched Leroy and Katherine. They couldn't keep their hands off each other. They were so much in love. Her thought about Charlie and how much he missed her. He couldn't see life without her in it. He had made up his mind what he was going to do when he returned to Ream Field.

When the wedding was over Punky visited with his old classmates. They talked about all the good times and trouble they had in high school. They had all gone separate ways. Mike asked him when he was going to get married.

"Soon I hope, if she will have me."

"Who is she?"

"Her name is Charlie and she works for Sikorsky Helicopters."

"Where did you meet her?"

"She was assigned to me on the carrier to find a problem with our helicopters."

"I didn't think they let women aboard ship."

"This was an exception to the rule."

"Will she be with you in the Navy?"

"I've decided to get out. I ruined my career in the Navy. Did you see me in the newspapers?" Punky explained about the mission and how everything happened. Mike told him how sorry he was that it happened.

"I think I would be wasting my time in the Navy. Watching Leroy and Katherine in love made up my mind. I'm going to take a job with Sikorsky Helicopters. Then I am going to ask Charlie to marry me."

"Well good luck."

"How is, the ranch and your family?"

"Everything is fine. You will have to visit us sometime."

"Gary, how has it been with you? What are you doing with a wolf?"

"Punky it is a very long story, but to make it short Wolf saved my life and now we are a team. I have a business where we hunt anything that is lost. You lose it and we find it."

Gary handed Punky a business card. It read The Hunter. "For example we hunt missing animals and people. The Wolf is better at tracking than most dogs and works with me."

"Do you hunt children when they are lost?"

"Yes, but I don't charge for that."

"It's good seeing you again. I heard you were missing for a long time yourself."

"That's where I met the Wolf."

"I hope to see you again soon. If you come to California look me up. I'll be working for Sikorsky Helicopters."

"I thought you were in the Navy."

"I am, but I'm getting out."

"Why are you leaving the Navy?"

"That's a long story too."

"One of these days we need to get together and swap stories."

"I'll hold you to that."

Charlie was back from her assignment in Norfolk, Virginia. She was walking down the hall to her office and saw the janitor finishing a sign he was painting. It read P. Wilson. She stopped and starred at the sign. No it couldn't be Punky. Dan walked by while she stood staring at the sign.

"I hired a new consultant while you were on assignment." He turned and walked on down the hall. He has a smile on his face.

Charlie couldn't wait any longer. She was shaking from anticipation on what she would find behind the door. She hadn't seen Punky in a long time. She tapped lightly on the door and opened it. She entered the room and stared at the man sitting at the desk.

"What took you so long coming home?"

Punky what are you doing here? How did you—?"

"Dan called me, I got out of the Navy and I work here."

Punky walked around the desk and opened his arms. Charlie went into them as they kissed. It had been a long time since they had seen each other. The kiss lasted a long time.

"Sweetheart we can't do this on company time."

"No, but we can do it after five. I'll pick you up on our way out. She pecked him on the lips, "I love you."

"I love you more."

X   X   X   X   X   X   X   X   X   X